KEEPING PROMISES

A HIGHER ELEVATIONS NOVEL

JODI PAYNE

BA TORTUGA

Keeping Promises
Copyright © 2021 by Joci Payne & BA Tortuga

Edited by LC Hinson

Cover illustration by AJ Corza
http://www.seeingstatic.com/
Cover content is for illustrative purposes only and any person depicted on the cover is a model.

ISBN: 978-1-951011-44-4

Published by Tygerseye Publishing, LLC
March 2021
Printed in the USA

KEEPING PROMISES

By Jodi Payne and BA Tortuga

Jeremy M. Dunn III has the single dad thing down, so the last thing he wants to do is call his ex-husband to ask for help with their two kids. They didn't part on good terms, and they've barely spoken since the divorce. But with a cast on his arm that goes up past his elbow, Jeremy has no choice. He needs a few days to figure out how to bathe their daughter, make school lunches and parent their son one-armed, and there isn't anyone else he can ask for help.

Former rodeo cowboy West Belen was already on his way back to his kids, and to Trey ("the third", his nickname for Jeremy). He made a promise to try again, and he means to keep it, so when he sees his chance to move back into his family's life, he grabs it like the brass ring he knows it is. He's determined to be more than an "every other weekend" dad to his children, and he doesn't want to keep on living with regret about how he and Trey ended.

Jeremy still desires West, but he isn't sure he can trust West to be responsible and available. West still thinks Trey is the hottest thing he's ever seen, but he has no idea how to convince the man he's ready to settle down. The two of them have never had trouble butting heads, but now they need to learn to work together to make a home for themselves and their kids where they both belong.

THE HIGHER ELEVATION SERIES

All true standalone titles that can be read in any order.

Bigger Than Us

Keeping Promises

Home Free

Heart of a Cowboy

CONTENTS

As always, to our wives.

1

"Kiddo. Kiddo, you awake?" Hank's voice jolted West upright from where he'd been dozing in the old recliner he'd moved near the hospital bed they'd put in the sunroom so Hank could see out the window and watch the hummingbirds.

"Yessir. You hurtin'? I can get Gretchen." The little hospice nurse was on it. She lived two houses down, too, so it took her no time to show up.

"No. No, I just wanted to talk to you." The hand that had been whole and strong three weeks ago was a sack of bruised bones, and West took it so carefully.

"Anytime. Anytime at all." Hank had been his best friend, his mentor, his adopted father for as long as he could remember, and time was getting short. They could both sleep when Hank was dead.

"You're a good man." Hank stared at him, gray eyes seeming to blaze with light, and West thought maybe that was what happened when the best of them was being called home.

"I try. I'm not feeling all the way on that, you know."

Hank shook his head. "No. You've been dealt some shit, but you have managed it. All of it."

What was he supposed to say to that? "Thank you."

"If you could go back and change anything in your life, what would it be?"

He rolled his eyes at Hank. "I would have bet on me two years ago in the finals."

Hank swatted his hand. "I'm serious, boy. Tell me. It ain't like I'm telling."

West took a deep breath. He knew the answer to this one. He'd known it for two years, two months, three weeks, and four days. "I would have told Trey no when he asked for a divorce. I would have stuck like a burr and kept my kids and my husband and damn the consequences."

Hank bobbed his head at him like a big, dying bird. "I hear you. I couldn't have had a family like y'all did. I never will now."

Shit. He didn't say anything to that because he didn't have anything to say. Hell, he'd lost his whole life—his kids, his husband, his house. He was working a job that was Friday through Sunday, and those were the days he could see Lukas and Ava. He got to keep his truck, his child support payments, and the knowledge that his ex hated him enough to make sure he had to choose between rodeoing or his babies.

Shit, why did he even want Trey back?

He guessed because he loved the son of a bitch.

"So, go make it right."

West looked up, just utterly confused. "What?"

They were divorced. That meant it was over.

"Go home and fix it. You have a chance. You survived that last bad wreck; you can do this."

He rubbed the back of his head, that heavy scar back

there. "Oh, Hank... Trey don't want me no more. He hates everything about my life."

"So change. If you want it—them—bad enough, do what you have to. Those babies need you, even if Jeremy Fancy Pants No Fun doesn't."

He started chuckling. Jeremy Fancy Pants No Fun. That was going down in history.

"Promise me, kiddo. Swear you'll try. Don't—don't end up dying with your regrets."

"Hank—"

"Goddamn it! I'm dying. You give me this. I'm never going to get to see those babies again. Promise me you'll try."

"I swear to God. I'll try." West felt his face try to crumple, because he didn't want to figure out how to be a man without the person who taught him how to cowboy up. He kept it together, though, because it was their way. "I promise, Hank."

"Good boy." Hank sighed, that light fading as he closed his eyes. "Know that I love you, West Belen. You are my son, just like as if I'd borned you."

"I love you, Hank. I got your back." Even though this was a trip West couldn't make with Hank right now, he was here 'til the bitter end.

"I never doubted that for a second. Just hold my hand a minute and pray for me."

So West did. All the way until Hank wasn't holding on anymore.

"You did what?"

Jeremy shook his head and tried not to glare at the nurse fussing with his IV. "Remember I told you I was going to paint the kitchen?"

"Jeremy Dunn the Third versus a cane-back cafe chair." Drew laughed. "Loser."

"It has a wobbly front leg." He'd managed to go thirty-two years without breaking a single fucking bone. He wasn't pouting. He was not.

Drew snorted, and he could picture the exasperated look on his best friend's face. "Then why were you standing on it, idiot?"

"Fuck you."

His nurse gave him the side-eye. "Watch your language, please."

"Sorry." He shrugged at her.

"Where are the kids?"

"Annie has them. She's had them a couple of times before." He wasn't sure what he'd have done if his neighbor hadn't been home.

"She's keeping them overnight?"

"I—maybe? I'll be home later today, but it's my right arm..." Four years of high school sports, rock climbing, and all of his idiotic shenanigans in college, running and mountain biking all over Boulder...and he shattered his elbow falling off a stupid fucking chair.

"Your right arm? Jer, how are you going to—I mean, maybe..." Drew sighed, and Jeremy's stomach sank as he realized what Drew was going to say before he said it.

"No." Nope. No way.

Drew sighed. "You have to—"

"I'm not fucking calling him."

"Jer—"

"What?" He shouted. "Did I hear someone yell 'shark'? Sorry, what? You have to go? Okay, man. Enjoy your honeymoon, get a great tan."

"Don't be an ass, Jeremy." Drew shouted back over his babbling.

"Talk to you later! Bye!"

He hung up.

Yep. He hung up on his best friend for not quite suggesting that he call his ex-husband for help with their kids.

Because he knew Drew was right.

Jesus, he'd gone off the deep end.

He looked at his phone. It was great of Annie to take them for the night, but she wasn't going to keep the kids long. She had a life and four hundred boyfriends and a day job.

West was their father after all, and it wasn't like Jeremy had asked him for anything since the divorce. Nothing. Ever. Maybe West could come take them for a few days until he figured out how to scratch his butt with his nearly useless left hand.

He pulled up West's number and frowned at the picture, feeling sick that he still thought that smiling vortex of chaos in a cowboy hat was handsome.

"Fuck." He hit the number and dialed.

"Trey." No hello, no what's wrong, just that nickname that he hated.

"Hey." He could hang up. Say he butt dialed West by mistake. The idea of asking his ex for a favor was making the bile rise in the back of his throat. But he tried to imagine giving four-year-old Ava a bath left-handed while trying to keep from jostling his right arm and decided he was going to have to suck it up. *Fuck.* "So...listen, have you got plans the next couple of days?"

"Why? What's wrong? Are the kids okay?" West's voice was sharp, clear, and focused. God, he remembered being the center of that focus.

"Yes, they're fine. I'm... I'm in the ER." He let that hang out there a second since West hadn't asked if *he* was okay.

"I'll be there in four hours. I was doing a signing in Raton." West's voice got quiet. "I got to bounce. Family emergency. Yeah. See you." Then West was back. "What's wrong?"

A signing. Still in the limelight. Some things never changed.

"I broke my elbow." *I got into a fight with a rabid dog... I was barreling down this crazy trail on my bike... I went rock climbing and man, it was a close one.* "I...fell off a fucking chair." He rolled his eyes. Drew was right; he was an idiot.

"That hurts like a motherfucker." West didn't laugh, but Jeremy knew that bastard was grinning. "Who has my babies?"

Asshole. West had broken every bone in his goddamn body. Twice. "*Our* children are with Annie, next door. I'll text you her number if you want it. They'll be fine with her for a while."

"Okay, good. Do you need a ride home, or should I just come to the house?"

"Let me know when you get up here, and we'll see if I'm home yet." Annie had a key, but no way was West going to wander around his house and pack up the kids unsupervised. His lawn might get mowed, but the kids would be covered in mud, and there'd be no beer left.

"Fine. I'll see you in a few." And just like that, the line went dead. Infuriating asshole. Seriously, if Jeremy hadn't needed him...

"Ow!" He dropped his phone.

"Sorry. I need to get your sling fitted." The nurse picked his phone up and handed it to him.

"Thanks. Sure." He nodded and sat up so she could reach, the simple move making him a little dizzy. He tried to text Annie's details to West, but texting with one hand, and left-handed at that, was a pain in the ass and it took him forever.

"Jeremiah M. Dunn, the Third." A doctor came in, grinning broadly and reading his full fucking given name off an iPad. "That's quite a name."

"It was my father's." Ha-ha. So funny. "Jeremy works."

"Jeremy. Got it. How are you getting home today?"

Fuck.

3

S hit Marthy, West didn't have one single solitary muscle that didn't hurt. It was a pretty drive up to Boulder, but less than fun in the pouring rain. He climbed out of his truck, his back popping and creaking.

Still, he was fixin' to see his babies, in the middle of the week, and he never once missed a chance at that if he had a choice. Ava and Lukas were his whole motherfucking life, no matter what their asshole father said.

Speaking of, there was Trey, sitting on a bench on the front porch with one arm in a bent-arm cast cradled in a sturdy sling. The paint-splattered T-shirt and beat-up jeans was a look he hadn't seen in a while. Trey was usually in a tie when West picked the kids up on Friday afternoons.

Trey hauled himself off the bench and ran a hand through wavy red hair that was longer than usual and fell right back across his forehead. "Lousy fucking weather, huh?"

"Yup." He'd been in it for hours, but he'd still made it in record time. He forced himself not to give Trey a once over.

That body wasn't his to look at no more. Not yet, at any rate. "What did the Doc say?"

"You know, the usual. I basically can't do anything but wipe my ass for a month." Trey sighed. Oh, that had to have ruffled him up. Trey didn't sit still for anything. "Can't drive, can't shower, can't run, the list goes on."

"Fun." Yeah, he remembered that. He'd broken both arms coming off a bronc, and it was awkward as all fuck. Looked like he didn't have to find him a hotel right now. He could stay right here. Help out. Drive Trey out of his mind. He grinned at the thought, then bellared, "Where are my babies?"

"Daddy!" Ava's happy cry rang out, and he opened his arms for his baby girl. She was a cowboy, through and through, and she launched herself at him without a hint of fear.

Lukas was seven, which meant he was far too old for such displays, but he still got a happy grin and a hard hug. "Dad's hurt bad."

"I saw that. I'm here now, y'all. We got this." He kissed Lukas's forehead. "I missed y'all like a lost tooth."

"You're taking us with you? I have school tomorrow. Do I get out of school now? Yay!"

Ava pouted. "But I want to go to school tomorrow."

Trey glared at him like it had been his idea. "Nobody is getting out of school."

"You mean I can't take them to the wilds of Borneo where the headhunters roam?" He growled playfully, tickling Ava. "Have I ever told y'all about my adventures in headhunting?"

"Headhunting?" Lukas jumped right on that. "Like hunting heads?"

"He's joking, Lukas. Tell him you're joking, West." Trey moved past him with a hiss. "Jesus. I need to sit down."

"Can I see your cast, Dad?" Ava chased after Trey.

"Yeah! I want to see your cast. Why did you get blue? Didn't they have anything cooler?"

Trey snorted and got hold of the arm of the couch, looking pretty pale. "Easy guys. Let me sit."

"Y'all chill. Ava, go upstairs and grab your dad a pillow. Lukas, can you get him a Coke from the fridge?" He waited for a second, then arched an eyebrow when they stood there like goats staring at a new fence. "Now. Get a move on."

The kids scattered. Ava took off up the stairs at a run, and Lukas headed for the kitchen.

Trey arched off the couch a little and pulled a pill bottle out of his pocket. "Thanks. This thing fucking hurts. I know, I know. You've broken two arms at once and a leg and had a hip thing and your foot...this is nothing for you. Tough guy. Whatever, it fucking hurts."

"Did I say anything?" He rolled his eyes and pulled off Trey's shoes, putting them near the door. When Ava brought the pillow, West got Trey settled and well-padded.

"Got your Coke, Dad."

Trey looked at the bottle of meds. "Can you please open this for me, West?"

"Surely." He got the Coke open, got the pills open and put one in Trey's hand, careful not to touch. No touching.

If he started touching, he'd either fuck the man or hit him.

Either way, he was screwed.

He made sure Trey wasn't going to say anything to him, then he headed to the kitchen—his fucking kitchen, dammit—and put the pills on top of the fridge before he started exploring.

They needed a brisket, some hamburger, Sprites, Dr Pepper, orange juice.

"Daddy, what are you doing?" Lukas asked, want lines in his forehead.

"Making a grocery list. Are there any grits? Swiss cake rolls? Pop-Tarts?"

Lukas looked at him seriously. "Dad says we don't eat that crap here."

"Your father lacks imagination. Wanna help me make an order?" He was retired, and he was hungry. Trey was altogether too friggin' law-abiding. "Also, I need to grab my bags out of the truck."

"Are you staying, Daddy?" Lukas was cautious like Trey and had Trey's eyes too. "For real?"

"Can you keep a secret?"

Lukas nodded, eyes huge.

"I'm staying. I can't miss y'all anymore." He was going to buy a house, next door if he could manage it, and he was going to be a full-time dad. He'd done good for himself with investments in bucking bulls, a couple of oil properties in west Texas, and one weird-assed western wear store chain. He could do this.

"Yes!" Lukas hugged him hard around the middle, unruly red curls about at his sternum now. "I can help you get your bags."

"Good deal. I'll take the basement, yeah? That way we can stay up late Friday night goofing off." The basement was finished, and he could make it work.

"Yeah? I can stay up past my bedtime?" Lukas went for a fist bump. "We can make popcorn and watch a scary movie."

"We so can." He could find something suitable for seven, surely. He'd look it up on his phone. "First, bags. Second, groceries. Third, we order something amazing for supper, fair?"

"Fair." Lukas took off for his truck.

Ava was sitting close to Trey watching *Paw Patrol* as he passed by. "Is Lukas okay? He just ran through here."

"We're good. Grabbing some stuff from the truck." *La la la—not asking permission—la la la.*

Trey was onto them when they came back through though. "Just a couple of nights. That's it. Just until I've got this figured out." When he and Lukas kept right on walking, Trey called after them. "It's my weekend."

Lukas gave him a big ol' wink and whispered. "Secret."

"Good man." He wasn't above just screwing with Trey's brain. These were his babies too. And he had ended up with every other weekend for two years—two!—when his motherfucking ex knew he worked Friday through Sunday.

The basement was finished, but it obviously hadn't been used for anything in a while. The pool table was draped with a sheet and had boxes stacked on it. The little mini-fridge was pulled out from the wall and unplugged. There was only one working lightbulb.

But the roll-out couch looked as comfy as ever, and the big TV was still there. Dusty, but there.

"Lord have mercy, we need to spruce this up. This can be a cowboy cave, huh?"

"Not a man cave?"

"Nope, because we can't leave Miss Ava out. That would be evil." Good thing he had a bunch of his shit in the bed of the truck under the camper top. "Remind me to order lightbulbs, son."

"Yes, sir. Lightbulbs, Pop-Tarts, Swiss rolls and...grits!" Lukas was smart, and he had a memory like an elephant.

"Very good. Sprites and Dr Pepper, brisket. You want potato salad?"

"Yuck."

"Potato salad is the food of the gods, but I'll give you a pass this time." He could make mashed.

"Can I get gum?" Lukas's look was wicked. "Bubblegum."

"On one condition—I find it anywhere besides your mouth and the trash can, and that includes your baby sister's hair, and I will blister your butt. Fair?" He didn't spank the kids; he didn't have to, and both kids knew it.

"Yes, sir." Lukas nodded. That was that, and he knew he wasn't going to have to repeat it. Lukas headed for the stairs. "Is there more in the truck?"

"There is, but let's get your father settled and get shit ordered, okay?" He needed to get a snuggle with his girl-child too. He bumped against Lukas. "So, school? Rocks still? Miss Franks still sweet on you?"

"School is good. Boring. I got another A on my math test on Monday. Miss Franks likes me, but she keeps giving me extra reading because I finish before everyone else." Lukas shrugged. "She says that's a good thing, but I don't see how it's fair."

"It's better than being bored, right? I'd rather read than sit with my head down and my thumb up anytime."

"I guess." They tromped up the stairs to find Ava and Trey sitting exactly where they were before. On the couch with the TV on.

"Daddy!" Ava hopped up, grabbed her hairbrush off the coffee table and ran to him. "You have to do my ponytail Dad can't. He's broken."

Trey snorted and shook his head.

"I will so do it. I've done real pony's tails, you know." He leaned down and hugged her tight. She smelled good, and her dark hair reminded him of pictures of when he was small. "Have you been good, m'ija?"

"Yes. I'm good. I made a paper butterfly in school today. I can't bring it home because it has to dry."

Lukas hopped up on the couch with his Switch.

"Did you finish your homework?" Trey asked in a parent voice.

Lukas didn't look up. "I don't have any."

"You don't?"

"I did it at school."

Trey nodded. "Okay. Did you put the recycling out yet?"

"Not yet."

"Lukas." That was a warning shot. Chores first, then games.

"In a minute Dad. Geez."

"Boy, get your butt up and take out the damn trash. You know better than to talk back."

"You're—" Lukas started to get his butt in trouble, and West cut that shit off at the pass.

"Your goddamn daddy. I'll throw that machine in the garbage, you take a tone with me. Take. Out. The. Trash." Jesus, his head hurt, and he needed a beer.

Lukas stared at him, tears starting to form.

"No waterworks. No arguing." He forced himself to breathe and keep his voice calm. "The sooner it's done, the sooner we can order Pop-Tarts."

Lukas took off for the garage.

"Pop-Tarts? Really, West?" Trey sighed. Again. Maybe he should start keeping count. "Keep your voice down too, please."

Patience, man. You are here. You got your kids. He can't do a thing about it. "Pop-Tarts. Really. I might buy two kinds."

"Some people never change." Trey got up carefully as

Lukas came back inside. "There's chicken marinating in the fridge and broccoli in the crisper. I'm going to bed." He kissed Ava on the cheek, gave Lukas a hug, then looked right at him, brown eyes flashing. "You're gone by Friday. Lay off the beer."

Trey turned and made a pathetic attempt at storming off, hauling his ass up the stairs.

West chuckled softly. Oh, wasn't that just the cutest thing? He turned to the kids with a grin. "So, Pop-Tarts. Swiss cake rolls. Brisket. And we're so ordering in supper. Pizza? Wings? Tacos?"

4

Jeremy was up early. The only reason he'd slept at all was because he'd taken his pain pills, and they knocked him on his ass. But he was up now, he'd managed a sponge bath and pulled on sweats. His T-shirt was a little more challenging, but he'd figured that out too. Nothing could be as hard as trying to undo the top button of his jeans with his left hand last night.

And he'd had to pee so bad.

There was no way he'd have asked for help. He'd have slept in them before he asked West for anything else.

He helped Ava get dressed—she was only four, but she was good about it. Her leggings were a little crooked but they came home from preschool crooked every day, so he decided to be Zen about it. Brushing her teeth was a little more complicated, but they managed it, both of them giggling.

Lukas poured them each a bowl of cereal, and he got the milk, noting the chicken still sitting untouched right where he'd left it.

Asshole. Friday was pizza night. Now he was going to

have to cook. West had no respect for routines at all. He was going to have to figure something out today. A nanny. Someone to come in Friday night after West left. Maybe sooner.

Yeah, sooner.

"You have about fifteen minutes buddy. Is your lunch packed up?"

"No, Daddy didn't remind me."

"No problem." Yet another routine West never fucking paid attention to. And his ex wondered why he didn't want the kids with him on a weeknight. Jeremy pulled out the lunch boxes and started putting them together. He did Lukas's first because he had to get on the—

Oh, shit.

Mother. Fucker.

Lukas had a bus, but Ava needed a ride to preschool, and he wasn't allowed to drive.

"Damn it."

"Dad!" Lukas gasped.

"Oh, don't pretend like you haven't heard worse from your other dad." Jeremy closed Lukas's lunch box. "I'll...be right back."

God fucking damn it. He was going to have to ask another goddamn favor. And he might have to wake the bastard up to do it.

Why did he never have an air horn when he needed one?

He knocked on the basement door. When there was no response, he knocked louder. Then a lot louder.

He threw the door open, mouth already open to scream, when he saw West in nothing but the tiniest pair of shorts on earth, covered in sweat and doing burpees, headphones in.

Jesus, that was hot.

He watched another second, then made himself back up and close the door. That was not his to look at anymore, and it was trouble he didn't need. He stalked back into the kitchen. "Lukas? Can you go ask Daddy to come up here, please?"

"Okay." Lukas hopped up and ran.

He looked at Ava. "Daddy's going to drive you to school today, baby. Okay? I can't drive yet."

"Okay! Daddy can take me in his truck!" She beamed at him. "We are going to have a sleepover tonight in the basement. It's going to be so much fun."

"It so is!" West was in jeans and a sweatshirt, boots in hand. "Y'all ready for school, my sugarbutts?"

If looks could kill West would be six fucking feet under. "You can grab her car seat from my car."

"Ooh. Thanks, Dad! I don't have to hurry to get one for my truck. Keys?" West smiled at him. "Son, you want a ride too?"

Oh, bullshit. "He'll take the bus."

"Dad..."

"You're taking the bus, Lukas. Get your sneakers on."

"Okay." Lukas pouted but grabbed his lunch and shoved it into his backpack.

Jeremy pulled out his phone. "West, I'm texting you the address for the school. You've got a little time; she doesn't have to be there until eight thirty."

"I know where my kids go to school, Trey." That wasn't light at all. In fact, that was dead serious.

"You remember? Good. Then you won't get lost." He tossed the keys to West for the car seat and helped Lukas on with his jacket. "You ready for a good day, buddy?"

"Yep. A good, boring day."

He laughed and opened the front door. "Get out of here. I love you."

"Love you. You too, Daddy!"

He watched Lukas run down the block and then closed the door.

"...my angel baby girl!" West was singing to Ava, making her laugh like no one else could. No one.

"You are silly, Daddy."

"I am! I am the silliest Daddy of them all." West nuzzled her neck, and Jeremy knew what that stubble felt like.

If he was honest, they were so cute together. Why did West have to be such a turd? West was a good father; Jeremy had never contested that...not before the divorce, never once during. He knew West would walk through fire for their kids, just like he would.

Feeding them a vegetable now and then wouldn't be a bad thing for him to do, but West loved those kids.

"Kiss your father, m'ija. I'll pick you up after school, and we'll plan our evening of fabulousness."

Jesus, he didn't even want to know.

Ava came to him and kissed him happily. "Love you!"

"I love you, baby. Sit straight in your car seat and keep your seatbelt on, okay? Or it's back to the baby seat for you."

"No baby seat!"

"Nope. No baby seat. Because you are not a baby." He gave her another kiss. "Eat your lunch. Have a good day."

"Do I get a kiss too?" West's bright blue eyes were dancing, laughing at him.

With his fist maybe. He raised an eyebrow. "When you get back I'll be working in the den so keep it down."

"So no pole dancing in the front room. Got it." West scooped Ava up. "Next week, we'll have Happy Meals for lunch one day. You and me. Sound good?"

"There is no next week. You're leaving Friday, remember? I'm getting a nanny. Friday the kids go to school and you go home."

"I want a Happy Meal!"

"Friday." Jeremy walked around them. He needed coffee.

"No nannies. You need someone to take care of them, I'm here. I'm not budging. No nanny." There it was again, that dead-serious tone. "Come on, m'ija. Let's ride!"

"Yeehaw!" Ava laughed as West scooped her up.

Yeah, he needed someone to get with the program. The kids needed their routines, especially Lukas. They needed bedtimes and not mid-week basement sleepovers. They needed veggies, not pizza.

West was definitely budging. They were going to have to have a talk. Later. After coffee and some Tylenol.

He'd only just sat down with his first cup when his phone rang. Oh. This should be good.

"Hey, Natalie." His sister was not much of a morning person. "What's up?"

"I have an early meeting. I thought I'd check-in."

She was driving. He could hear the road noise. "Bored in the car?"

"You know it."

"Well, I'm fine except for the broken elbow, two pins, and the full-arm cast." *Boom.*

"Oh." There was a long pause. "Wait. What? You broke your elbow? For real?"

He laughed. "Yes. For real. I was painting the kitchen—damn I need to finish that—anyway, I was painting, and I... fell and landed on it. Yesterday. But that's not even the worst part."

"There's more? Did a lion break into the house and eat Ava?"

"Way scarier. West is here. As in staying here. To help with them. He's driving Ava to school right now. Don't drive off the road." He couldn't believe it himself. "It's a fucking nightmare."

"Jesus. Jesus, Jeremy, the ex? Seriously? You're going to stroke out."

"I had to call someone in a hurry. I can't...it's my right arm, I can't do shit. I couldn't put Ava's hair up. I can't give her a bath. I'm useless." He growled. "I think homicide might be more likely than a stroke." Assuming he could pull that off one-handed.

Natalie snorted, then her merry laughter filled the air. "Oh god. I love this. You're stuck with the hot, crazy ex for how long?"

Hot and crazy just about covered it. And she hadn't seen West doing burpees in his skivvies. "Until I have him arrested?" Hey, that could be fun. "I told him Friday, but he's trying to make plans for next week. I'm hiring a nanny and throwing him out on Friday if I have to beat him with my cast."

"Oh, I would pay to watch that. Seriously, I love the idea of you freaking out because Mr. Fast and Dizzying is there." She was so not helping. "You want me to book a flight out?"

Christ no. She'd be on West's side.

"He's still gay, Nat. Single, I think. But still gay. I got this." Fast and dizzy? More like impulsive and insane. "And I'm not freaking out."

He was totally freaking out.

"I'm just trying to keep some order in this house, and you know how he is. There are Pop-Tarts on my counter." He picked them up and tossed them in the trash. "Were."

"Uh-huh. Because order is important. Lots of order. All the order. Order order."

"Whoa! Whose side are you on?" He looked at the Pop-Tarts for a second, then signed, fished the box out and put it in the recycling. "No, you know what? Don't answer that. I have to go. I'm working from home this week."

"You should take a day off, bro. Sleep. Rest. Breathe and heal."

"Yeah. I should. I'm not going to, though. Talk soon. Love you. Drive safe."

He hung up, so he didn't have to argue that point. He needed to keep busy with West in the house. Sitting around watching TV was an invitation for bad things. Things like conversation. And West loved to talk.

He took another sip of his coffee and then went on a hunt. He threw out another box of Pop-Tarts, some chocolate cakey things, and all the leftover pizza, then hauled the bag one-handed to the can in the garage.

Take that, Mr. Midnight Snacker.

He took his coffee and some cantaloupe to the den. Task number one; hire that nanny.

———

WEST GRABBED a couple of sausage biscuits and a coffee from McD's and headed back to the house. He had no doubt that Jeremy the Uptight Asshole had thrown away his snack foods.

Good thing the real stash was in the basement. This morning's plan: finish painting the kitchen and get the rest of his shit downstairs. Then he could just plant himself on the front porch with a good book and tell every single nanny Trey hired to fuck right off.

He wasn't going to lose a second with his babies.

And if he had to, he'd call in a lawyer.

West's phone rang, and he hooted when he saw the name that popped up.

"Nat! Hey, girl! How's you?"

"Hey, Sundance! I'm fantastic. I just heard you moved back in!" Nat had always liked him. Always, always.

"I did, and that son of a bitch brother isn't moving me back out, Nat. I'm sticking like a burr."

"Now, now. I love that son of a bitch brother of mine, so let's not get nasty. But good for you."

"I love him too. And my kids. I want my family back." He'd answered the things that Trey'd bitched about most: not being around on the weekends, being hurt all the time, always being gone, and leaving Trey to deal with the babies. He'd retired. He'd invested. Now he was going to be so far up Trey's ass the man would never be free of him.

"I know. You've done all the right things." He thought maybe Nat had cried over the divorce more than he had "Have you told him you want him back?"

"He knows." He had to know. West had been perfectly clear, dammit, but he hadn't been ready to give up the rodeo. Not yet.

"Yeah? Well, he's definitely got a nanny on the brain, so maybe knowing isn't enough. He loves to complain about you. I can't believe he'd spend that much time thinking about how much he hates you if he didn't still love you." Nat was a good ally. "You know I'd love to see you guys work it out. And not just for the kids."

"We will, and there ain't gonna be a motherfucking nanny. I'll take him to court again first." No way. He was here. He was their daddy. He'd take care of them.

"That's what I like to hear." Nat laughed. "Good luck. Keep in touch!"

"I will, Sister. Love you, ladybug." He had to smile. Had to.

Hell, he was still smiling when he headed into the house and stripped off his shirt to finish painting.

Nanny. He'd bite Trey first.

It wasn't ten minutes before Trey was shouting. "Do I smell paint? West?" Trey stormed into the kitchen. "What are you doing?"

"Did you hit your head too?" He thought it was pretty fucking obvious what he was doing. He had a paintbrush in one hand, he was painting with it...

"I didn't ask you to paint my kitchen. I don't need any favors from you." Trey put an empty coffee mug down on the counter and took his time filling it carefully with his left hand.

"Nope. Not a one." The temptation to point out that his happy ass had dropped everything to get here last night was fucking huge, but he'd save that one.

Painting the wall, la la la.

He wondered if he could flick paint in Trey's cup from here.

Sigh number twenty-seven, and it was only day two. "Shut up." Trey put the pot back and opened the fridge, took out the milk, wrestled it open and poured some in his coffee. "Don't drip paint on the floor." Trey leaned against the counter and sipped, watching him. Watching. Him.

He kept his expression pleasant. If he'd learned anything in his old age, it was that calm dogs bit, still bulls dropped to the bottom of the chute, and Trey hated him. He knew how to breathe through it and wait it out.

Also, if Trey pissed him off, he'd pour this whole can on the man's head.

"I better get back to work." Trey pushed off the counter,

sounding worn already, and it was only nine thirty. "Looking good though." Trey threw the grudging compliment over his shoulder as he left the room.

"Thanks, baby." He didn't say it loud enough to be heard, but he meant it with his whole heart.

And that was that. The house was quiet for a bit while he painted, and Trey worked. Every so often he'd hear Trey on a call. It was strangely normal. It reminded him of when Ava was just new, and Trey worked from home a lot. She'd nap, and he'd work around the house, Trey would warm up bottles, and he'd feed while Trey took a call, he'd pick up Lukas at preschool—the same one he'd dropped Ava at this morning, thank you very much—and Trey would start dinner. When it worked, it worked.

But when it didn't work? Man. It was ugly.

The doorbell rang just about noon and he could hear Trey on the phone, so he answered it, finding a pretty young lady standing there.

"Hi. Are you Mr. Dunn? We talked on the phone." She smiled sweetly. "I'm here for the interview?"

"I'm sorry, honey. The position was filled. The kids' dad came home to take care of them. Thank you for coming by, though." No. Fucking. Way.

"W...what?" She blinked at him, looking shocked. "We just got off the phone an hour ago."

"I know. I just showed up. He wasn't sure I was going to make it." West put on the drawl and the best harmless yokel expression he had. "He fell, you know? Broke his elbow climbing a ladder. Between you and me, I think he might have hit his head a little. As soon as I heard, I got on my pony and rode. Thank you for still stopping by, though. If I hadn't busted my butt to make it, he'd have needed a hand."

"Oh—uh." She shrugged, smiling slightly. "Well. That's

disappointing, but I understand. Glad you made it." She backed away a couple of steps. "Hope he...feels better soon. Bye." She looked over her shoulder at least twice on the way to her car.

"West? Where'd you go? I'm expecting a—"

Trey caught him closing the front door. *Whoops.*

"Was someone...who was at the door?"

"A little girl that was lost." He stared Trey down. *Come on, buddy. Try me.*

"A—" Trey strode past him and opened the door. "Was that...hey!" Trey waved at the car already backing out, then watched it drive away. "Was that my nanny?" The door slammed closed. "Did you just send away my fucking nanny?"

"Well, baby. I wasn't aware you needed one. You need someone to wipe your ass for you?" Oh wait. He was going for chill. Easy, not evil.

One of Trey's eyebrows shot up so fast it was a wonder he didn't sprain something. "I need someone to help me with the kids after I throw your ass out on Friday. Possibly sooner. You had no right to do that."

"No." He wasn't having some stranger do this when he was here. Trey could fight him.

Trey squinted. "No? Jesus Christ, West. You don't get to say no. This isn't your fucking house, or your fucking visitation time."

The madder Trey got, the easier it was for West to slide into the pocket. Dogs. Bulls. Trey. He knew this, and when he spoke, he was calm as a summer day.

"We can be decent about this or nasty, but I won't have a stranger taking care of my kids. I'm staying." And if he had to buy the house next door and split custody down to the millisecond, he would.

Trey took his time answering, rubbing his forehead and walking toward the living room. "Decent. I called you, didn't I? I called you because, yeah, you're their father. You should be the first person I call for help. But I didn't invite you to waltz in here like a king and take over with pizza and Pop-Tarts and undermine—" Trey took a deep breath and puffed it out, then sat heavily on the couch, bringing it down about six notches. "I don't know what I was expecting. It's not like you're not still *you*. Although it's ironic that back when I wanted you to stay you wouldn't, and now that I want you to leave you won't."

No, he had needed to work. He had needed to ride while he could. He had needed to save his pennies and invest and be in a place where he could hold his own. He was still him, and he hadn't changed. Trey had, but West was here and, irony or not, he had just needed a reason. One reason to come home.

This was it.

He stood there, willing his boots to sink into the floor so deep that no force on earth could move him.

"West. The kids have a few rules on school nights. A snack and homework right after school, a decent dinner at the table, bed for Ava at seven thirty and at eight for Lukas. Baths and stories before bed. That's it. Weekends after homework, all bets are off." Trey leaned back in the couch. "Can we just agree on that at least?"

"No problem. I'm going to finish the kitchen." West forced himself to just walk off like it was the most casual thing ever.

In his head, West was roaring with pain. He'd never encouraged Lukas to slack off. In fact, he was the one that brought books. Every other week, he brought books and books. He'd never once treated those kids badly. He'd never told them to be bad, he didn't smoke in front of them, he didn't drink in front of them. He was a good man, and he was a good daddy.

But Trey didn't see that. He saw rodeo trash.

Hank would be telling him that he was a newborn fool right now. Probably was flipping Trey off in Heaven. He wondered if Trey even knew Hank had lost his battle. Hell, he wasn't sure if Trey even remembered who the old bullfighter was.

West climbed the ladder and got back to work.

He'd have thought that would be the end of it, but no, Trey stuck his head in the kitchen a few minutes later.

"Um. So, Ava needs to be picked up at three unless you want to leave her in aftercare. You're authorized to sign her out. You and Drew. And I know you promised them a sleepover tonight so...a promise is a promise even on a school night. You guys have fun."

Trey's sigh was different this time. Heavy. He stared at the floor for a second, then he nodded like he'd decided something and left.

He took a shaky breath. *Okay, God. I'm here. I'm going to do this. Lay Your hands on me. I need it. Amen.*

Round one to the cowboy.

5

Friday came, it was dreary day, and there was still a cowboy in his basement. Jeremy was pretty sure that was a country song.

He and West had worked to keep the peace since they'd had it out on Monday, and the rest of the week was fairly uneventful. Of course, keeping the peace meant they'd both managed to talk to the kids, but hadn't said more than a handful of words to each other.

And this morning, the words that he'd wanted to say, that he should have said for his own sanity, stuck in his throat, and he never said them. He couldn't, and he didn't want to examine the reasons why.

So, yeah. West was still in his basement, and until Jeremy could put Ava's hair in a ponytail himself, it looked like things were going to stay that way.

But it was awkward as hell.

He'd thought about packing up all of West's shit while he was driving Ava to school and locking him out, but that seemed...psychotic.

Sure would have been satisfying though.

Instead, he poured himself a cup of coffee and tried to find patience for the all bets are off weekend ahead. West could literally come up with anything.

West came in, a toolbox in hand and headed down to the garage without even looking at him. Well hell, what was broken out there?

Don't follow him. Don't. You'll just end up fighting about something. Jeremy didn't want to fight. It was the reason he'd been so damn quiet all week. He was afraid to open his mouth and start something he didn't have the energy to finish. But the devil on his shoulder had already won. He grabbed a bottle of water from the fridge and followed West to the garage.

In the week West had been here, the garage had been completely reorganized, and there was a little pink bike with training wheels on the workbench, along with a dozen of his half-finished projects done.

"You've been busy." He set the water bottle down for West, partly his excuse for being there, and partly...well, maybe an olive branch.

"Yessir. You need some help?" Those pretty blue eyes dragged along him like they were touching him.

"No. The arm feels a lot better actually. I haven't taken anything for it today. I just... Okay, I'm just nosey and wanted to find out what you were up to out here." He rolled his eyes. Nothing like a little honesty to make him look like an idiot.

"Working. I'll get to working on the shutters next, but it's a little wet for that now."

This piece of West he remembered. Always in the middle of a project, always three more to do. He never needed to make a honey-do list because West had it done before he could think to ask. "Cool. Thanks. I'll get out of your way. It looks great out here. The bike is cute."

"She wants to ride so bad. She's so jealous of her big brother."

He nodded. "Yeah. It's been on my list. I just haven't had time yet. She's funny right? I caught her trying to get on his bike once."

"She's a cowboy. I bet she figures this thing out in a few days. I'll take her skiing this winter."

She'd love that. He knew she would. Lukas was hot and cold on winter sports, but Ava? She'd try anything.

"So when are you riding again? Not this weekend I guess."

"I'm not, no. I'll stay in the basement over the weekend. The kids know to get me for anything that needs doing. They're excited about hanging with you and taking care of you."

Well...shit.

"You don't have to hide in the basement, that's...I mean, thank you, but that's...not right." He really didn't want to have this conversation. He just didn't want to be an asshole. "It's pizza night. You still like olives?"

"I do." West watched him—it wasn't ugly, it wasn't aggressive, but it was maddening because Jeremy liked it.

"Good. Okay." He should have told West not to look at him like that, but he didn't. "See you later, then."

"I'll be here, baby."

Oh.

"West." Oh, no. He shook his head. He wasn't ready for that at all. The sudden ache in his chest stole his breath and it was so intense he rubbed at it like that might fix it. What made it worse was he didn't know what it meant; hurt, angry, happy, terrified...maybe all of it.

It was time to go. He wasn't going to try to figure it out standing *here*. He turned around and headed back into the house.

He heard soft whistling, the sound so fucking familiar and right, and then the sound was lost, buried in a deluge as the skies opened, drenching him in a second.

West appeared at his good elbow, moving him fast. "Come on, baby."

He let West hustle him inside while he focused on keeping his cast dry, but once they got in out of the weather, he put space between them fast. Several feet of space. He told himself he was breathless from the mad dash up the driveway, but he was a runner, and he couldn't even make himself believe it.

"Thanks. I...didn't see that coming." That was a fucking understatement. He took another step back. "I better get a towel."

"I'll grab you one. Hold on." Jesus, the wet and running cowboy was a glorious sight.

"They're in the—" *He knows where they are. He lived here. Lives here?*

Didn't he have a conference call or something? He'd been meaning to clean out his desk forever. Dust the bookshelves...something. Idle hands and all that. Right now, his idle hands were twitching for some cowboy.

"Here you go." One towel wrapped around his cast, another was draped over his shoulders, then West started unbuttoning his shirt.

"I can do that." But he didn't stop West, he just watched his ex-husband's face, admiring the little bit of stubble there.

West stripped him off and dried him, then knelt down, encouraging him to take off his shoes.

He snorted softly. "It's just water, honey. I'm not going to melt."

"Probably not, but we shouldn't take the chance." West's grin was wicked, that face right where Jeremy wanted it.

"What are you up to, cowboy?" As if he didn't know. As if he didn't remember that look or West's wandering hands.

"I was taking off your wet clothes so you can dry off baby." West opened his fly. "You're still the prettiest son of a bitch ever."

"Whoa." The burn in his gut and the sudden ache in his balls woke him up, everything snapping into sharp focus. He reached down and jerked his fly back up. When he stepped back, he tripped over his shoes but managed not to fall. So fucking graceful. "No. Nope. Bad Cowboy."

"Be careful now." Christ, West moved fast. "You're fixin to lose your towel."

He snorted. "Yeah, you'd like that."

West laughed, husky like he remembered from years ago. "I'm not *dead*, baby."

No, that was for sure. West was very much alive, and way, way too close. He reached forward, spreading his fingers out over West's chest, working them into the fabric. He was being pulled in so many directions he didn't know what he wanted. "You're wet too."

"Am I?" Like West didn't know.

"Yeah." This wasn't right. It felt good, but it couldn't be right. He swallowed and gave West a little push. "You better go change."

"Yeah, I better." West put Jeremy's shirt in the washer and grabbed a Dr Pepper from the fridge, leaving him just standing there.

"Shit." He'd planned to kick West out on his ear today.

and instead he'd let West stay and let...*that* happen. Did West think he was that easy?

Was he that easy?

Maybe. But he knew what he was headed for if they went there. He'd loved West like no one before or since. It had been deep and real. And no matter what his dick wanted, his heart couldn't take losing that all over again.

He kicked his shoes out of the middle of the room and went to get changed.

6

West stayed in the basement or outside all weekend, helping Lukas with his homework or Ava with her bike. He installed a real fridge in the basement and a little cooktop, replaced the TV, and re-caulked the entire bathroom. He'd ordered him one of them purple mattresses and the lumber to build a little storage closet.

"Daddy, can I play Barbies down here with you? Dad is napping, and Lukas doesn't want me."

"Sure, baby girl." It was hard to be the four-year-old who was still wild while her brother was fastidious as all get out. Genes were a thing, he guessed. "Come on down. I would love to play."

She came barreling down, leaping for him, and he caught her, swinging her around. God, she was perfect. Both his babies were.

He had a soft spot for Ava though, because she was his. Lukas had all Trey's red hair and responsibility, and Ava had his eyes and his cowboy genes.

"Barbie is mad today. She wants to ride her bike some more but it's raining again."

"I know! What's up with that? I think it's fixin' to start snowing in a few days. Maybe next weekend we'll take a drive up to Estes before they close the roads next month." It would be a good day outing, and Trey wouldn't lock him out if he took the kids with him.

"Snow! I like snow. Dad likes snow. He's a good skier. But he said you were going to teach me!"

"Yep! This winter. We'll have the best time. We'll make snowmen and drink hot chocolate together. Then next spring? We'll start going out and riding together."

He had a buddy that was marrying a gal out on Arapahoe. She had a big old horse property, and she was happy to board three horses in exchange for ownership of four fine cutters. Josh was picking them and the rest of his shit up in six weeks.

Not a bad timeline, all in all.

Ava plopped herself in the middle of his bed. "This is a big bed. Dad has a big bed. How come two daddies don't share a room like a mommy and a daddy? Elise's mommy and daddy have one big bed in their room."

Because your father made an ultimatum, and I respond poorly to threats. "Because Elise's folks are together, and me and your da aren't. We're divorced."

She looked at him confused. "But you live here now so why are you still diborced?"

Oh, that one was easy. "Because grown-ups are stupid, baby. Never grow up. Stay little forever."

"I can't do that silly Daddy. Dad's not stupid. He's good at math, and he can read! Even better than Lukas!" Her eyes were wide. "Really."

"Yeah. Yeah, baby girl. He is. Me? Not so much." He chuckled and grabbed a Barbie doll. Some things weren't for children, and why two men that had been so hard in love weren't anymore was one of those. "What's this one's name, m'ija?"

"Today she's Linda."

"Her name changes?"

"Well, yeah. Yesterday she was Gina, but Gina had to go work. She'll be back in two weeks."

"Ah." Made sense. "Did you know *linda* means pretty in Spanish?"

That had been his mama's name. Mama'd never met the kids, which was a shame. She would have loved them.

"It does?" Ava was very pleased about that. "Teach me more Spanish words. What's...cat?"

"*Por supuesto.* Cat is *gato*, and dog is *perro*." He tickled her, making her giggle. "*Y tu, m'ija, eres una niña.*"

"M'ija wants a gato! Ah!" She wriggled and twisted. "Can I have a gato, Daddy? A little gray one."

"You have to get your da to say yes." That was all their problems, wasn't it? "But if he does, then we'll talk about it."

"Okay! Let's go see if he's awake!" She stood up on the bed and tugged on him.

"No, ma'am. No one likes to be woke up from their nap, and Da's still hurtin' some. You come on and play with your babies, and we'll watch some TV before I go upstairs and make y'all hamburgers." The last thing he needed was Trey pissy because he got woke up.

Ava looked at him, and he could see the wheels turning as she weighed whether this would be worth getting into it with him or not. Whether this would be a fight she could win. It was all there in her little frown. Then the little cloud lifted, and she plopped right back down on the bed. "Okay, Daddy."

"Thanks, baby girl. Love you." He kissed the top of her

head and turned on Disney Junior. "You want a juice box? I got some down here for you."

"Yes, please. Is it apple?" She focused right in on the TV, as always.

There was a solid thud over their heads. "Fuck! Dammit!"

Ava's eyes went wide. "Uh-oh. Is Dad hurt again?"

"You hang here, missus." He sprinted up the stairs, double time. "You okay?"

"Stop! Hang on. I dropped a Coke. It went everywhere." Trey sighed. He didn't know what number sigh that was; he'd lost count. "Can you get the mop? I'll—get the fridge."

"You sit. I'll clean and grab you a drink. Lukas, come help your father get sat down!"

"I'm reading!"

"I'm fine! I was just trying to open the fucking thing. I don't need to sit." Trey reached for the paper towels but ended up with a long string of them trying to get one off the roll. "Fuck!"

"Dad!" Lukas stared at Trey, wide-eyed.

"Chill, buddy. You've heard the word before. Go on back to your reading. Burgers for supper tonight."

"On the grill?"

"Yeah, I got that little overhang fixed so I can grill in this rain." West started wiping up the mess. This first, then the fridge, then the mop. Christ, it went everywhere.

"Sorry, Lukas. Now, listen to your father, and go finish your reading."

"Okay."

Trey watched Lukas go. "I'm a disaster. You fixed the awning?"

"Yep."

Trey wasn't the most...handy son of a bitch ever, and he

worked while the babies were at school, so West fixed things.

"Thank you. That's been busted for... I don't even know. It wasn't a high priority because I rarely grill." Trey was scrubbing the counters and cabinets. "The kids love it when you do it, though. Lukas talks about your chicken all the time."

"We grill out a lot together." Because they spent a lot of weekends in motels and campgrounds, they had to. It was fun, though, camping and running around and laughing.

"I forgot how handy you are to have around." Trey stopped scrubbing a second and looked at him. "Do you...do you think you could have a look at that banister on the back steps?"

"Sure, baby. It's supposed to stop raining tomorrow. I'll fix it." No big deal. Zero. Just sure, even though his heart was going a million miles a minute in pure joy.

He poured Trey's Coke and got the mop.

"Thanks. Did you find the leftover pizza? I ordered one with half olives and nobody eats them but you so...it's in there. Breakfast of champions, right?"

He chuckled and nodded, even though he didn't eat a lot of pizza since he'd found out he had an ulcer. Trey didn't know that, though, so he'd eat some for lunch tomorrow. "Thanks. I'll make burgers tonight. You want tater tots?"

"Oh, man. I haven't had tater tots in forever." Trey sat to drink his Coke, looking a little stiff. "You want me to make a cucumber salad?"

"Sure. Sure, I was thinking I'd start the burgers at five." He cleaned the floor before he went to rub Trey's shoulders. He couldn't fucking stand there knowing the son of a bitch was hurting.

"Oh. Hey, you don't have to..." Trey groaned, relaxing,

the sound so familiar. "Oh, wow. That's...that feels great, honey. I've got a spot right by your thumb."

"Here?" He found the spot and dug in, forcing it to let go. Oh, that would feel better.

He got another groan, and Trey's head rolled forward. "Fuck, yeah. So much better. I didn't realize how tight that was. Is this going to feel like this the whole time? Or does it get better?"

"You need a couple of rub downs, but it'll help, I swear." He kept rubbing, then blinked. "I left Ava downstairs. I'll be right back."

He bolted downstairs, finding her sound asleep on his bed, thumb in her mouth.

Trey appeared at the top of the basement stairs. "All good?"

"Yeah. Yeah. She's fine. Sleeping. Should I wake her?" He looked up a Trey, forgetting for a second that he was supposed to be friendly, not loving.

"No, no." Trey came down a few steps, talking softly. "She plays hard. She never has trouble sleeping at night. She gave up napping a while ago because her brother doesn't. You know how she is."

"I do." He covered her and dimmed the lights a little, forgetting for a second that Trey hadn't seen what all work he'd done down here.

"You fixed the lights." Trey came farther down and looked around. "Jesus, West. Is that a new bed? When did you bring that in? And you turned the little bar into...almost a kitchen? You've really moved in."

Yeah. Yeah, he really had. He wasn't leaving either. "I won't bother you. You don't come down here."

Trey glanced over at him, brown eyes even darker than usual. "I'm in your space. Sorry." Trey turned and started up the stairs. "If I thought you were a bother, you wouldn't still be in my basement."

"I just want my goddamn family back," he whispered. He'd given everything up for this shot. He hadn't expected to do it this week, but he'd been on route to Boulder for next weekend.

Trey turned around to look at him. "I don't know what that means. But it sounds tough to do if you're hiding in the basement." Trey started up again. "I'm going to put that salad together."

Okay. Okay, that was good, right? That felt better than "I hate you, get out."

"Sounds like a plan. You want help peeling the cukes?"

That shit was hard one-handed.

7

West was right about the weather. Jeremy could almost smell snow coming. West had always been smart about things like that, maybe because where West came from weather mattered in a way that it didn't when you grew up in the suburbs.

But while the air outside was getting colder, inside the last few days had been surprisingly warm. West seemed to take to the weekday schedule, and the kids settled down. Mornings were good, but bedtimes were better. Jeremy was pretty pleased with the routine.

Tonight had been his turn to tuck in Ava, and West had Lukas. He didn't know what they'd read but it made them both laugh, and Jeremy had loved listening to it. How could he not?

West had gone straight downstairs as usual after tucking Lukas in, and he'd missed his opportunity to ask West to open a bottle of wine for him. He had been off the painkillers for days, and he really wanted a glass.

He looked at the wine bottle and then at the opener and convinced himself pretty quickly there was no way he was going to be able to do it himself. The last thing he needed was another emergency room visit. He could knock, right? Just ask a favor?

Sure. It was just a favor, and it wasn't late. He picked up the bottle and the opener and started to go, but before he'd taken two steps he turned around, set the bottle down, grabbed two Solo cups out of the cabinet and hung them over the neck of the bottle. Why the hell not?

He got to the basement door and knocked on it with the bottom of the wine bottle.

"Hold up. I'm nekkid."

Oh. Oh, that was a temptation and a half.

"No worries." And honestly? West could take that however he wanted.

West opened the door, wearing nothing but his itty-bitty workout shorts. "Hey, baby. Sorry, I was fixin' to jump in the shower. You okay?"

"Yeah. Sorry to interrupt, I just... I wanted a glass of wine, but I can't open the bottle." He shrugged and lifted the bottle in his hand, ignoring the little voice telling him to chicken out. "I was going to knock and ask, and then I thought maybe you might like to join me. But if you're getting in the shower then—" It was cool. He'd been drinking wine alone for a couple of years.

"Sure. I haven't had a glass of wine since...a long time. Hold on." West went downstairs and stripped off like it was nothing, letting him see that taut, firm body before West pulled on a pair of sweatpants.

He had a feeling this might have been a very bad good idea. He followed West down the stairs. "I would have brought wineglasses, but I couldn't carry them, so we have super fancy red Solo cups." It wasn't until he'd hit the bottom of the stairs and West was blinking at him that he realized that West had probably intended to come back *up*.

"Good deal. Come sit. Welcome to the basement." West winked at him. "I retiled the bathroom."

"And you built a closet."

"Yeah."

"And cleaned off the pool table." He held out the bottle so West could open it and then went to check out the bathroom. It was tiny, but it did have a stall shower. "Damn, honey. You do good work."

"Thank you. You like it? I thought Lukas would love this when he was a teenager. Not having to share a bathroom with his sister." West handed him his wine.

"Thanks. I like how you think." Even the assumption that if Lukas were down here, that would mean West would...not be.

He sipped his wine, loving the dry, bitter flavor. "You spoil the kids." He didn't mean that in a bad way, but having a room with your own bathroom, TV and a pool table as a teenager was a pretty sweet deal.

"Yeah, I know. I can't help it." West shrugged, cheeks heating. "It'll be a great room for him in ten years."

"You're a tough act to follow, sometimes." He took a seat on the roll-out couch, which West wasn't using as a bed, propped his cast on a pillow, and put his feet up on the trunk they used as a coffee table.

West didn't answer him, just shook his head a bit and perched on the pool table, wine in hand. "I'm glad you like it."

Okay. So they weren't going to talk about that, then. They could talk about West. "So, what were you doing before I called you? You said something about a signing?"

"Yeah, at a western wear store. I was working my way across to here from San Diego."

"Sponsor?" That seemed like how it worked most of the time. Boots or something.

"In a manner of speaking, I guess." West shrugged and shot him a grin. "I own a chunk of 'em."

What the hell? "A chunk? Of what?"

"The western wear chain. The stores."

"You own a retail chain? A real one? *You?*" He stared at West. It wasn't that West wasn't smart enough or resourceful enough, it was just hard to believe that he was involved in anything that...permanent. And it was frankly hard to believe that West had that much money.

"A part of it, yes. I own thirty-five percent." One of West's eyebrows went up. "Contain your excitement."

West was so defensive. He wanted to talk, but he didn't want to fight. "Sorry, I'm just surprised, honestly. Congratulations."

"Thanks. Thanks, I—I wanted to...I mean, investments are good, right?"

He cocked his head, interested in this development. In as long as he'd known West, Jeremy never heard the word "investment" come out of West's mouth. "Really good, yeah. Stable income is good for you, and good for the kids. It's great."

"That's what I figured." West sighed, and the sound went right to his soul. "I wanted something that I understood. A couple of investments that will keep things going."

He nodded. "I think it's a good move. From what I remember, bull riders have uncertain futures."

Speaking of riding, when was West heading back out? It was October. There would be a smattering of events before the finals, right?

"How's your year going? You seem healthy." He'd seen West in peak health, in the hospital, and everywhere in between.

West stared at him, and for a second there was something that looked like betrayal, like agony, but it disappeared. "I'm fine as frog hair, baby. Looking forward to Halloween."

"God, with all of this going on, I'd almost forgotten that was coming up. It's a weekend this year...a Friday. Are you going to be around?"

"I told you, I'm not going anywhere. Ava wants to be Elsa. Lukas wants to be Harry Potter. I'm going to be a yeti."

"Harry Potter? Last we talked it was Captain America. Next week it will be Darth Vader." He grinned. "You will be a very good yeti, I am sure." Since the divorce, he usually took the kids around early, and then spent the rest of the evening handing out candy in a Mickey Mouse wizard's hat. He'd never dressed up himself, he just...didn't love it. "I'm glad you're dressing up. The kids would probably rather go around with you anyway."

"You like looking at the kiddos and their costumes. I love taking them around. They...they're growing up damn fast." West swirled the wine around in his cup like the secrets of the world were written there.

"Really fast." Jeremy didn't need the secrets of the world; he just needed some answers. This cowboy looked like West, talked like West, had West's swagger...but something was off. There was something he didn't recognize. And every time he started to poke at it, West deflected it handily.

He patted the couch next to him. "Why don't you come sit?"

"I'd love to." West sat with him, moving nice and easy. So he wasn't broken, right? Not dying...

Jeremy sat up, took a big sip of his wine, then set it down. He was going to need that hand. He reached out before he lost his nerve and curled his fingers into West's.

West held on, that calloused hand wrapping around his.

He just sat there for a bit, letting himself get used to how that felt. West's grip was confident, like West always was, but careful too, and that was new. He caught West's gaze, holding his wild cowboy there a minute. "So, talk. What am I missing here? I called you, you showed up, and you've... stayed. I'm starting to like having you around again, I know the kids love it. What's up?"

"I told you, I'm staying. I want my family back." West wasn't any better at talking about things, and Jeremy knew West—the son of a bitch wasn't stupid. He thought about things, felt things so deeply, but Jeremy had to mine for every nugget.

Jeremy believed that; he'd seen it. West had been making a real effort. Routines were never West's strong point, but he'd been working at it. He'd done things around the house like it was his...his *again*. He'd certainly moved in like he meant it, even without Jeremy's blessing.

Getting his family back would mean West would have to fix what he couldn't fix before. And that meant...

Damn.

"West...are you riding? At all?"

West chuckled softly, the sound strangely harsh, squeezed his fingers. "No, not since we lost Hank. I took a bit to be with him and announced my retirement six weeks ago."

Hank. Oh, fuck.

"I'm so sorry, honey. I didn't know about...fuck, I'm sorry."

He'd checked out of bull riding when West had left. He

just couldn't watch, and it hurt too much to even follow online. After a while, it got easier. It wasn't that he didn't care; it was more that he didn't want to know.

And he had a bad feeling Hank's death was everything about the reason why.

"What happened?"

"Cancer. He took a hit that knocked him out, and in the hospital they found he was riddled with it. He didn't make it but three and a half weeks." West sounded so matter of fact, but Hank had been West's mentor, his father figure, and his friend since West was a teenager.

He squeezed West's hand. "It must have been awful. I just... I know what he meant to you. I can't imagine—" *I can't imagine how much it hurt.* West had never talked with him on that level. Jeremy always understood when West was hurting, but West wasn't good with words that way. West could say everything he needed to with...with a hug or a kiss or...in bed.

"Yeah." West took another drink of his wine. "I haven't told the kids yet. They haven't asked after any of the guys, so I figure they aren't real to them here so much."

Well that was obvious enough. There hadn't been one second of rodeo on since West showed up. "It hadn't been... I...stopped watching a long time ago. Obviously, or I would have known about Hank and...about you otherwise."

"It ain't nothing, baby. It wasn't like you were a fan." West stroked his fingers, drawing shapes, and he remembered that, how he used to know what West was telling him. "The kids spent a lot of weekends with Hank and some of the guys. We got a condo in Estes—me and Hank."

"I remember Hank fondly, you know. I was a fan once. I

hope it was a good service." He didn't know why that mattered but it was true.

"It was real simple. He didn't want much. I dealt with all the shit before he went. Then I started working my way home."

"And then I called. Funny how things work out that way." And here they were. He let go of West's hand, just long enough to get another sip of wine and then took it right back. "Do you think we can do this without hurting each other all over again?" He wasn't worried about the chemistry; what had happened—almost happened—between them was proof enough they still had that.

"I have no idea." West never lied to him, even when Jeremy needed him to. "I want to come home. I'll stay down here if that's what we need, but I want to be here with y'all."

"Y'all" included him; he heard that. He felt it too, in the slightly tighter grip West had on his fingers. "You've been great around here. I appreciate everything you've done. And you've been great with the kids too." He tried not to say, "but what about me". West had made a move; he was the one who turned it down.

"Thank you." West lifted his hand, kissed it. "I won't make things tough. You got my word."

"Okay." This one-handed thing was for the birds. He let go of West's hand and combed his fingers through West's thick, dark hair. "Can you make it easy, though?"

"I'm still a cowboy, baby." That was a non-answer answer, but the kiss wasn't. The kiss nearly killed him, the touch of West's lips enough to make him shake.

It felt like yesterday; like it hadn't been years since they shared this. His heart starting thumping against his ribs and he flushed like a teenager in love.

He remembered the little touch of his tongue he used to

keep West interested. He slid his hand to West's nape and held on, opening and letting West explore.

West's groan filled his lips, the sound pure hunger. It would take nothing—nothing at all to just give himself over to their need.

He'd known what he was doing when he knocked on that door tonight. He'd known they could end up like this. He didn't know it would be this intense.

He decided not to fight it.

"Yes." Just in case there was any question. Just in case West wasn't sure.

"Oh fuck..." West blinked at him, then surged up, the kiss going from heated to fierce, West fucking his lips like there was no tomorrow.

He wanted it now. Jeremy wanted that piece of himself, that piece that belonged to West to come alive again. He moaned as he began to tingle and ache. He leaned back into the deep couch and tucked his cast tight against him, keeping it out of the way.

West put their cups on the table, then moved to stretch out on top of him. "You're still the hottest bastard on earth."

Then that hand cupped his cock, reminding him that West Belen knew him inside out.

He gasped, pressing up into West's touch. The weight was just right. "Fuck."

"Mmm...Want to love you until you can't think. Until you can't—"

The doorbell rang.

"Was that...?" He took a breath and tried to focus. Who the hell stopped by after eight on a weeknight without— "Oh, shit. That's Drew."

"Okay. You want me to answer it?"

He grinned. "I'll get it. I'll tell him to come by tomorrow."

He pushed West up as the doorbell rang again. "I'm sorry. Don't...just hold that thought. I'll be back."

"Be careful with your elbow, baby." West chuckled softly, shook his head. "Go on before he lets himself in."

He hurried up the stairs, straightened his sweats, and finger combed his hair, then went for the door.

Yep, it was Drew. "Hey, newlywed!"

"Hey, honey! I wanted to check-in on you. I brought you rum cake and rum balls and some rum. Brought the kiddos some goodies too."

Oh. Presents. "That's a lot of rum." Well, he couldn't just run Drew off; that would be rude. "Come on in, but just for a minute. Okay?"

"Sure. Sure, Nick's unpacking, so I thought I'd check up on you, make sure you were okay." Drew headed for the kitchen and started putting things away. "I'm picking us up burgers on the way home. So? How are you feeling?"

He pointed to his cast. "It doesn't hurt as much anymore, just kind of aches. I'm getting the pins out in about ten days, hopefully." Then it would be another cast for a couple of weeks. It was never ending. "How was your trip?"

"Lots of wonderful sun, sand, and sex. The perfect honeymoon. Who ended up watching the kids? Did your folks come?"

"No. I ended up calling West." *And you're interrupting...* He went for a smile and a shrug.

"Oh, man." Drew's eyes went wide. "Oh, honey. I'm sorry. Was he decent to you, at least?"

"He's been great. He's been staying in the basement." *Awkward.* "He's...here now. In the basement."

"In...like staying-staying? Like moved in staying?"

He nodded slowly. "He retired. It's kind of a long story. Can we have coffee this week?"

"We need an entire brunch, Jeremy. With cantaloupe."

He laughed. "I missed you. I'm glad you're back. It's been something. Good though. Good. Promise." Better than good at the moment. "Thank you for the presents. I'll make sure the kids call you tomorrow."

"You call me. You." Drew came to him, kissed his cheek. "Be careful, honey. You know how he is."

"I thought I did." He gave Drew a hug and a grin. "And now I have rum if I need it!"

"You do." Drew kissed his forehead. "Talk to you tomorrow."

"Night, you." Jeremy walked Drew out and closed the door with a sigh. Okay, that didn't go too badly. Drew seemed more like he was ready for gossip than worried. Back to the basement.

Unless maybe West wanted to come upstairs.

It was a school night, dammit. He was going to pay for this tomorrow.

West came up with the cups and the bottle of wine. "I heard him go. Thought you might want this."

He smiled, feeling a little flirty. "Me? Who needs it more right now, me or you?" They'd gotten wound up twice, now.

"Are you suggesting I might need something to kill the ache in my balls, baby?"

Listen to that. West's voice was rough and dry, so hot it commanded his attention. "Drew brought rum if you need something stronger. He says I should be careful. Should I be careful?" Jeremy was teasing and stepped in close enough to West that he'd know it.

"Probably. I'm a big, mean bastard." West's hands landed on his waist, sure and heavy.

Big. His rodeo cowboy. Right.

"So mean." He pressed his prick against his West's thigh

and leaned in for another kiss, having very little trouble picking up where they left off.

"Fucking evil." West licked his lips, teasing him. He wanted West to kiss him like before.

West could play, but he knew how to fix his cowboy's little red wagon. "Don't tease, honey. I *need* you."

"You want me to go up or do you want to come down? I want somewhere with a locking door." Good cowboy.

"Up." He tangled his fingers with West's and tugged gently. "The lock you put in is still there."

"It's sturdy. Meant to last forever." West eased him up the stairs.

They'd rarely used a word like forever because they'd focused on tomorrow when West was riding. Bull riders didn't ride forever. They couldn't even be sure they'd be riding next week.

"Forever, huh?" He loved West's possessive touch and the way West crowded against him when they reached the upstairs landing.

"Yeah. Kiss me." West palmed his cock, rubbing him hard.

A needy sound escaped him and was cut short by their kiss. He couldn't stay still and rocked into the touch. He found his balance so he could reach between them and return the favor, fingers molding around the impressive bulge in West's sweats. It fit right into his hand, just like he remembered.

West humped against him, and it was a lit match to gasoline. No one had ever loved him like West; no one else ever would. And West knew it.

"Honey...bedroom." Kids. They had kids. They had a forever lock and they needed to use it because he wanted

West out of his sweats. He was dying to get his hands on his cowboy.

"Uh-huh." West nodded, their foreheads together as their gazes locked. "I still love you. I still need you. You have to know that."

Love hadn't been their problem.

He stayed steady, made sure West heard him. "I love you. We need you. I want you to stay."

West kissed him, softly this time. "Come on, baby. Let me make you feel good."

Jeremy felt good; he wanted to burn the way only West could make him burn. He wanted to scorch the last few years away. He led West into the bedroom, which he'd changed completely since the last time West was in it. He hadn't been able to sleep in their bed. He'd stored it in the attic with the second dresser and the old rug and started over.

West glanced around, then locked the door and started helping him strip down, hands hot where they eased his clothes away.

"You... I want to see you." He shoved a hand into West's sweats, fingers finding what he needed easily. "I want to feel you."

"C-careful of your arm!" West bucked, the motion gratifying as fuck.

"This is the good one, honey. I only need one hand for this." He gave West a squeeze, putting pressure on the head as he circled it.

West bared his teeth, head thrown back as he drove toward Jeremy's touch. Jeremy had forgotten how goddamn sexual his cowboy made him feel. He'd always felt powerful rather than vulnerable when he was naked with West, and

West had always been beautiful to him, scars and all. He could watch his cowboy's face enjoy this for days.

His cast was inconvenient, but he could be careful. It was more that he was better at this with his right hand. Still, West didn't seem to notice. He let go long enough to push at West's shirt—he wasn't going to be any help getting West naked. "Off, huh?"

"Uh-huh." West stepped back and stripped off, standing there, hard and proud. West was leaner than he'd ever been, sculpted and tanned, that fuzzy belly rippled over the fat, heavy prick.

He may have licked his lips.

"Jesus, honey. You're still fucking stunning." He drew his hand from West's shoulder, across tight pecs, and down over muscled abs.

West hummed softly, stretching up tall. "Fuck, that's good. I missed you."

He explored, hungry fingers finding scars he remembered and ones he didn't, some fading, some seeming very new. "I want to be patient, but..." Jeremy wanted to relearn all of it, but he was aching.

"You don't have to be. Stretch out on the bed. You want my hand, my mouth, or my ass?" Oh, West didn't offer that often.

He felt his eyebrow shoot up, interested. "Are you kidding?" Maybe West would ride even.

"Did I laugh?" West met his eyes, bold as brass.

He took a hard kiss and then stared right back, never afraid to go toe-to-toe with his cowboy. "Come ride."

"You got stuff in here?" West helped him settle down on the bed.

He nodded and pointed to the nightstand, watching

West move, graceful as a cat. "Ever hopeful." He'd be surprised if the box of rubbers was even open yet.

"New box?" West asked, the expression on the tan face a little vulnerable.

"Old box. Just...untouched." He'd tried to date, but he'd been celibate as a fucking monk since the divorce.

"Me too."

There was no way his surrounded-by-lonely-cowboys ex hadn't gotten some. No way.

He snorted. "Yeah, okay. It's not like I'd be mad, honey. We weren't a thing anymore."

"I'm not a liar, Trey. You ought to remember that."

He did. "Did you fend them off with a cattle prod?"

"Fend who off? For fuck's sake, Trey, I spent all my time on the road, with the kids, or at work. You know that."

Lord.

"That was meant to be a compliment. If I met you on the road tomorrow, I'd let you get me drunk and fuck me in your truck all over again. Hey." He caught West's arm. "Single parenting sucks. Do you want to fight or fuck, honey?"

"Single parenting does suck, and I don't want either. I want to love on you, but I'll totally take a fuck." West reached for him and jacked him, nice and steady.

"Yeah." West's hands were so good, they still had all the little spots he liked memorized. He knew they had things to hash out, but he didn't want to think about any of that right now. "You can love on me. I'd like that." He grinned. "And you can leave that box unopened because if you haven't, and I haven't...?" They'd ditched condoms after Lukas was born.

West chucked the box across the room, making Jeremy bark out a surprised laugh as it hit the dresser and spread rubbers everywhere.

"Kiss me, you loon." He pulled West down, careful not to pin his arm between them. West's hand kept stroking him like he wasn't going to pop off, just from having that hand on his dick.

Jesus, he didn't know which way was up. He just knew he wanted more patience than he had. He found West's prick, thumb gliding through the already leaking and slippery slit.

West bit out a cry, the sound muffled in his lips. Jeremy loved the way West's eyes went wide, the need shining from them.

West was right there with him, and he let it be what it was. He hadn't needed anything this badly in ages. He rocked his hips, groaning as he pushed through West's grip. "Fuck, West."

"Uh-huh. Fuck West." West waggled his eyebrows as he sat up, reaching behind to slick himself. Oh, no fair. Jeremy couldn't see. "Does that feel good?" He did like the little furrow in West's brow. "It won't feel as good as me."

"You sure about that?" West was beginning to pant a little, his eyes crossed. "Damn, baby, I want you."

"Come on, then." If he'd had to put money on how this moment would go, he'd have lost the bet. In a perfect world, he'd have had two arms and would have been holding on tight. Not that this wasn't fucking incredible—he was going to get to watch West, stroke him off—it was just so different.

Maybe different was good. Maybe a new foot was what they needed.

Maybe he should stop thinking now.

West totally helped with that plan, because the teasing son of the bitch rubbed the tip of Jeremy's cock over that tight little hole. Everything else in the whole fucking world went away.

He gasped and caught West's hip in his hand, digging his fingers in hard as he fought not to roll his hips up. West might need to take it slow at first.

"Be careful of that elbow." West rubbed again, then again, and it made him want to scream, but nowhere near the sounds that tight ring of muscles scraping along his cock threatened to draw out.

His elbow was the last thing on his mind. His toes curled, his ass clenched, and he arched his back; pretty much every muscle he had was screaming. But he wasn't. Jeremy wasn't going to wake anyone up if he could help it. God, it had been so long he'd almost forgotten what sex felt like.

He hadn't forgotten what sex with West was like, though.

West leaned back, rocking and taking him, inch after inch. His lover was gleaming, and he'd never felt anything tighter around him. Ever.

When their bodies finally came together, West's ass to his thighs, he lifted up just a little and let out a long moan as he slipped in just that tiny bit farther. "Fuck. Oh, fuck." When they'd first separated, he'd had fantasies about this, but the reality was so much better. Way fucking better.

West rested there a moment, muscles rippling around him, then blessedly, they began to move, West riding him, nice and slow.

"You feel so good." He palmed the head of West's cock and gave it a swirl, then slid his hand down to the base and got a good grip.

West nodded, his teeth bared. Jeremy swore he could feel the touch of his hand in the way West gripped his cock.

It didn't take them long to find their rhythm. They moved together, West riding and that gorgeous cock pushing through his fist. He rocked up to meet every move

West made, quickly climbing higher, feeling himself begin to lose control. West was beautiful—wild and giving, he was always a generous lover. West offered him everything, not holding a bit of that need, that pleasure from him, and by the time West began to bounce hard, grinding on him, it was damn near over.

Jeremy sucked in a breath and stroked West faster, working his thumb around on every pass. When the head was good and slippery, he found that little divot and drove through it, pressing his thumb down hard.

West grunted, ass tightening like a fist, and shot, spilling over his belly.

"Jesus!" He bucked a couple of times, West clinging to him and unmovable, then shouted and curled up off the bed as he dove right off the cliff after his cowboy.

West's hand landed on the headboard, the stacked body trembling above him.

He gulped air and reached for that muscled chest, touching, tracing, making sure it wasn't a dream. That was his cowboy, it really was. This had really happened. Jeremy looked up, still breathless but trying to catch his lover's eyes. "Honey."

"Yeah, baby. R-right here." West panted, lips parted as their gazes met.

His smile grew slowly as he caught his breath. "Welcome home."

8

"Daddy? Daddy, this isn't your bed. You sleep downstairs." Ava shook his shoulder, and West fought to open his eyes.

"What?"

"You are in the wrong bed, Daddy. You got to get up."

In the—oh fuck him. Seriously?

"Sorry, baby girl. I fell asleep." *I fell on your father's cock and passed out from orgasm.*

She tugged the blanket, and he grabbed at it. "Come make breakfast, okay?"

"Ava? I told you to let Daddy sleep, baby." Trey came hurrying into the room dressed in familiar sweats and a T-shirt. He knew that had to be driving Trey crazy. "Ava, come out of there. Sorry, honey."

"No. No, Daddy doesn't sleep in here. This is your room!" She frowned at Trey thunderously. "You are *diborced*! Daddy is stupid and sleeps downstairs!"

West fought to keep his face straight.

Trey gave her a look. "Ava. We don't call people names,

remember?" Trey grinned over her head at him. "Not even your father."

He stuck his tongue out at Trey. "I'll throw my sweats on and be right down to help your dad. He's broke, you know, so he needs me a little."

"Mm. Useless." Trey returned the gesture, only the tip of his tongue lingered on his upper lip just a second, and Trey waggled his eyebrows. "Would you mind, though, honey? I'm supposed to be on a call in a few. I just need some coffee."

"No worries. Superdaddy to the rescue!"

That made Ava giggle and shake her little finger at him. "Silly Daddy."

"I know. Go on, baby girl. I'll be right there."

"Superdaddy!" Trey shooed her out so he could get his naked ass out of bed.

He grabbed his sweats and his T-shirt and went to the bathroom to do his business. He tried not to notice how Trey had erased him completely from the upstairs. He wasn't much of a presence downstairs, but up here? He didn't belong.

Hell, the tile was different, the shower was different. Even the toilet was new.

West sighed softly, washed his face, and then headed down to do the morning thing. Breakfast, school, McD's, then work. He thought he'd build a woodshop, and he needed to make sure the fireplace was ready for winter.

"Morning, Daddy." Lukas said as he walked by without looking up from the book he was reading. "I got a Pop-Tart from your little kitchen."

"Don't tell your da. You want some eggs too?" Fuck a doodle goddamn doo.

"Do I have time? My bus is soon." Lukas closed his book and hopped off the couch.

Trey was making coffee in the kitchen, and Ava was sitting at the kitchen table looking at him expectantly. "Waffles!"

"How about an egg wrap? You can eat that and walk." He nodded to Ava. "Waffles it is."

He grabbed a pan from the rack. He could make Trey a couple of wraps too, easy peasy.

"Awesome. Thanks." Lukas sat with Ava but stuck his nose back in his book.

"Is that homework, Lukas?" Trey asked leaning on the counter.

"Yeah." Lukas shrugged. "I'll get it done."

"Weren't you reading last night?"

"That was fun stuff."

Trey sighed. "I don't even know how to argue with that."

"No arguing. Mornings are for eating and coffee." He put two frozen waffles in the toaster, started Lukas's wrap. Oil. Eggs. Salt and pepper. Cheese. Tortilla. "You want a couple, baby?"

"Sure. But just one, please. I'm not working out with this elbow thing." Trey's hand ghosted across his ass.

"No? You sure did last night," he muttered under his breath, knowing Trey could hear him. He flipped Lukas's egg wrap, handed Ava her cut up, yes honey, no butter waffles.

"Thanks!" Ava dug in like she hadn't eaten in a year. She loved breakfast.

Trey's eyes were all over him. "What's your plan today?"

"I thought maybe I'd start a workshop or clean the fireplace." Eventually he was going to have to start breaking things so he could fix them. "You got something for me to do to...I mean, for you?"

"Uh...no. I haven't thought about it, but I will." Trey refilled his coffee. "I may come up with something by lunchtime."

"I'll be home by then. I'm going to get some lumber." He rolled up Lukas's breakfast and wrapped it in foil. "Here you go, son. Get a move on."

Then he starred the whole thing again, adding mushrooms and spinach this time.

"Thanks, Daddy!" Lukas gave him a quick tight hug, then the same for Trey.

Trey watched Lukas gather his things, then followed him to the front door. "Have a good day, bud. Love you."

"Love you!" Trey watched as Lukas took off at a run for the bus stop. As always, the front door didn't close until Lukas was out of sight.

Ava put her plate on the counter. "Yummy. Can I have strawberries?"

"Do you deserve strawberries?" he teased, flipping Trey's wrap, before he grabbed the berries from the fridge. "You are my little strawberry."

"No, Daddy. I'm your cowgirl. Your only cowgirl."

"That's right. My one and only cowgirl."

"Spoiled rotten cowgirl." Trey tickled her, but not with the usual abandon, obviously watching out for his arm. "I gotta run to my call, honey. Would you mind running that in to me when it's done?"

"Spoiled brat." He winked at Trey and nodded, waving him off. He handed over strawberries and then slid the wrap from the skillet and rolled it. "Finish up, girlfriend. It's time to get ready for school. It's library day, right?"

"Uh-huh."

"Okay, I'm going to take this to Dad, and then brush my teeth, and get dressed. I'll be right back." He dropped off the breakfast, and then disappeared. He'd never belonged in Trey's office. It was practically perfect in every way.

Sort of like the new master.

He shook his head and ran downstairs. He belonged down here still. Maybe he always would. Maybe...

"Shit, stop thinking. One good fuck didn't change anything. Maybe y'all can be nice to each other, but you can't believe that he thinks you're more than you are."

He got dressed, brushed his teeth, and grabbed his boots, his keys, his gimme cap, and his wallet.

There was nothing of him upstairs but those kids, and he'd be smart to remember that. He lived in the basement and the garage right now.

Ava had found her rain boots—not that it was raining—and her pink cowboy hat, and was waiting for him by the back door, looking very proud of herself. "Da says be waiting."

"You look fabulous. You got socks on?" Those rainboots could get cold without socks.

"Yes, sir." She plopped down on the floor and tugged her boot off. "See? Red!"

"I love those. Still wanting to do *Frozen* for Halloween?" He helped her get her boot back on, then swooped her up.

"Anna!" She threw her arms around his neck and rolled her eyes. "Everyone wants to be Elsa."

"Yeah? Why, do you reckon?" He loved learning how her mind worked.

"She's magical and pretty." She squirmed out of his arms as they reached his truck but looked at him with mischievous eyes. "But Anna is smart."

"Anna is smart. And she's funny and brave and loving.

Also, I like her freckles." He popped her in her car seat. "I like Woody best, though. Him and Buzz are buds."

"To infinity and beyond!" She giggled, so pleased with herself, then started singing that little song about friendship, rocking in her car seat.

"I do love you, baby girl." He loaded his happy ass in the truck and headed out, leaving worries and questions and baggage at the house. He had a plan, his best girl, and a date with McDonald's coffee.

West thought he could figure it out.

9

J eremy sat on his conference call, finding it hard to care one way or another about whether the city's newest housing ordinance was illegal. It wasn't like him to not care; he was the king of caring. He was the guy who made other people care. He was an activist by nature and legal practice.

His back ached, his elbow was sore, he was tired, and he was about to throw his phone and go eat some worms.

Natalie was right. He needed a goddamn day off.

He made up an excuse about having to research something and tabled the discussion early. He wanted more coffee, some fresh air, and he wanted to figure out a way to take a long, hot shower.

The coffee part was easy. Tugging his coat over one arm and tucking around his other one was challenging, but he managed that too. He left his phone on the kitchen counter and ducked out onto the deck to sit in the sun and think about paying extra after he got the pins out for a waterproof cast.

Suddenly, he could hear West singing like a goddamn

bullfrog and banging away at something like the world's happiest cowboy.

For a second he forgot that they were divorced. This moment felt exactly right. West puttering and fixing something that probably really didn't need fixing, and him sipping coffee and pondering something that should be work but wasn't.

But they were definitely divorced, and it wasn't normal anymore. He just couldn't get his head around his cowboy... retired and not riding, investing in a retail chain. It was good for the kids, but what else it was beyond that he just didn't know yet. Were they together now? They'd been apart so long that it felt like last night, even though it was amazing, was reaching for something. He didn't think they'd quite gotten hold of it.

The sun went behind a cloud and the chilly fall air drove him back inside once his coffee was empty. He set it down and followed the sound of West's music, hoping getting his eyes on the cowboy would help him figure this out.

West was filthy, sitting on the hearth, cleaning out the fireplace. Jeremy was fairly sure West was yodeling.

"Okay, the warbling like a frog was always kind of endearing, but the yodeling I didn't miss." He grinned and sat carefully on the sofa, which West had pushed much farther away from the fireplace in order to lay down his plastic tarp.

"You lack the appreciation for my dulcet tones, baby. Who cleaned this last? They sucked."

"I pay a guy. He does the woodstove and the flue too." He was pretty sure Nicky didn't suck, but nobody ever treated someone else's house like their own. "He mows the lawn, plows in the winter..."

"Is he the hot little twink that mows with his shirt off to try and tempt you?"

"He's hot and taken, honey. He married Drew three weeks ago." He was pretty sure Nicky wasn't going to be mowing with his shirt off anymore.

"Ah, so he seduced the best friend instead. Good for Drew. Best wishes and all." West winked at him. "Were you the best man?"

Yeah, that was pretty much how it happened. "Of course. I'm the best man in town." He winked right back. He didn't say that if Drew hadn't been on his honeymoon, he would have asked Drew for help instead of calling West. "It was a nice event. Lots of people, very fancy."

"Cool. I bet you looked fine." West leaned back into the hearth, showing off that flat belly. "I brought you tacos."

"Oh, yum." That would be worth the calories. "Thank you." He got up and eased himself down next to West, then slid his fingers under West's shirt feeling naughty with no kids in the house. "Which is dessert, cowboy or tacos?"

"You got time for dessert, baby?" West's belly rippled under his fingers. "Because I can so free my time up for snacking."

"I think I'm going to take a couple of days off. I hated work this morning. And sitting in that chair is murder on my back." His team could manage a couple of days, and it wasn't like he couldn't be reached if they did need something. He kept exploring. West was leaner than the last time he'd gotten this view. Harder.

"Yeah? You need me to rub you down, baby. Those slings are hard on a body. I know." West stared right into him. "I'm fixin' to get you dirty…"

"I was dirty before you got here." He didn't give a shit. He wanted what West's eyes were telling him.

"Oh, I think I make you a little more filthy." That laugh filled him up and made him shiver.

He laughed too, feeling his cheeks heat up. "Yeah. Maybe a little." His cowboy had no shame.

"A little? Come on now, you know I can make you scream." West rolled up, head coming dangerously close to the metal of the fireplace.

Fuck. Now he had a full-on blush. "What am I supposed to say to that? You can drive me out of my mind when you want to." He narrowed his eyes. "But I remember a few tricks that make you crazy too. Last night you went off the rails, and you know it."

"I did. I still want you. Still need you." West's abs worked hard, vibrating as he held himself up.

The want was clear in the way West's gaze held him. He lifted his hand off West's belly and stroked his fingers over West's jaw instead. His cowboy had never really been a talker, but he had to know. "What do you mean when you say you need me?"

West shook his head. "What do you want to hear? I been working my ass off to be what you asked me to be. You got to keep our life, our family, our home, and I did everything you asked. You're the man I love. That enough?"

Ouch.

He'd meant that as a simple question, but it was obviously anything but simple to West. He searched West's eyes for another second, then sighed and pulled his hand away. "Right, this was all my fault. I walked with away with everything, and I'm the bad guy. I forgot."

He put some space between them, suddenly wishing he hadn't given up smoking after West left. That was telling, wasn't it?

"I never said you were the bad guy. I never said you

walked away. That was me. I said I worked hard to do all the things you said you wanted. I still am. Working, I mean." West blew out a harsh breath. "I'm sorry, baby. I feel...real exposed."

Wow, okay. That was unusually honest for West. He puffed out a breath of his own and tried to relax. "Yeah. Me too. This is hard, and it's confusing, and I shouldn't be asking you questions when I feel like crap. I'm sorry. It sounds like you have something really good going."

"I do." West looked right at him, like *right* at him, but it didn't feel like a judgment. "You want to spend the afternoon together? I'm done here, there are tacos, and I could rub your back after I clean up."

"I do. I want to know more about what you've been up to. And I will never say no to those magic hands." He'd pretty much ruined the moment, but maybe they could get it back again.

"Well, the fireplace is ready for the winter, which is good, because it's coming soon, I think." West stood up and started stripping down, getting naked like it was nothing.

"You know, if you did that a little more slowly it would be way hotter."

It made him incredibly happy to watch that flush climb up West's perfect belly. "Yeah? I'll keep that in mind. I'm going to carry all this to the back, then run my clothes downstairs."

"You want some help?" he asked, but then he snorted a laugh. "Not that I'm all that able to help right now."

"That's why you called me."

Jeremy got a lovely view of West's sweet, tight ass as he bent to gather up the plastic.

"Can you get the door, baby?"

"Sure." All this time and he still loved the way West said

"baby." Some of it was the accent and the affection, but most of it was that slightly possessive tone. "I got you." He moved past West and tugged the door open, something that actually was harder than it looked. Turning a doorknob left-handed took some brainpower for him.

The wind blew in icy cold, and West gasped. "Oh fuck me, that's bitter!" The gust grabbed the edge of the tarp, dragging it across the deck, sending a mess and clothes and tools everywhere. "Motherfucker!"

"Whoa. Go get something on, honey. I got this." Jeremy dashed outside going after the tarp first to pin it down.

"Careful, baby! Don't you hurt yourself!" West came running out, prick bouncing away as he gathered up tools and clothes. "Fuck a doodle doo! That's ice in the air!"

If Annie looked over her fence, she was going to get an eyeful.

"You have lost your mind?" He basically stood on the tarp to keep it from blowing off and watched West run around like a loon. "Will you get your frozen ass inside? You're going to get blue balls for real."

"You w-w-wouldn't warm them up for me?" West's teeth were actually chattering. Silly Texan.

Good thing the fireplace was clean; they were going to need it. He started doing his best to gather up the tarp. They could just toss it in the garage and make it pretty later, right? "Yes! I will! Hurry it up. You weren't made for this weather." Settling in Boulder had been a discussion with a capital B.

West ran the tools and clothes into the mudroom, then ran back out to grab the tarp from him and shove it in the trash can. "In. In. In in in."

He was fairly sure his cowboy was turning blue.

It was windy, but once the door was closed, he wasn't really all that cold. "Come here." He tossed Ava's blanket from the couch at West and pulled his cowboy into him, forgetting for a second about the cast. "Jesus, you're an ice cube. You're cute in lavender moons though."

"God, I love the way you smell." West nuzzled into his jaw, breathing hard as the tight body shivered.

He inhaled as he rubbed West's back to warm him, shivering for a different reason. "You too. You may not be riding but you still have that rough cowboy smell." He knew what he meant; it was West. A little sweat, a little natural musk...that. Masculine. Delicious.

From here he could see a huge scar traveling along the back of West's head, splitting his scalp. That was new. That was new, and he'd never ever seen it. West almost always had a hat on.

He turned his head and kissed West's temple. "What did you do to your head? Did you fall? Get kicked?" He kept his voice calm, even though he didn't feel so calm looking at it. It had to have been bad.

"Little bit of both. I bucked off Satan's Bride, and she caught me with a hoof on the way down and tried to scalp me."

"How bad was it?" He pulled West toward the bedroom for a hot shower.

"It was a bit of a pain. I—I don't know how much truth you want to know, baby."

He stopped walking and stared at West. "You missed your weekend with the kids. I remember now. You said you were taking a trip. What was that...seven or eight months ago?" He'd been so mad.

"I'd been in a coma for three days. I woke up on Tuesday. They wouldn't let me out in time to drive back here, and I couldn't fly. The pressure on my skull."

"You should have told me." That came out reflexively,

and when West cut his eyes over, he sighed. "Yeah, okay. Never mind. Do you have any...are you okay?"

"I am. I got a hard head, you know? I slept at Hank's for a week, then came to my condo and recouped, watched the skiers and shit."

He blinked. What condo? "Your...you have a condo? You? Like a real one that's not on wheels?"

West rolled his eyes and stuck his tongue out at Jeremy. "Up in Estes, yeah. It's a little three-story ski-out deal. The kids like it better than a hotel."

"Three story?" What else was West not telling him? "You're full of surprises, today. Anything more I should know? Struck oil? Won the lottery?"

"Own a quarter of a bucking bull outfit. Hank left me everything, and I'm bringing my horses up in the spring."

Holy... "What? Hank left you...what horses? Bringing them up where?" Who the hell was this cowboy? The only thing West had owned two years ago was a beat-up truck and bag full of rodeo gear.

"I got a bunch of cutting horses and some riders. My buddy's marrying a little gal up here that's got a horse property, and I'm trading the cutters for boarding so that I can teach the kids to ride." West gave him a smug little look. "Keep up, man. Don't the kids tell you anything?"

He squinted at West. "Sure. I assumed you were taking them to visit friends or they were making up stories."

West shrugged and then turned to start the water. "Do you think I'm going to need to go pick the kids up early?"

"Lukas has a bus, so if school lets out early, he'll be on it. But if you want to pick up Ava early you can. Do you think we're getting more than rain? I didn't look at the forecast." He was so jealous of West's ability to shower.

"That was ice on the air. I'll check when I get out." West

slid in the water and grabbed the soap. "I may have to run out to the Walmart in Lafayette and buy some clothes and all tomorrow. I'd thought I'd take the kids to Estes, but I need to get snow tires put on for that and I don't want to go up in shit weather."

He watched West shower, all the soapy suds running over tanned skin, until the glass fogged up "Yeah? I'll take the ride with you. I need to get out of the house." Not driving was making him crazy.

"Are you sure you can survive a Wallyworld, baby?" West was teasing him now, just being a turd, but it didn't feel mean, just silly.

He snorted. "You'll protect me."

"I will. I might even take y'all to get a burger." The water turned off and then West stepped out and grabbed a towel, steam lifting off his skin. "I should have gone downstairs so I could get dressed. I'll be back in two shakes. Get settled, and I'll grab the tacos."

"Okay." Jeremy's fingers slid along West's warm, damp skin as he walked by. "I'll see you there."

West sprinted down into the basement, the big door shutting with a thump.

What the hell?

He didn't sprint. With his luck he'd trip and break something else. He still couldn't believe he'd broken anything. Him. King of Careful. He grabbed his coffee mug when he got downstairs and put it in the dishwasher, then peered out at the sky. He could go for some snow, he loved it.

West was back up in a minute. "Man, better. I was froze before I got all the way down. And that door! I need to check the spring. It shuts *hard*. Someone could get hurt."

"I wondered why you were running like something bit you. You could have taken my robe if you were cold, dork."

"I didn't want to be...It's yours. Thank you, though." West grabbed the tacos from the oven and the bag of guacamole and sour cream from the fridge. "I got three beef and three chicken."

"Sounds good." Didn't want to be what? So what if it was his? "I'll start with a chicken. Thank you. You want a beer?"

"Yeah, but not until I pick up my girl." Right, driving in bad weather didn't scare West per se, but there was not a more careful driver on earth if things were icy or snowy.

"Our girl." He winked. "And it's preschool. You can pick her up any time you want."

"Yeah, let me check the weather, and if it's going to get worse, I'll go get her. You're sure about Lukas? That the bus is safe?"

He smiled. The bull rider who got his head kicked by a bull was worried about his son on a school bus. "You can pick him up too if you want."

"I might. We can maybe have a lazy afternoon together." West looked at his phone. "We're safe until one-one thirty. Let's share our tacos, and then we could run out, get stuff for your stew, hot chocolate? Celebrate the first snow?"

West looked so hopeful, so vulnerable.

It was the easiest thing in the world to agree to. "Sounds perfect. You can start a fire in your nice clean fireplace, and we can play a cutthroat game of Candyland."

"I'd love that." West waited until he looked up, then his cowboy kissed him hard enough to steal his breath. "Thank you."

He nodded, feeling dazed for a second. "You're welcome. I'll take another one of those if you don't mind."

"All you have to do is ask." West cupped the back of his head, tilted him, and planted another kiss on him that made him feel like there was no one else on earth West wanted to be with.

He hummed softly into the kiss and tried to make sure West knew it was more than welcome. He hadn't considered this as a possibility—trying again, living together, sex—any of it. But West had obviously had it on his mind for some time. He was doing his best to catch up.

And that was one of their problems, wasn't it? West lived at a different speed—not steady, but incredibly slowly, then a lightspeed jump, then slow again.

"My cowboy," he whispered when the kiss ended. "I didn't realize how much I missed you. I guess I've just let the kids be enough. I'm glad you're home."

"Me too. Y'all are my soul." West kissed him one more time. "Eat your tacos, and let's go to the store and get our babies."

His soul. Someone had done some thinking. A lot of thinking. He'd do some too; they were important enough to try. "Hand me a beef one?"

10

West stood at the back door, bundled up, looking out at the snow and the early morning sun shining off it.

The little storm had ended up dumping two feet on them, and it was still falling.

Trey had made stew with his help, he'd made popcorn and cocoa, and they'd ended up sleeping together upstairs in Trey's room.

He'd woken up early and come down to make coffee and bundle up. He wasn't sure he belonged upstairs, but he wasn't sure he didn't so...

He stood at the window, remembering Hank, Hank's last day, how he'd promised to fix his family. He wasn't sure why Trey had married him, but he was going to do everything to change himself so that Trey wanted to do it again.

Lord have mercy.

"Daddy?"

He turned, finding a grin for his boy. "Hey, son. How goes?"

"Good. Good. Last night was cool, huh?"

"Yessir. Last night rocked. What do you want to do today?"

"Look at all the snow!" Lukas ran to the window. "Snowman. Snowball fight. Snow fort."

"Yeah? Rock on. I think that sounds fun." He sipped his coffee. "I'm thinking about building on to the garage, making a workshop for you and me to use together."

He knew his boy loved robots. He had introduced Lukas to *Robot Wars*, and he thought it was something they could figure out together. Maybe. It had to be less disastrous than LEGO.

"A workshop? Cool." Lukas had on monster slippers and a thick robe and looked kind of like a little kid and a big one at the same time. "You can't build in the snow though, Daddy, you'll freeze."

"Yeah, we'll have to plan it together. That'll take time." He sat on the sofa and patted the cushion. "We'll have to decide all sorts of things, buddy. Storage and size, furniture, all sorts of things."

"What are we building? Can I learn to use your table saw?" Lukas sat and leaned on him.

"Yes, eventually. We have to start learning about saws and such." He smiled, his world feeling warm and solid. "I was thinking about us learning how to build a robot together."

Lukas sat up, eyes wide. "A robot? A real one?"

"Yeah. Why not? We can figure it out together." It might take eight years, but a man needed to have projects with his son.

"I'll get robot books at the library next time we go." Lukas nodded. "We'll learn. We're smart."

"You're smart. I'm determined. Together, we're amazing." He grinned, matching the expression on his boy's face. "So, wanna sit here and watch *Robot Wars* until your sister wakes up and we make waffles?"

"Yeah!" Lukas grabbed the remote and handed it to him "Dad likes it too, you know. We watch it sometimes."

"I do know that. He's the one that introduced me to it.' He carefully didn't meet Lukas's eyes. "You're okay with me being here, huh? Because I mean to stay."

Lukas didn't move a muscle, and his voice was very quiet. "Like, stay forever?"

"Like forever and always. I retired from riding. I'm home for good. I mean, I might have to go to a signing every so often, but I bet you can come with me for that kind of thing."

"Wow. So you're going to live here...and Dad is okay with that?"

"We're working out the details, but I will promise you this, even if I can't live here—and your dad and I are serious about me staying—but if I can't, I will buy a house in this neighborhood and we'll be together." He glanced at his son. "But I'm here. I'm here for robots and library day and Christmas and baseball and snow forts."

"Cool." Lukas nodded, and he could see the wheels turn and the clouds lift in his son's eyes. "That's going to be awesome." He got a bright smile. "Wait until you see me pitch."

"I can't wait. You can give me a sample with the snowballs, right?" His grin wouldn't be held back, because Lukas needed to know that he wanted to be here, with them, be their daddy.

"I want to throw snowballs too!" Ava came padding in, dragging her moon blanket and Jonesy, her stuffed rabbit. She climbed right into his lap and settled there.

"We'll go out and play soon. Snuggles and waffles first. Snuggles and waffles are super-duper important."

"Mhm." Ava dropped her head on his shoulder. Not long ago she'd have popped her thumb in her mouth, but Trey had pretty much put an end to that habit. He wasn't entirely sure he wanted to know how. "Blueberry waffles?"

"Oh, there's an idea. Blueberry waffles." Trey appeared in PJs and a robe and smiled at him. "I should get a picture. You guys look so comfy."

"We are. We're planning our day—waffles, snuggles, snow forts, possibly a movie with popcorn." He winked up at Trey. "Mornin', baby."

"Count me in on all of it." West thought maybe Trey was about to come kiss him but then stopped himself. "I'm going to make some coffee. You guys want cocoa?"

"Yes, please!" The little chorus made Trey laugh.

"You got it."

"Do you need help?" West didn't want to move—he was warm and surrounded with his babies—but he would.

Trey smiled at him. "No, honey. You three stay put. I'll bring it and we can have a slow morning. Sound good?"

"We're going to make robots, Dad. Not today. We have to build a workshop first. And learn how. But Daddy wants to do it too."

Trey glanced at him, one eyebrow arching curiously. "Yeah? Robots are incredibly cool."

Ava gave him the side-eye. "Girls can make robots too."

"Girls can make robots too. Girls make cool robots. Lukas will have to see if there are plans for robots for kindergarteners." Look at him being all on top of kid power.

"LEGO robots maybe! I'll look at the library, Ava. Okay?"

Ava beamed at her big brother like he'd hung the moon. "Thank you, Lukas!"

Lukas nodded to her. "I got this. No worries."

He met Trey's eyes, hoping that his ex could see that he could fit here, again.

He got a wink and a slow nod. "I'm going to get our drinks guys. I'll be right back." Trey disappeared into the kitchen.

"Uncle Nicky will come plow today I bet. It's cool to watch."

"Is it? He's the man who married Uncle Drew, right?" Hopefully he wasn't tempted to eat the poor man for lunch. It could happen.

"Yeah. Dad says they're a good couple. Whatever that means." Lukas shrugged.

Ava squinted at him. "What does that mean, Daddy?"

"It means they love each other and they..." He frowned and searched for words that made sense. "You know how peanut butter is good and strawberry jam is good, but peanut butter and jelly sammiches are great? It's like that."

"Like cookies and milk." Lukas said, sounding sure of himself. "I get it."

"Elsa and Anna!"

"Everything always comes back to *Frozen*, West. Just in case you hadn't figured that out." Trey awkwardly handed off two cups of cocoa. Ava's was in an adorable, tiny, two-handed mug.

"All roads lead to Disney." He began to sing a crazy medley of "Let It Go," "The Bear Necessities," and "You're Welcome."

"Daddy!" Lukas sounded appalled.

"That's not how it goes! That's weird, Daddy!"

Trey returned with two mugs of coffee balanced by the handles and handed him one. "You heard her."

"I did. Weird is my middle name. Cowboy Daddy Weird,

just in from the basement!" If you couldn't be a total goofball with your kids, why be a dad?

Trey sat in what had always been Trey's chair, a comfy monster that lived where he could watch the snow fall and the fire at the same time. "The basement has gotten quite a facelift since you arrived. I'm impressed."

"Daddy can make anything. He just cuts and cusses and hammers, and it's there!" Lukas sounded amazed. "He *made* a closet."

"He did. He made the cabinet in my office, and the bench out by the big tree out back...he made the garage."

"The whole garage?" Ava blinked at him.

Trey nodded. "The whole garage. He had a little help, but not much."

"And we're going to make a workshop together now." Lukas stared at Ava. "*Just* us. You're too little."

Oh good lord and butter.

"Lukas!"

"Hey. Baby, I can't help with my arm either, so you and I will make cookies instead. Okay?"

Ava glared at Lukas smugly. "We're going to make cookies."

Lukas opened his mouth, and West met his son's eyes, winked. "We have to plan and plan first, right? And you can come to the library and the lumberyard with us. Today? Today is playing in the snow."

"I don't think I'll be much good in the snow, but I'll come out and tromp around." Trey sipped his coffee and West felt him watching, but the look was warm, not judgmental.

"You can take pictures for posterity." He hummed over his coffee. "Thank you, love. This is perfect."

"You called Dad your love," Ava pointed out, and West nodded.

"I did."

Lukas leaned close to Ava. "Daddy is staying. He told me. That means they're in love."

"Are you in love with my Dad, Daddy?"

He wasn't going to lie to her. "With all my heart, baby girl."

Trey didn't say anything about that, one way or the other. "Would you mind starting a fire? It's chilly in here. I can start the waffles."

"I can do both. I volunteered." He gave Lukas the remote and stood. Time to get to work. Fire, food, then he'd wear the babies out.

"Thanks, honey." Trey stood with him, then gave him a peck on the cheek before heading for the kitchen. "My vote is *Princess Bride* later!" he called over his shoulder as he left the room.

Lukas rolled his eyes. "Again?"

"He likes the big wrestler." West chuckled under his breath.

Ava tugged on his sleeve and whispered. "He kissed you."

He nodded and whispered back. "He did. He might like me too. You think?"

She nodded. "He likes cowboys I bet. Not wrestlers."

"From your mouth to God's ear, my girl. From your mouth to God's ear." And if not, then he'd just work harder. He was taking this buckle, no matter what. "Now let me make a fire for us."

11

"Thanks for picking me up. It's not exactly on your way to anywhere, I know." The cafe he and Drew were hanging out in was warm and smelled like cinnamon and coffee. He'd left the kids with West to give them some time together without him.

"No problem. How are you feeling? How's the arm?"

"It's just a little sore. It feels good except when I do something stupid like bang into something. I don't know how I got this far in life being such a klutz and never broke anything." Drew looked great. Like, great. Tan, smiling, fit. "You look amazing."

"Thanks. I am. It's been a wonderful few weeks. It changed things—getting married."

"It does that." Getting divorced did too. Getting back together with your ex? That was an adjustment and a half. He picked up his coffee and sipped it.

"So..." Drew stared at him expectantly.

He puffed out a breath. This was why he'd called Drew, right? To talk it out, see how insane he was. "So. I called him because you told me to. So this is all your fault."

"Well, he is their father too, right? I didn't expect him to move in."

"I didn't either, but he had plans I didn't know about." He leaned forward. "Drew. Hank left him everything. He has some western wear stores, a condo in Estes, horses...and he's retired."

One well-manicured eyebrow lifted. "Did he have a breakdown or a stroke or something? And who's Hank again?"

"Right, sorry. Hank was his...gosh. His mentor, friend, maybe like a father figure almost...they were really close. He got cancer, and he died not too long ago." Jeremy actually wished he'd known. He didn't know Hank well, but West had to do all of that alone. He couldn't imagine. "Anyway, I guess he had some money. And apparently my phone call came just as West was on his way back here anyway to—" He shrugged. "I don't know what. Get us back I guess."

"Well, maybe it's good he stopped playing around and decided to be a responsible person. Are you taking him back?"

Too late? "In my bed, yes. In my...everything else? I think so? I want to. But with the kids...it's just hard. I want to know it's right. I want a crystal ball."

"Well...I mean, people don't change, do they? Not the base of who they are. The outside stuff, sure, but not their makeup." Drew played with his cup, moving it around and around on the table.

"Well then I have my answer." West was everything he wanted. West at his base was generous, a gentleman, an amazing father. West at the core was his. "He can be a little wild and unpredictable, but he loves all of us." And he knew how he felt. It was guarded, but it was there.

Drew chuckled softly, eyes dancing. "A little wild? Are

we talking about the same man? He is the man that jumped off your roof into the snow on a dare..."

He laughed. "Yeah, we're talking about that guy." That had been more of a prank than a dare. West had hardly ever seen so much snow in one place. And he'd never been more glad not to be in on something. "He's a little wiser now I think."

"I hope he is. I know he hurt you, and I will go castrate him for you."

"It's funny what you figure out when all the fighting is over." And now, everything they'd fought about seemed to have evaporated. "It just seems too good to be true sometimes."

Drew leaned back in his chair, nodding like he agreed with Jeremy, which was unique in and of itself. "What's he going to do, if he's not doing the rodeo? He'll have to get a job, right? He's too young to just hang around the house all day and expect you to support him."

He laughed. "At the rate he's going he'll be supporting me before long."

"Are you sure you're talking about West? Your ex-husband West?" Drew shook his head. "I mean, I never thought he was bad or anything, but he's not...a self-starter."

"I checked it out on the internet, and his retail stores are apparently a big deal. And has a thirty-three percent share. You can actually google him. *Him*. As owner." Not that it wasn't hard to believe, he understood Drew's skepticism.

"So...what happened? Why now? Why did he manage this *now*?"

He'd thought about that. Obviously the condo he didn't know about. and the retail stores hadn't happened overnight. "Maybe it was losing Hank? I guess I should ask him, huh?"

"I would. I mean, I'm not suggesting it's nefarious, just that, well..." Drew pursed his lips like he was weighing his words.

He looked at Drew squarely. "Just that what, Drew?"

"Well, if one of the problems was that he didn't talk to you, didn't keep you in the loop, you guys have to work on that."

"Yeah. You're right." This was why he needed to talk to other people. He just wanted West, he wanted it to work, and it was hard to see details through that. "Want to babysit this weekend?"

"I need to talk with my husband, but I think it can be arranged. If West lets us, of course. He's a little protective of those babies."

"I'll convince him." They needed to talk and not just in bed. "You said...husband." He grinned.

"I did." Drew's entire face lit up. "When does it stop being cool?"

"It never did for as long as we were happy. I was always proud of him. Proud he was mine." He shrugged. "Nicky's a sweetheart. Was the honeymoon amazing?"

"It was." Look at that blush. "Seriously. I thought—but we never fought. We stayed in bed for hours, played on the beach, ate—we had *fun*."

"You thought what? That you'd make each other nuts?" On a random Tuesday, sure, but hopefully not on a honeymoon. "It sounds like a perfect vacation."

"It was. Where did you two go again? Did you have a honeymoon?"

"Uh...we went to Disney for a few days, but mostly because it was near an event in Anaheim. It was fun, though. Honestly. Neither of us had any money back then, and we just goofed off and rode roller coasters and drank a lot of beer." He had zero complaints. He'd loved every minute of it.

There was a bit of quiet, and it was heavy in that way that meant Drew was going to say something important. "That really sounds like fun. You might consider doing that again—having fun, I mean. You haven't in a long time."

"We had a good time with the kids in the snow yesterday. I wasn't able to do a lot, but Ava kept bringing me snowballs to throw...with my left hand." He hadn't been able to hit anything or anyone, but it was adorable anyway.

"Did West freeze?" Everyone here loved West's fascination and worry about Colorado winters.

"He did okay, because he was running around a lot. But let's just say we need to take him shopping." West had borrowed some things, but nothing really fit.

"Oh yeah. That could be fun, dressing him in the boy's section of the department store."

"Oh." He laughed, but it was only sort of funny. "Don't let him hear you say that. He sometimes lacks a sense of humor about that."

"I do seem to remember that." That was a shit-eating look on Drew's face.

"You're going to get yourself in trouble." He grinned over his coffee and took another sip. "Speaking of which, I better get back soon."

"Worried about the kids?"

"No. He had the kids on his own in motels and crazy places every other weekend for a couple of years. That I worried about. Sitting in my house? That's a piece of cake." He sighed. "*Our* house. I guess it's ours again. God, this is weird."

"You know you can make him leave, right? I mean, he's not forcing his way in, is he?"

"Well, he made it hard to say no, and he's pretty settled in now. New bed in the basement, and he's fixing things around the house every day. But he went to the grocery store and he handles the kids before school...he's handy to have around." Handy. West was way more than handy. "I mean, I like having him around."

"That's cool. Hell, you two might find you're better off as...co-parents. Roommates. Not these wild, passionate lovers. Just friends. People do that, right? Just share a family and a house?" Drew winked at him, playfully. "Make him pay rent, though. Draw up a lease."

"Shut up. People may do that. I'm not those people. I'm not having a hot cowboy as a fucking co-parent. He's either in my bed or not in my house."

Oh. That was supposed to be flip and funny, but it wasn't something he'd totally thought through before he said it, and it wasn't off-base. Something else to add to their conversation.

And if he meant it, he'd better start thinking about it as theirs, because that hurt that stemmed from West ending up with a truck and child support payments—which the man was still paying faithfully—while he kept the house and the kids wasn't going to heal until he did.

"We'll never be able to be roommates. We're not roommates now. That ship sailed not long after he moved back in. I can't keep my hands or my eyes or my mind off him."

Drew's lips curled up, the expression just bordering on smug. "Good, because god knows that man looks at you like you're the center of the earth."

"You're maddening, Drew. I can't tell if you're trying to defend him, play devil's advocate, or warn me off." Not that it mattered, he was much clearer on things now.

"I'm trying to be your friend, man." Drew reached over and squeezed his hand. "I'm just wanting you to do what you feel is best."

"I know. And I only sort of know what that is. I know what's best for me. I know it's probably best for the kids, but if he—if it doesn't work out, Lukas and Ava are going to be devastated. On the one hand, he's done everything I could have asked him to do. On the other hand, we're a couple of years older and each have a lot of baggage to unpack." A lot. Some they probably didn't even realize yet.

But the kids were the most important thing. At least he knew they agreed on that.

No one could fault how much West loved them—he took them to the library, to the park in the snow, to the trampoline park. Hell, he'd kept Ava home from preschool just for a 'spa day'.

"We'll figure it out. I want to, I know he does."

"Then I'm crazy happy for you."

He smiled. "Thanks. But...*you*. I'm way happier for you. Especially since I made the introduction." He snorted. He didn't make any introduction. Drew just sat on his deck shirtless every Saturday afternoon for weeks while Nikki worked. "Sort of."

"Uh-huh. I worked for this. You know how many sunburns I lived through?"

"You tanned eventually. I miss having you around every Saturday eating everything in my fridge." Jeremy stood. "Come on, newlywed. Take me home."

"Well, you figure out when you want us to babysit, and I'm in. I'm rooting for you both."

"This weekend. Friday night maybe. Talk with the hubby and let me know? I really appreciate it." They stepped out into the chilly air. He loved fall. It was cold but not winter, and he loved the crisp air and early sunsets.

He planned to have a good talk with his cowboy after sunset on Friday. Maybe they'd watch it together first.

12

"Daddy! We're going to have a sleepover at Uncle Drew's!"

West caught Ava as she threw herself down the basement steps. "I know! I hear he's so excited!"

West wasn't absolutely sure what was on Trey's mind, but whatever it was, he intended to make it end well.

"He has a dog. Her name is Sandy, and she is big and pretty, and she loves to play."

Trey's voice travelled down the stairs. "Ava! Lukas? Uncle Drew is here!"

"Give me a kiss, girlfriend, and have a good night."

"You'll be here tomorrow?" Her worry broke his heart.

"I will pick you up in the morning!"

She stuck out her pinky. "Pinky promise?"

He hooked their pinkies together. "You got my word, m'ija."

She gave him a soft kiss. Then squirmed to get down, trotting back up the stairs. "Love you, Daddy."

Lukas appeared right after she left and waved down at him. "See you tomorrow. Love you."

"Love you, son. Be good!" He waved and finished getting dressed in jeans and a sweatshirt. He'd just showered after cleaning out the garage, and he'd change if he needed to. He headed upstairs in his stocking feet, searching for his man. "Where you at, Trey?"

"In the den. You want to put on a fire? I'm looking at take out." He found Trey on the couch with his iPad. "What are you in the mood for?"

"I'm easy. You know what I like." He wasn't picky, when you got right down to it. "Something you can eat without getting frustrated, hmm?"

He'd already laid a fire, so it didn't take much to get her blazing.

"Thai? Or Greek? You want gyros?" Trey was watching him. "I hardly ever made a fire on my own."

"No? I love a fire." He made sure they had enough wood for the night. "I love gyros. Can we get all the dips with it?"

"Oh yeah. They have grilled veggies too." Trey tapped the screen. "I love a fire. I was just too busy to sit and enjoy it. But with you around again...well, it's one of the things I'd forgotten how much I appreciated."

"I have a cord of wood being delivered next week, too. So we don't run out. Especially on the weekends."

"Thanks, honey." Trey beckoned with his one hand "Come sit with me?"

"I'd love nothing more." He snagged a quilt on the way by, pushing right up close to Trey's good side.

Trey tucked his arm over West's shoulders, keeping him warm in more ways than one. "Thanks for letting me send the kids off. I wanted us to have some uninterrupted time, just us. We haven't really had time to be together, to talk about things."

"I'm right here and listening." Hopefully they were good things.

"Hopefully talking too?" Trey laughed gently. "But I'll start. It's been good having you home. You're spoiling all of us. I don't think I've cooked a full meal since you walked through that door."

"I'm glad. I wanted to make things easier, not harder." Well, he'd hoped to make some things hard. The thought made him chuckle, but he knew that Trey knew what was funny.

Trey rolled his eyes. "I don't think I'd be functioning without you around. Hard or otherwise. And that last bit's been pretty damn good. When you decide to come upstairs."

What did that mean? He came every time Trey called, like a dog to a whistle. "I...when I decide?"

"Well, yeah. You just seem a lot more comfortable down in the basement than...pretty much anywhere else in the house."

West shrugged a little, and his cheeks went a bright and hot. "I'm just trying to—I mean, it's your place, baby."

"Honey." Trey shifted his arm and turned a little to look at him. "Lukas told me you were either going to stay here or buy a place in the neighborhood. I don't want a lover who lives in the basement."

"I don't want to have to live in the basement." It didn't suck, but it was lonely as fuck, and he ached to belong.

Trey's smile was kind and affectionate, and he got a gentle kiss. Trey stayed close, looking in his eyes like he was trying to see beyond them. "If you're moving in here, back in with me—with us—I need to know this is it. You're home. You're not leaving us again."

God, he didn't know how to say all the things he wanted to say. And he had to swallow over and over to keep himself from bursting into tears like a moron. "I ain't going no-nowhere."

"Oh. West." Trey inhaled sharply and swallowed just as hard. "That's all I want." This kiss was messy and full of things Trey probably wanted to say too.

West grabbed the back of Trey's neck, holding on tight, and he dove in, letting Trey feel all his need, all his fear and joy and all that shit he didn't understand. He wanted to come home.

"Missed you," Trey said between the kiss and a harsh breath. "Love you."

"I love you too." He sucked in air, the world a little fuzzy around the edges. "I want to live with you."

"Let's get your ass out of the basement then." Trey leaned into him. "And upstairs where it belongs."

"I wasn't sure—" Trey had all but erased him in the entire house.

"Why not? What is it?" Trey slowly combed gentle fingers through his hair.

"It was like I disappeared," he whispered. He'd never believed Trey would file for divorce. He'd never believed Trey would go through with cutting him off from his babies. "You must have hated me pretty bad."

"I've never hated you. Not for a second. But I was parenting alone, taking care of you when you were injured… I was hurt. I didn't feel like I had a husband." Trey sighed. "It was better to choose to be alone than just live that way."

"I'm sorry. I was doing my best." It just hadn't been good enough. "Maybe this time I'll do better for you."

"I know you were. You always worked hard. It's not that you didn't try, it's just that it wasn't working. None of us were happy. I didn't want to live in this house without you. Not before the divorce, and it was even harder after."

West nodded, but he wasn't sure what to say. He wasn't sure making Trey happy was a possibility, and he was sure he wasn't willing to give his family away. He was smart enough to know that he'd only had so much time to make money, and he'd had to do it.

What else did rodeo cowboys do, if they didn't have a ranch to go home to?

Trey's voice was soft and his tone uncertain. "You didn't disappear, West. I—I pushed you away."

"Yeah, and I guess I let you. I shoulda fought harder." He should have stopped wallowing and told Trey that he would not just go, dammit. This was his place too.

He hadn't felt strong enough then.

"Well you are now." Trey laughed. "I mean...you just came through that door and dug your heels in. I was mad. For a minute there, I was thinking about having you hauled out."

"No, I was coming home. If I had to buy the house next door and torture you, I was on my way." He grinned at Trey, and he knew he looked smug, but he didn't care one bit.

Trey grinned back. "You were going to be a little asshole, huh?"

"No. I was going to show you that I was real and here and fucking necessary." And he prayed that it was true, that he could be...Trey's.

"So far, so good." Trey kissed his temple. "Are you going to be happy? Not riding I mean?"

"I'm going to have to be." His body wasn't up to it. Shit was sore all the time as it was. His back hurt every day, one finger didn't straighten, and one of his ankles might as well be bionic. Retirement was inevitable, no matter what.

He just chose to do it, rather than have it done to him.

"Okay. Well, hopefully we'll be worth it."

"I didn't retire for just you, baby. It was time. There's only so much a man's body can handle. There was only so much mine could handle. Roughstock's a young man's game."

Trey pretended to look horrified. "Are you saying we're *old*?"

"Fuck yes, baby. You fell off a ladder, remember?"

"Shit, you're right." Trey's eyes popped open wide. "You're going senile! It was a chair."

Don't laugh. Don't even. This was too much fun. "Head injury, remember. I got me an excuse..."

"Yeah, well—"

The doorbell rang.

"Ooh. Dinner. Saved by the bell." Trey hauled himself up with a groan and then laughed. "Okay. Don't even say it..."

"Poor old dude. Are your balls saggy?" Oh. Oh god. If looks could kill, he'd be dust.

"Did they taste saggy?" Trey tossed the comment over his shoulder as he went for the door.

He lost it, tickled as a man with a feather up his ass, but not before he managed to get out, "More dusty, baby."

"Oh yeah? Well, it had been a while." Trey opened the door, took the bag of food with a thank you, and closed it again with his hip. "Man, this one-armed thing is a pain in the ass."

He grabbed bags and locked the door with his free hand. "Where do you want to eat?"

God, it smelled good.

"Uh...well, how about the floor in the den? We can stay toasty with the fire and put on the TV while we eat?" Trey shrugged. "I just need a table."

"Sounds perfect. You want wine?" He got the bags on the

table, then supported Trey on the way down. He kissed the top of Trey's head, a little stupid in love.

"Hm. Maybe a beer?" Trey smiled up at him, not looking old at all in the firelight. "Wine with gyros sounds weird, doesn't it?"

"Baby, every glass of wine I've ever had has been with you. If you say beer, beer it is." He liked a glass of wine, but for him, that was intricately entwined with his Trey.

He grabbed napkins, two Shiners, and the church key before going to settle on the floor with his man.

"I don't remember the last time I—no wait. I do. The last time I sat here and had takeout was with you." Trey wrestled with his gyro to get it open. "You might remember it too. We did s'mores in the fireplace, and I tried to set the couch on fire."

"I remember that. We laughed our asses off." He helped Trey unwrap, and then set to opening all the dips and munchie bits. "There was chocolate in inappropriate places."

"Yeah, I wonder how that happened?" Trey laughed. "I'd burn a marshmallow again if you'd let me." Fingers tangled with his and Trey gave them a brief squeeze. "You're not a guest here anymore, okay? Just in case you need me to say that."

"I love you." Just in case Trey needed him to say that.

"I love you, crazy cowboy." He got a quick peck. "Grab the remote and pick something. Is there an event tonight?"

"There should be bull riding for sure. They're ramping up for their finals." He wasn't sure if it was televised, but he found an event on one of the little cable channels. "Ta da!"

"Sweet. Who's hot right now?" Trey took a big bite of his gyro and chewed, looking pleased with himself, probably for not dumping it everywhere.

"There are a couple of young kids—Terry Miles, Jimmy Redbone, Zeke Hamilton. I think Tapper's going to win the buckle though. One more time." Him and Tapper had had a couple of mutually beneficial hand jobs back in the day, but Tapper was happy with his boy toy.

"Tapper Young? He was smoking hot from what I remember." Trey sipped his beer.

"Still is." And twice the cowboy he was. The man just wanted it more.

"Not as hot as you, though." Trey gave him a flirty grin.

"You're full of shit, but it's nice to hear. Thank you." In fact, it was sort of fabulous to hear, because Trey was the one he cared about.

"You always say that, and you're wrong. I'm not full of shit. Later tonight, since we have a childless house, I'll prove it to you. I'll prove it in every fucking room if you need me to."

"Damn, baby..." His cock went from 'gee I love you' to 'oh fuck me now' in a heartbeat.

Trey nodded, looking satisfied. "You believe me now?"

"Eat your food." He hid in his beer, but yeah. Yeah, he guessed he did. "Want a some of this bread in this gray stuff?"

"Sure. Lay it on me." Trey tilted his head and opened up, asking for a nibble like a baby bird.

"With pleasure." He set up the perfect bite and fed his lover, scooting closer so he didn't make a mess.

Trey took the bite in his teeth, drew it in and chewed it slowly, eyes on West the whole time. "What is that? It's really good."

"I don't know." He didn't care. What he did care about was that he was close enough to lean in and drag his tongue along Trey's lips.

"Mmm. Hey, honey." Trey's tongue met his and circled it.

He groaned, luxuriating in the long, slow kiss. This was delicious, and it was all he wanted on earth. "Hey, baby."

"You still hungry for dinner?" Trey's fingers slid over his thigh and tucked in tight against his hip.

"It'll keep." He cupped Trey's cock. "I want you. I want to suck you off, fuck you until you scream. Then do it all again."

Trey arched right into his hand. "I can't wait."

He worked Trey's fly open, wiggling down to put himself in the perfect position for that sweet cock. He was ready to stop talking for a minute, prove that he was someone Trey could want.

"Oh...like *now*. Oh hell, yes." Trey leaned back against the couch and helped wiggle his sweats lower. "I love your mouth."

"Still, hmm?" He liked that, yes he did.

"Still." Trey spread to give him more room. "God, I feel... sneaky or something. Sex in the den like we don't have kids. Like we're twenty-five again."

He wouldn't go back. No way. He wanted to be right here, right now, today. Today knowing that Trey wanted him back. "You smell like mine."

"I am. You're the man I want." Trey's eyes were lit up and focused on him. Staring right at him. "You."

"Good." He'd done everything to get his family back. He'd made changes, he'd gotten his shit together, and he'd fought. Dammit. He rested his cheek against Trey's belly and lapped at the wet tip of Trey's cock, gathering the familiar, salty flavor.

Trey hummed and played with his hair. "I can't believe this is us again."

"Believe it. I won't lose y'all again." This was his life, dammit. He opened up, taking in just the tip.

"Good." Trey hissed and those busy fingers froze for a second, pressing into his scalp. "Good..."

Yeah. Hell yeah. He bet he could get begging, a scream. Pure need.

Trey gave him a little push, asking for more but not nearly impatient enough yet. "Want it, honey."

West didn't stop, but he slowed down, letting himself focus and tease. If Trey wanted it, he could beg for it.

Trey tensed. "What...you don't have to tease, I'm ready."

"Just loving on you, baby." He hummed softly, tongue sliding over the heavy shaft.

Fingers tightened in his hair and Trey rocked up toward him with a growl. "Let me feel the back of your throat, honey."

Fuck. He grunted and took his lover down to the root, swallowing hard and giving Trey what he asked for.

Trey gasped. "Oh, fuck." Trey curled forward at first and then straightened up with a groan. West could feel his lover's control slip. "Fuck, yeah."

He slapped the shaft, then traced the heavy vein with the tip of his tongue as he rolled Trey's balls. West was loving this. Loving Trey's hunger and knowing it was his fault.

And he knew Trey so well. He knew just where to tease, where to be gentle, when to go harder. He got Trey breathing heavily and fighting to stay still, and he knew any second he'd get what he wanted.

"West. God, West. I need...*please*."

He stopped playing then, letting Trey fuck his throat, pushing down even as Trey bucked up. Christ. His man was hungry in a way he only remembered.

Trey shuddered and those hips went still. He was rewarded with a crazy sound, wild and needy as Trey shot down his throat.

That was it. West pushed his hand down into his jeans, jacking himself off, fast and hard.

Trey reached out and grabbed his arm. "Wait, honey. Wait. Jeans. Off. Pull 'em down."

He groaned, but he did what Trey asked and shoved the coffee table away to strip down.

"Up on the couch. I got you." The way Trey touched and tugged and helped move him, anyone would have thought the man had six hands instead of one. And his ass hadn't been settled on the couch for a second before Trey's mouth was on him, taking his aching cock in deep.

"Baby!" One hand landed on Trey's head, the other flying up in a weird parody of riding before he slammed it down on the back of the sofa.

"Mmm." Trey hummed around him, sucked and swallowed and showed him no mercy, driving him toward his climax.

"Don't stop. Don't stop, I fucking need you." He didn't hold back, slamming up into Trey's lips.

Trey took it, took him, everything he had to give and didn't let up for a second.

The whole fucking world spun, the lights behind his eyes perfect. He groaned, his balls drawing up so tight they throbbed. "Soon."

Trey grunted, hand snaking up under his shirt. It found his nipple and pinched it hard.

That was all she wrote. West shot so hard he shook, his bones rattling.

Once he'd relaxed some, Trey released him and

collapsed in his lap, breathing deep and heavy. "Damn, honey."

"Uhn." That was a good response, right? Surely so.

Trey rolled to lean heavily against the couch again, holding his cast against his chest. "Jesus." Trey exhaled loudly. "Wow."

"You okay? Your arm? Elbow. You know." He was trying to focus. He wasn't brain dead. Nope. Not him.

"Yeah. Just...you know. Pinned it." Trey didn't sound any clearer than he was. "'M good. Really good."

"Yay." He closed his eyes and let the low, deep groan that wanted out escape.

Trey chuckled and that red head tilted and rested on West's knees. "I remember why I married you. I mean, you're nice and all, but your mouth is so close to Heaven you can make fucking angels sing."

"You may have married me for my mouth, but you got with me because I was exciting, and you were slumming with the redneck." He stroked Trey's hair, loving on his man.

"So naughty." Trey laughed. "That, and nobody lands a bull rider. Nobody. I didn't believe for a second it would last longer than one night."

"No? I knew I wanted you bad. You got those eyes, baby." He'd seen them and had immediately been caught.

Trey turned his head and kissed West's knee. "I'm glad that hasn't changed."

"It hasn't. As mad as I have been, it hasn't." And he'd fought hard to be what Trey needed.

"I got mad too. I stayed mad for a long time." Trey turned his head, craning his neck to see him. "Some of it was probably because I couldn't shake you. I wanted to but I just...part of you never left."

That was because he wasn't erasable. No matter how hard Trey tried. West was here, if in no other way as those babies' daddy. "Nope. I was lurking in the corners."

Trey nodded, lying back down again with a sigh. "That's why I redid the bedroom. I couldn't sleep in it...in our bed. I couldn't even shower without—"

"It's okay, baby." It wasn't, but saying so didn't help anything. It didn't matter.

Trey shook his head and hooked an arm around his calves hugging them. "The furniture is all in the attic. We could—well, *you* could bring it back down if you want to. I'm useless carrying anything right now."

"You'll be back to normal soon, no worries." That was how life worked, for the most part. Everyone healed somehow, even if you healed twisted.

"New normal." Trey let him go and hauled up onto the couch with him, then shot him a grin. "You look great with your pants around your thighs."

"You mean you're okay with my naked butt on your sofa?" he teased. How many times had they fussed at a little Lukas about rubbing himself on the couch?

"It's your sofa too. But if you'd like me to make the rules, I could totally get into that." Trey laughed and leaned in, nipping at his chin.

"Dork." He leaned in with a laugh, kissing Trey hard. "I ain't so good with rules. Suggestions, sure."

"Only because a suggestion is something you can easily ignore." Trey blinked at him, eyes shining in the firelight. "Hey. Thank you."

"Hey. I love you." He took another kiss, just sort of luxuriating in it. "You know, once we eat, we should go take a long bath together."

They used to do that, once upon a time. Have long, lazy baths that were just steam and water and time together.

Trey's smile was like a reward. "Oh, can we? I'd love that. I really would."

"We'll wrap your arm up in a trash bag, and I'll wash you." West waggled his eyebrows and did his best pervy uncle expression. "All over."

"Mm. Me and my super sexy trash bag." Trey sighed. "I'd be more mad at it, but it made me bring you home."

"It'll be right as rain, baby. Soon." He should know. He was good at that whole injury deal.

"I get the pins out and a new cast next week. I'm going to ask for a waterproof one because I'm about ready to give them the arm for a shower." Trey chuckled and sat up, hunting the rest of his dinner.

"That will make a world of difference. One arm showering is for the birds." He leaned down and put things together for Trey, offering it over. God, he loved this.

"Thanks, honey. Sorry I'm so high maintenance."

It was all he could do not to laugh out loud. Trey had been high maintenance since the minute they'd woken up in the same hotel room. It was part of the package.

"You're mine, and I'll keep you." And that was that. No one on earth could do what he did, dammit. No one ever would.

"I didn't get to see anybody's ride, did you?" Trey hadn't done anything to straighten up and still looked all flushed and disheveled as he took another bite of gyro.

"Baby, we haven't ridden yet." West knew what Trey meant, but he wasn't interested in watching what he'd given up.

Trey reached for the remote and shut the TV off. "After our bath."

"Looking forward to that, are you?" He fed Trey another bite of gray spicy goo.

"I am. Even with the garbage bag. I haven't had a bath since the last one I took with you."

As he recalled, they hadn't had much time for them after Ava was born.

"Babies are hard work." He thought maybe they should have waited a little longer between, until he could retire, but he couldn't imagine a life without his baby girl. "But you did a good job."

Trey glanced at him and then looked away. He wasn't sure what that strange, sad smile was supposed to mean, and Trey didn't say anything to explain it. "I think this might have fig in it."

"Fig, huh?" He wouldn't know a fig from a handsaw. "Like as in Newtons?"

"As in Newtons. Butthead." Trey shook his head. "Don't make fun of me or I'll make you drink wine again."

"Fig fig fig—man, that word damn near sounds dirty. You ever noticed that?" He took another bite, enjoying the hell out of the sweet-sour stuff.

"It can be. Figging. Google it." Trey waggled his eyebrows.

"Aren't they sticky?" This was sticky. Fig Newtons were sticky. He really thought slick was better for dirty than sticky.

Trey laughed so hard he snorted his beer. "It's not—it's ginger, it's...never mind. Oh my god. I love you."

"I love you too. Dork." He liked ginger well enough. Especially in cookies. Ooh. He got Trey's Christmas cookies this year...

"Are you all done, honey? Still eating like you're riding. You want to clean up?"

"Am I?" He hadn't noticed. He hadn't eaten with the family much. "I always thought as soon as I retired, I'd eat fried chicken and mashed taters every day."

"We'll have that tomorrow night." Trey hauled up off the couch with a groan. "Man, you about did me in with that mouth."

"Good." West gathered up the trash, whistling away. He was full and warm, happy and fixin' to soak in the tub. "You want to bank the fire?"

"It would be nice to leave it glowing until the morning I'll give it a shot, see if my left hand can handle a one-handed poker." Trey snorted.

"I bet you figure it out. You're a bright guy." West put the few leftovers in the fridge and took out the trash.

When he got back, Trey was lingering, waiting for him at the bottom of the stairs. "You want to bring anything up from the basement?"

He just—just—avoided the urge to do the happy dance. "I do. I'll grab some shorts and my toiletries and my robe. I can get the rest tomorrow?"

Trey's smile was playful. "You can do whatever you want, honey. It's your house."

If his fucking day got better, he might just bust. "Well then, I'll...clean out the basement bathroom and grab my first load."

"Go for it. I'll start the water." Trey crooked a finger at him. "I want a kiss first though. For the road."

"You can have all the kisses." He walked right into Trey's space. "You've made my dreams come true, you know."

"You're the only dream I've ever had." Trey tucked him closer. Their kiss was intense, fueled by truth.

West wasn't sure he was going to make it upstairs and through a bath. He didn't need to shoot again, but he didn't want to let go. Not now. Not ever. He felt like Christmas had come early, and he could believe again.

Not only that, but if he stopped kissing Trey for even one second, West was scared he was going to burst into tears.

13

Weekends were much more fun with West around. There were still chores and errands, but Jeremy loved the way he and West fell so smoothly back into the way they'd always done things without even discussing it. As far as he was concerned, it was just further proof that this was how they were meant to be.

One of his favorite things was Sunday breakfast. It was unhurried, usually West did most of the cooking, and they all ate together. Sometimes waffles or pancakes, sometimes bacon and eggs. Today looked like some kind of breakfast burrito.

"That smells amazing." Jeremy was still in his robe and pajama bottoms, feet toasty in slippers to keep them off the cold floor.

"Thanks, baby. Are you ready for Halloween week?" West was stirring veggies and warming tortillas, obviously relaxed and happy to be doing so. "Starting Monday I think we have something with the munchkins every day through tricks and treats Thursday. They're going to be exhausted."

"It's like that every year. No respect for school nights."

But he knew West loved Halloween; everyone in the house knew it. "Is anyone ever really ready?"

"Nope." And look at that deeply satisfied look one West's face. "Wanna watch scary movies all week? I'll let you hold me when I get wigged out."

Trey snorted. "Sure. Sounds like the perfect excuse to keep my hands on you all week long."

Lukas wandered into the kitchen in a giant sweatshirt and fleece pajamas and looked at them as he headed for the kitchen table.

"Morning, bud."

"Morning," Lukas answered, still squinting at them suspiciously.

Ava was playing with her dollhouse in the den, and she'd been up long enough she'd already had a snack. But Lukas had started sleeping in a little. Well, if you considered eight o'clock sleeping in.

"You want breakfast tacos, son? I made some without peppers for you and your sister." West headed to the stove and poured up a mug of hot cocoa for Lukas.

"Yes, please." Lukas gave West a careful smile as he accepted the cocoa. Jeremy had noticed Lukas had been a little off the last week or so, but he hadn't figured out why, nor had he wanted to push his son too much about it.

"Are you looking forward to this week? Still happy with your Harry Potter costume, bud?"

"Yeah. Yeah, I guess. It'll be good."

West's nostrils flared. Jeremy swore the man had radar when anything was wrong with one of the kids. "You feeling okay, boy?"

"Sure. I feel fine." Lukas sipped his cocoa but didn't look up from it.

Jeremy watched him. "Did something happen at school?"

"Huh? School's fine, Dad." He heard the "duh" even if Lukas didn't say it. And he didn't, as a rule, because Jeremy hated it.

"Uh-huh. So, you looking forward to your Halloween carnival deal?" West started building tacos like a machine.

"Yeah. It'll be cool. I always get a ton of candy. Last year I got a five-dollar Amazon card too. Daddy helped me buy a book."

Okay, that was more normal. Maybe he was overreacting. Maybe Lukas was just tired.

"Why are you guys acting so weird?"

Or, maybe not.

"We're acting weird?" He'd thought Lukas was the one who was off.

"Uh-huh. You're all touching and stuff. And Daddy's sleeping in your room, not the basement."

West blinked, but just kept making tacos.

Chicken.

"Well, Daddy and I have decided to get back together." Lukas was too smart for anything less than the truth.

Lukas frowned in that way he did when he was working out a math problem. "Together like Daddy's staying here? You're not buying another house, Daddy?"

"No. Your dad and I talked, and we want to live together, love each other, be a single family again." West's gaze was heated, proud.

"Why? Do you love each other again?"

Jeremy laughed softly. "Yes, buddy. We do." He wanted to say it was complicated; that it had never been about love. But how could he tell a seven-year-old that? How could he explain that love wasn't always enough? He couldn't. Grown-up issues were for grown-ups. "We love each other very much. And we love you."

But Lukas was smart. Smarter than both of them. Lukas seemed satisfied by some of that, but Jeremy could see the wheels turning as he put pieces into place. "No fighting anymore?"

"Son, everyone fights some, but I ain't leaving y'all again. If we fight, we'll work through it and make up." West brought the food over, then he sat and met Lukas's gaze. "I messed up when I left. I had to work. I didn't know what else to do, you know? I didn't have any way to support y'all. I busted my butt, and I do now."

How come West hadn't said that to him?

"You work *hard*, Daddy." Lukas said that like he knew it, deep in his little boy soul.

Jeremy nodded. He had married a bull rider, after all, hadn't he? Walked right into that life with his eyes closed. Maybe West had tried to tell him. Maybe he hadn't listened. Maybe neither of them had *heard* the other.

He'd been playing the what if game for two solid years.

"He does work hard." Jeremy set two mugs of coffee down on the table and stood behind West a second, resting his hands on those strong shoulders. "Nobody is perfect, bud. We're just going to try to do better."

"Good. Good, it's good, being together. Are we still going to ski up in Estes, Daddy?"

"Sure, son. The condo is still there."

"Maybe I'll come when my arm is better." Skiing didn't seem to be in the cards this winter. Maybe by the spring. He gave West's shoulders a squeeze and sat, digging into his breakfast. "I'm not half the cook you are, honey. Thank you. This is so good."

"Thank you, baby. Ava, come eat! And you should come

anyway. There's a great view and it's nice, because there's no pressure to do anything but relax and chill." West shrugged, the move familiar as breathing. "Besides, it's not real until you see it."

"That's true. I guess I—"

"Breakfast!" Ava practically dove into West's lap.

Jeremy laughed. "Yours is over there, baby. In your seat."

When Ava didn't move, Lukas didn't miss a beat. He just took her plate and pushed it over to her.

West kissed the top of Ava's head, holding her like it was the easiest thing in the world.

"Roll mine for me, son, so I can eat it?"

Lukas nodded and fixed West's food so he could eat one-handed.

He wanted to watch this. He loved it, the way parenting came so naturally to West and how simple the love was between the three of them. He was a little jealous sometimes, if he was honest, but it had always been this way. West was the fun dad, and he was the practical one. The guy that made sure they had their homework done, their vaccinations up to date, and their baseball uniforms still fit. What mattered most, though, was the kids weren't missing out on anything.

"What are you going to do today, Daddy?"

"I am going to sit on my butt with your dad. What are you going to do today?"

Ava looked cute and thoughtful for about two seconds before she took a huge bite of her breakfast. "Can I watch a movie?" she asked with her mouth full.

"A Halloween movie!" Lukas seemed to like that idea. But Jeremy doubted what Lukas was thinking of would be appropriate for Ava to watch.

"How about we watch Disney Halloween, and *then* we'll

talk about another movie." West offered Lukas a wink over Ava's head, and the argument that was about to hit eased back.

There was little his son liked better than to be in on some secret.

"Disney!" Ava, who was as big an eater at four as anyone in the family, stuffed in her last bite and slid off West's lap.

"Chew, baby," He said softly, scooping her right up. "Finish chewing and then I'll let you go get ready for your movie."

Ava rolled her eyes and made a big show of chewing, tilting her head back and forth. When she was finally done, she opened up and stuck her empty tongue out to prove it.

He let her go and she took off like a shot. "She is so your daughter." Jeremy laughed and took another bite himself.

"You know it." West grinned at Lukas. "We'll watch something scarier during her nap, kiddo. Fair?"

"Fair."

"Brilliant. I'm going to watch both. Daddy needs me to hold his hand so he doesn't get scared." He winked at West.

"Absolutely. I might need hugs." West managed that with a straight face.

"You can sit in the middle, Daddy. We got you." Lukas got up from the table and took his plate to the sink.

"Lucky you," he mouthed at West behind the kid's back.

"You know it, baby." Wicked man. Wicked, evil, wonderful man.

"Dad?" Lukas came back over to the table. "What happens if you get mad again?"

"If I—" Oh, boy. "Like Daddy said. We'll talk it out and fix things. Don't you worry."

"You're not going to make him go?"

Jesus. That was a hell of a loaded question for a kid. "No,

bud. Listen, we're still learning things too, you know. Grown-ups don't get everything right the first time."

"Shee—oot. Some of us, it takes a couple three tries." West put the dishes in the dishwasher like their son wasn't asking the hard questions.

"Listen." He took Lukas's hands and looked at him. "We love each other, and we love you. You should ask all the questions you want, but if you can't or aren't ready to? Just remember that. That's most important. Okay?"

"I just want to be a family again. With both of you. I want to build robots, and you'll be there."

"We are a family again. That's for sure. I don't know anything about robots, but Daddy does, and I'm sure I can learn *something*. As soon as I have more than one arm again, anyway." He winked at Lukas, grinning.

"You should use the right tool for the job, or you get hurt," Lukas pronounced, and he could *hear* West in that tone.

"My smart boy." He kissed Lukas's forehead. "Why don't you go brush your teeth and put on some clothes...don't forget to change your undies, okay?"

To West's credit, he didn't start laughing until after Lukas was headed upstairs. "Oh, good lord. Don't hurt me."

"Go ahead and laugh, but you don't do his laundry. There was one week he didn't have a single pair. Not. One. Pair." He tried not to make a gagging face.

"Wow. That's impressive. I let him go commando usually..." West waited for his mouth to open, then went, "Kidding! Kidding!"

"Oh, I wouldn't put it past you." He started cleaning off dishes and putting them in the dishwasher. "So that was interesting."

"I hate that he had to ask, but I'm glad he felt like he could."

"It was fair. He needs to know he can trust us." Jeremy hoped they were trustworthy. "This is complicated with kids, huh?"

"It is. I wish we could have..." West stopped and shook his head. "It doesn't matter."

He watched West, wondering if he should let that go and decided not to. "What is it, honey? You can say it."

"I just didn't think I could say anything to help you understand where I was."

"You just told Lukas without any problem. I understood that." He couldn't say how much it would have changed things, or if even he would have understood then but somehow, he did today.

"I couldn't say it then. I was broke-dick, and we both knew it. I needed to feel like I could offer you something."

"I was making enough; we'd have been okay." He knew he needed to tread carefully here.

"And what, baby? I just sat around here until I found a job at the Walmart?" West chuckled softly, but there wasn't any humor in the sound. "That would have driven us both bonkers."

"I wouldn't have understood. I didn't understand...who I married." He caught West with his one arm. "We grew up a little. That's good, right?"

"Yeah. It was a hard row, for sure. I told Hank..." West sighed. "Christ, I got me a headache. You want another cup of coffee?"

"Sure. And then I want you to talk, and I'll listen." He sat at the table again, eyes glued to West, watching how his lover moved and noticing the slight tension there.

"I don't know that I got lots to say." West came to sit with him, though, instead of just getting up and leaving.

It was funny how West had plenty to half-say though. "What did you tell Hank?"

"That I wanted my family back. That I was tired of working my ass off, missing weekends with my kids because some pansy assed judge didn't think what I did was a job. That I was getting old and busting my hump to become somebody you wasn't ashamed to be with."

"I...ashamed? I wasn't ashamed to be with you, West. I wanted...something you couldn't give me, but I wasn't ashamed of you." His lawyer wanted that judge, though, and had made him part of the strategy. Jeremy hadn't meant it to be as ugly as it turned out.

West shrugged one shoulder. "It was what it felt like. In my own circles, I was someone important, but outside of it? All I did didn't amount to a hill of beans. It's hard to give that up."

He understood that. He'd fallen for that swagger, the bravado, the little bit of celebrity feel. "I'm sorry that I made you feel that way."

West's mouth opened, closed, then opened again. "Thank you. I'm sorry I couldn't figure out what to say to make you understand where I was. I wasn't in love with rodeo, but I had to make enough money to become something else."

He tangled their fingers and held West's gaze. "Well, we fucked up. We have another shot, so we'll just do better. I never fell out of love with you."

"No. Fuck no. You're my Mr. Right Now over and over.' West winked at him, and they both laughed, the silly joke old, familiar, and fond.

"All right then. We need to get Ava dressed and her teeth

brushed, we need a fire, we need to get the rest of your things upstairs. It's time to walk the walk." He stood up, stopping to run his fingers over West's morning stubble.

"Slavedriver," West teased, leaning into his hand. "You wrangle the baby girl. I will make a fire, then get the boy to help me."

"Sounds good." He couldn't wrangle much else, honestly. He took his coffee with him. "Love you," he threw over his shoulder as he left the kitchen.

That was the first time they'd apologized to each other about everything. It felt good. It felt like they could let that go.

Now to get a hold of Ava.

14

West rubbed his forehead, sorting through his emails at the kitchen table. He was fixin' to have to make some decisions about finals. He had to promote the stores and sign autographs, meet with the marketing guys and make commercials. Hank's memorial was going to happen, and they needed him to speak. Dammit.

Maybe they could all go as a family—goof off, maybe he could take Trey out for a supper. Lukas would only miss a couple of days of school, and all the big holiday festivities would be happening after.

First though, he had to get through trick or treating with an exhausted four-year-old and a grumpy second grader.

"It's *cold*." Lukas stomped into his boots resentfully. "Nobody is going to see my costume under my coat."

It had snowed last night and dumped a foot plus in town, and no one was happy about tromping around.

But no one wanted to stay home either.

"Well, you have the robe and the wand and the lightning bolt—" Trey offered, trying to help.

"Can't I just not wear the coat?"

"You'll freeze your heinie off," he shot back.

"No, I won't! I'll be fine."

"Fine. No complaining, though, and you don't get to come back until your sister wants to." Lukas wouldn't last three houses.

Trey shot him a look but didn't contradict him. "Good luck. I'll be here, all nice and toasty, thinking about you freezing."

West fought his laughter. "I'm wearing my coat, for sure. Go get your sister."

Lukas rolled his eyes but stomped up the stairs. "I don't have to wear my coat like you do!"

"Little shit. Let me put his coat in my treat bag, real quick." There was no reason to ruin Halloween for a silly bit of stubborn.

"You're a good sport. A little bit of a pushover, but good." Trey helped him stuff the coat in. "Ava's going to pull her mittens off a hundred times. Try to come home with both of them?"

"Why doesn't she have those ones with strings? You buy the separate ones just to screw with me, I know."

Trey sighed. "She had some of those, I think they got left at preschool. And the little clippy things are trash, they just fall off. If you had any idea how many mittens we go through."

"That's your department, clotheshorse. I need new socks, by the by, and a cock warmer. Mine's fixin' to get chilly." He grabbed his hat, tickled as all get out. Teasing Trey was one of his life's great joys.

"I can get you the socks on Amazon at least." Trey poked him in the shoulder.

He craned his neck for a kiss. "Save tonight for me, baby. Hot cocoa and popcorn, scary movies and X-rated snuggles."

Trey's kiss was warm. "I'll put you on my dance card."

Ava and Lukas appeared, ready to go. She put her coat on without complaining. All she cared about was the candy.

"Have fun you guys! Stay on the sidewalk and listen to Daddy."

"We're going to have the best time!" Ava was lit up and joyous and totally West's little girl.

A cold blast hit them as Trey opened the door. Jesus, this was still fall. Winter was going to suck. They passed a handful of kids on the walk as they left. Everyone in coats. Trey was going to be busy.

"Which way first, y'all?"

Lukas pointed up the road, and Ava nodded. "This way, Daddy!"

"This way it is. Remember, we say thank you, and we only ring the bell if the lights are on."

"Yes, sir. And we don't go to Mr. Devin's house. He's mean."

"Yeah, he's mean!" Ava parroted, probably having no idea why. Mr. Devin, West remembered, didn't like that the bus stop was right on the corner by his house. Hopefully his light would be off.

"Fair enough. Let's go, y'all. It's snowing." And there was hot cocoa with a shot of whipped cream vodka waiting for him at home.

They got exactly three houses before Lukas started to pretend he wasn't shivering.

He wasn't about to ask, though. He'd offer the coat when Lukas learned his lesson a little.

"Trick or Treat!" Ava shouted, running for the next

house. Her brother followed, moving fast behind her, probably trying to keep warm. Lukas glanced at him after they'd finished, but hell if he didn't see that boy set his jaw and move on.

He chuckled softly. There was a line of cowboy in that child, sure as shit. Stubborn and a little stupid.

They only made it two more houses though, before the damp snow started to finally get to the boy. But still, Lukas didn't admit he was cold. "I guess I'm done. I can walk back. You don't have to go."

"Hey, you sure you don't want to come with us? Your sister needs you." He held out the coat without comment.

Lukas blinked at him, then took it and pulled it on. "Thanks, Daddy." He looked pretty sheepish as he said it and leaned into West for a second. Then he smiled and took Ava's hand, tugging her toward the next house. "Come on!"

Lord have mercy. He was a lucky son of a bitch. Cold and tired, but lucky as fuck.

A half an hour later he was carrying Ava. She'd buried her frozen nose into his neck, his toes were numb, and Lukas seemed more into eating the candy than getting more.

"I want to go home, Daddy," Ava whined in his ear. She was half asleep despite the cold.

"You ready, buddy? Sister is a popsicle."

"Let's go, Daddy. It's cold."

He nodded, and snow fell off his hat. "You got that right."

Trey opened the door as they trudged up the walk, warm light spilling out onto the front steps. "You guys look so cold! Did you have fun? Come in, come in!" Trey took Ava from him and she snuggled in, "Oh, I'm going to run her right upstairs, honey. You guys okay?"

"F-f-fine, Dad."

"How about you run jump in the shower, son, and I'll check your candy?" And warm up. God.

"Okay!" Man, Lukas really was cold to abandon his candy that quickly.

"Cocoa is on the stove." Trey winked at him. "I'll be back in a sec to warm you up, Daddy."

Everyone disappeared upstairs, leaving him frozen in the front hall.

He got his coat and boots off, then went to sort candy with bright red fingers. Lord, it was fixin' to be a hard winter. He was glad he wasn't sleeping alone.

"She went right down without a fuss. Little girl has had a long week." Trey came over and sat with him, reaching for a mini 100 Grand. "Did you have fun? Or are you miserable and frozen?"

"I am frozen, but we had fun. Someone was pleased I brought his coat." He winked at Trey, shivering a little now that his jeans were defrosting. "But he walked with Ava, was decent, no teasing her."

"We're lucky. They get along really well." Trey's stuffed the chocolate in and then took his hands, rubbing and warming them between his own. "Jesus, babe. You're a block of ice."

"Yep, the dangers of being a dad." Oh, Trey's hands felt good.

"You need a warmer coat. And gloves. A scarf. Warm boots..." Trey shook his head. "We're going shopping this weekend."

"Are we?" It warmed him through, the way Trey loved him, took care of him. "I reckon I need long johns too."

"Don't you have any for skiing? Oh. They're in Estes, I bet. So, long johns. Wool socks." Trey laughed. "Maybe we should just keep you indoors."

"Oh, there's a bunch of stuff at the condo—the guys bring shit and leave it. Ski pants, overalls—fancy shit." He loved Estes best in the summer when everywhere else was warm.

"Oh, good. Sharing a condo with cowboys." Trey rolled his eyes. "Maybe I'll hire someone to clean before we visit."

"Be nice, now. The guys always clean up." And he had this management company to deal with it, anyway.

Trey kissed his cheek. "They clean up, sure. It's what they do before they clean up that I'm remembering. You want some cocoa, honey? Slightly spiked?"

"Lord yes. And you do got yourself a point." He didn't want to think about that nastiness.

Trey levered himself off the couch. "Drinks. You want to tuck the boy in? We can have a grown-up night."

"Are we letting him have candy?" West wasn't sure what Trey's rules for this were...

"Of course, it's Halloween! Or... I mean, I think a little is fine, but if you—" Trey looked at him uncertainly.

"Baby, it's Halloween. Let the boy have...what's fair? Five pieces tonight? Ten? Ten seems like a lot, but..." No, ten seemed like a lot.

"Five is good." Trey nodded. "He can pick them out."

"Then after, I'll tuck him in." West tilted his head, listening for the water. "Is he out of the shower?"

"He's quick. He's not old enough for forty-minute showers yet."

"No. No, I don't even want to consider that yet, baby." West headed up to check, smiling as he found Lukas in his bed with his baby sister curled up with him, both of them sound asleep.

He snapped a picture and sent it downstairs while he changed into dry sweats.

Trey hearted the pic and sent back a picture of the bottle of vodka.

My hero. 2 minutes. Putting on easier access pants.

So good to me. He could hear Trey's laughter from the kitchen.

He checked on the babies one more time, then headed down for their Halloween. He was all warmed up, comfortable, and relaxed.

Now they just needed chocolate, vodka, something spooky, and kisses.

"Well, that was adorable." Trey held a mug out to him "You wore them out. Nice work."

"Thank you." He tested the heat of the drink with the tip of his tongue, then drank deep. Oh, yummy.

"You're welcome. It's time to get you warmed up, cowboy." Trey had bedroom eyes, and a bedroom voice to go with it.

"Oh, I do like the way you think, Trey. That I do." He pressed right up close to all those warm muscles and moaned, tickled shitless to be right here, right now.

"Mhm. Be honest. It's why you married me." Trey's good arm tugged him in so they barely had room for their mugs.

"I married you because you took me to the zoo in Denver." That had proved to him that Trey was willing to have fun and play with him.

"And you took me after the zoo in Denver. That was a good day." Trey laughed and steered them toward the couch.

"It was the polar bears. They were inspiring." There was a grand nest of pillows and blankets built up. "Oh, look at this."

"I think it started out as a fort. The kids do this when it's cold."

"Yeah, Ava had a bit of a need of it this afternoon."

Someone at school had told her about ghosts and damn near scared her into tears. He'd dealt with it, but she was in bed with Lukas, wasn't she?

Trey nodded. "She told me Katelyn was telling scary stories. That kid is going to be a handful one day."

"Either Stephen King or a serial killer. I can't wait to see." West chuckled softly. He wasn't sure what it said about Ava that she made friends with the scary ones. It was kind of cool.

"When she's a teenager, I'm going to blame everything on you." Trey was staying close, flirting. "Hey. You want to go up to Estes for Thanksgiving? The kids will have more time. And I might have my arm back."

Oh, that would be special. He'd have to call Roger and have wood delivered to the condo and clear the road right before. "You want to? I'd love that, and so would the kids. We can order a turkey and stuff from City Market there. I don't know if we have all the pots and pans to do a whole Thanksgiving supper from scratch there at the condo."

"Sure. We can order. That sounds great. And easy. More time for fun, right?" Trey waited while he rearranged the kids' nest into something more adult-sized before sitting with him. "Are you all warmed up now?"

"I could be warmer..." He chuckled and drew Trey into a kiss, letting himself sink into the chocolatey flavor of his lover.

"Mm." Trey hummed and practically leapt into the kiss, tongue darting out and tasting him. He moaned, deep in his chest, one hand cupping the back of Trey's head and dragged him in.

One-handed Trey was balancing a mug of spiked cocoa, and their kiss was tempting fate, but they managed not to spill anything on each other. Trey pulled back, blinking at him. "Yummy. Warm enough yet?"

"Getting there." West stole a sip of hot chocolate, then ran his hand along Trey's belly, loving up on his man. "You have a lot of tricker treaters?"

"I did. Not as many as usual, but I managed to give out most of the candy. They were a chilly but determined bunch. Did you see the dragon roaming around? His mom was smart. She made it big enough to wear a coat underneath."

"I did. Did you get the twins in the peas in a pod costume? Those babies were cute as all get out." Snug as little bugs, too.

"Oh yeah! There were. And their big brother was a knight. He was trying very hard not to be overshadowed by them. It almost worked." Trey chuckled and sipped his cocoa. "Thanks for taking them out."

"It's my absolute pleasure." He'd had a ball, and he loved being with those babies, seeing them have these experiences and make memories.

Trey set his mug down. "Hopefully you saved something sweet for me." Trey covered his hand and tugged it up to his lips to kiss it.

"Are you kidding? Trick or treat, baby?" He waggled his eyebrows, going for full-on naughty.

"Can't I have both?" Trey shifted and straddled his knees, dark eyes staring into him like they were daring him to say no. "I'm feeling greedy."

"You can have anything you want. You name it, it's yours."

Trey leaned down, lips brushing his. "I want...all of your Snickers bars."

He snorted into their kiss. "Shit, you can have my

Snickers-es-es and my Three Musketeers." He nipped Trey's bottom lip. "I'm so taking your Reese's."

"Mm. Peanut butter and chocolate. Best combination ever." They made out slowly, like kids on a date, but the heat between them was far more adult.

"No, baby. You and me—we got fire, but we're meant for this."

"Yes." Trey nodded, giving himself away with a soft, shuddering breath, fingers slipping under the loose waistband of West's sweats. "This."

That was the God's honest truth. The sex with them hadn't ever been anything but wonderful. Hell, the love had been pretty damn wonderful. They'd just missed on the respect bit a little, and the remember why y'all fell in love bit.

Trey wrapped hot fingers around his prick, and the thoughts dissolved in a pop.

"Warmer?" Trey's left hand didn't have any trouble giving him what he needed.

"Uh-huh..." His eyes crossed, and he moaned, their cave getting damn steamy.

Trey bent forward, lips brushing his ear. "I know what you want, cowboy. If I close my eyes, if I breathe you in deep, I can almost feel you inside me."

Oh, sweet fucking Christ. "Don't tease me, baby. I'm trying to be so good."

And he wanted to take Trey, so bad. He wouldn't hurt that elbow for love or money, though. He'd tried not to even think about it.

"Good?" Trey leaned back and stared at him. "Is good a thing? I'm not teasing. I want you."

"I don't want to hurt that elbow, baby." But he wanted that ass. Now.

Trey grinned. "So you'll have to have me sunny-side up."

If Trey was willing, he was able. "Bed, Trey. Now."

It came out way more like a growl than he'd hoped.

"Ooh." Trey braced a hand on West's shoulder and pushed himself up to his feet, grinning. "Sexy, growling cowboy is giving orders."

"Git your butt up them stairs." He swatted Trey, then turned off lights and made sure they were locked up. He didn't want to be interrupted.

Trey laughed and took his time, lingering at the bottom of the stairs as he locked up. "You're so mean to your helpless, injured lover." Now Trey was teasing. But Trey could play all he liked, the flush in his cheeks gave his man away.

"Helpless my ass." He finished and muscled Trey up the rest of the way to the bedroom, locking the door behind them. "We got too many clothes on."

West helped Trey with his clothes, then stripped down, dragging them both into the covers before they froze.

"Hey, honey." Trey wrapped one leg up over his hip, and rocked up, gliding their cocks alongside each other. "This is the treat part, right?"

"You know it. I've been waiting for you to want me." He was patient too, dammit.

"I didn't know you were worried about—I've wanted this. I've been afraid to ask." Trey rolled his eyes. "We're supposed to be better at talking now, right?"

"Yes. We are." And what was terrifying? They were. Damn. "We'll have a heart-to-heart. After."

"After." Trey rocked against him again, fingers on the good hand spreading out over his chest. "If I can actually talk at all."

Now he had a goal. Reduce lover into pile of goo. "You

turn on your good side, and I can snuggle right on up behind."

"Oh, that's nice." Trey did exactly what he said, rolling and offering him a perfect ass, shoulders expanding with a deep breath. Of course, now Trey was lying on his good arm, which meant he couldn't do...well, much of anything but wait him out.

That was a little glorious. He could play some. West started by dragging his hand down Trey's chest, just skirting those pretty nips.

"Mm. You're certainly warm now." Trey leaned back and made an awkward attempt to touch his hand, realizing he was pinned. "Hang on. This isn't fair."

"Hmm?" West nuzzled the hair away from the back of Trey's neck, intending to leave his mark. His hand kept sliding down, nice and slow, pinning them together.

"It's not—oh." Trey shivered against him. "I can't touch... anything."

"No?" Then Trey could feel and just let him drive a while. He'd been sweet and all, and he wasn't going to hurt his man, but damn—he wanted to push a little.

"Shut up. You're evil." That was the worst attempt at a protest ever. Even as Trey said it, that long neck arched for him, giving him room.

"Mmhmm." Evil. That was him. West dragged his teeth over the spot, even as he drew circles close to Trey's cock. He needed to get the slick and start opening his lover up.

"Jesus, West. Now who is teasing?" Trey rocked back just right, and his cock nested in between those sweet cheeks.

He didn't answer, but he did get his fingers slick. Now he was rolling Trey's balls, rubbing tiny circles over Trey's hole, and pulling at that bit of skin. He wasn't teasing. He was making love.

Trey's complaints dissolved, replaced with soft moans and heavy sighs. Every move was an offer, his lover's body begging him for more without Trey needing to say a word. There were words though, quiet, needy things—*please, and more.*

"West." The last words got his attention, they were delivered with a groan. "Fuck me, honey. *Please.*"

"Yes." He slicked his cock and replaced fingers with his prick, easing in with painfully slow rolls of his hips. West sobbed as he moved, pressing into his man.

Trey cried out as he pushed beyond the tight muscles and panted out a harsh breath. "Oh fuck, West." Trey managed to reach back over his head, finger scrabbling in his hair.

"Love you." More than life itself. He squeezed his eyes closed, focusing on their rhythm, on this ride. He let himself sink into it, into Trey and those needy little sounds.

"Yes." Trey nodded. "Love you." True to West's memory, Trey wasn't a passive lover. Trey arched back into his thrusts, moving with him, directing, demanding. His man had never been a mystery, it was always clear exactly what he needed.

He grabbed Trey's cock, using their motions to drive Trey into his hand. The low cries got louder, stronger, and he tightened his grip.

"Shit. Fuck, yes." That sent Trey even higher. "You feel so good. Oh, god I... I need this. Need you." Caught between humping into his hand and riding his cock, he felt Trey finally give up and just let him drive.

Trey had him, every inch of him, down to the root.

His eyes crossed as he tried to keep it together, tried to focus on loving on his husband and not how motherfucking good it felt.

Gulping air, Trey reached for the headboard and braced

a hand on it, using the leverage to press back hard against him. A second later, Trey shouted his name, muscles rippling and spasming around him as hot spunk spilled over his fingers.

Good. Good. West set his teeth against Trey's shoulder, driving toward his own orgasm now, pushing harder, spanking Trey's ass with his hips. It didn't take long, not with the heat surrounding him, those muscles milking him.

"Fuck...fuck, honey." Trey arched his neck, giving him that shoulder, abs working hard under his arm.

He rode out his orgasm, moaning deep as his hips began to slow. "Love." West loved every inch of his man.

Trey kept very close and took a few shuddering breaths. "I love you. I love you, I'm sorry."

"For what, baby? You hurtin'?" Lord, please don't let him have hurt Trey.

"No. For...forgetting how important this was."

Oh. He kissed the mark he'd left on the back of his lover's neck. "I'll never let you forget again."

"Thank you." Trey nodded and settled heavily against him. "Left me a mark, huh? It felt great."

"Yes." He blew a line of air against it. "You're mine, baby. All mine."

"All yours." Trey's sigh was satisfied. "I'm not going to forget that tomorrow. I'm going to feel you all day."

"When you stop, let me know. I'll remind you again." He was grinning like the goddamn Cheshire cat—wide enough that his fucking cheeks hurt.

Trey hummed a laugh. "I will do that." Trey rolled toward him, stretching out on his back, looking up at him with half-lidded eyes. "Kiss me?"

He leaned right over, licking at Trey's lips, begging his lover to open to him.

Warm fingers settled on his nape as Trey's lips parted for him, and Trey's little hum of approval was muffled between them. Trey was pliant, yielding to him easily, willingly. He felt like he could ask for the moon right now and he'd get it.

The problem was, he had everything on earth he needed.

15

The morning after Halloween was a little bit of a gift. The kids were always exhausted, and they usually slept in. Well, slept in for a four-year-old. But eight or nine was a dream compared to six a.m.

Jeremy was up at six anyway, because having kids had trained him not to sleep much past sunrise, but the house was quiet, and the den was warm. He curled up on the couch in his pajamas and pulled a quilt over him, waiting for the coffee to brew.

Quiet was golden these days, and it also meant he had time to think; about the kids, about West, about...*wow*. About sex with West.

About marriage. About family.

He looked out at the snow and sighed. He only had an hour or so, that was a hefty proposition. Especially before coffee.

Everything about West had changed—well, not everything, but all the things he'd asked for, West had done. It was wonderful, but he was also a little worried. What if

West wasn't happy? What if he changed his mind? What if—

"Morning, baby." West dropped a kiss on the top of his head.

He caught West's hand and looked up into eyes he knew so well he could map them. He should have said good morning but what came out was, "I love you."

"I love you too, baby. Do you need more coffee?"

"I haven't had any yet. It was still brewing." He started to get up. God, how long had he been sitting there?

"Sit. Stay. I'm going to grab us both a cup. You want cocoa in yours?" West took such good care of him.

"Thank you. That sounds great." He needed to get West a robe and some slippers for Christmas. The sweatshirt and thick socks worked, but they seemed so...temporary. Like West was visiting. And he obviously wasn't visiting anymore.

But he liked the view as West walked away, no matter what was covering that ass.

He needed to hire someone to bring down the dresser that had been West's, at least. It was time to stop living out of a suitcase. "Have you been upstairs in the attic?"

"To put down mousetraps, yes."

They had mice? It was a hazard, he knew, but he still hated them. "Did you see all the bedroom stuff is still up there? Ours? Your dresser and stuff?"

"I did. You want me to sell it?"

"Sell it?" He blinked, a little shocked. "No, honey. I was thinking we should bring it back downstairs."

West came back with the coffees, expression warm and happy. "Oh? I'd like that a lot. That one dresser was my granny's."

"I know." He knew. He knew very well. It was one of the reasons he moved everything out of the bedroom after the divorce. He couldn't look at it without it hurting. "I can't help right now obviously but...we should hire a couple of guys." He made sure to say *we*, to put some weight on it. We, us, he needed West to know—to *believe* he belonged here.

"I could—" West stopped and rolled his eyes. "No, I really couldn't. That thing is heavy. Let's hire someone. Ooh. Drew and his boy toy!"

"Nicky. His husband's name is Nicky." He rolled his eyes. "Nicky could do it. Drew would supervise and bake cookies." And if they told Drew there were mice in the attic, Nicky would probably come alone. "It took three guys to get everything up there. I'll just call them."

"Three guys? Were they pretty?" West snuggled in next to him. "Did you ogle?"

"Fuck, yeah." He grinned, and since his one good hand was holding coffee, he let West settle the blanket over them both. "I was newly single. I ogled everything. For all the good it did me. It wasn't your ass going up and down that ladder."

"No." West looked into his coffee with a bit of a frown, but he didn't say anything.

He ducked and tried to catch West's gaze, wishing he had two hands. "By which, I mean that I missed you."

"I know. God, I cried like a baby leaving here, knowing I was rodeo trash, and I could either pay my child support or see them some weekends."

These conversations were so hard, but he'd danced around them enough. "You weren't—you're not trash. I made you feel that way, I know. But you're not."

"I'm trying hard to be what you asked for, Trey. I swear to God. I'm going to be the husband and father you need."

Being alone had left Jeremy plenty of time for soul-searching, and he knew that was his fault; West, feeling like he wasn't good enough, always feeling that he had to live up to something. "West." He started to reach for West with his right arm and winced. "God, I hate this fucking cast." He sat his coffee down heavily on the end table and tried again with his left hand, tangling their fingers. "Listen to me. You've changed. I see that, and I understand why. And so have I. You're more than enough for me, for the kids. Don't try so hard, okay? Just be...you. This won't work if you feel like you're reaching for something all the time. You'll resent me and—I don't want to be something you have to work for. This is your family. You are what I need."

West searched his eyes, then Jeremy got a smile. "That's...that's damn nice to hear. I am loving this—loving you, seeing the babies, doing Halloween. I feel alive now."

"We're better with you here." The kids were so happy. He wasn't going to admit to West how often he'd felt like a failure because he wasn't enough for the kids on his own, but that didn't make it any less true. They'd missed their father.

Not only that, he'd missed West like a sore foot.

"I'm better here with you. I've never been so happy, baby. I belong here with you, loving you."

He thought maybe they had this. That if they paid attention this time it was going to work. And he was definitely paying attention. "Yeah, that loving on me thing does not suck."

"Well, not every time..." Oh, evil shit.

"Okay, so certain parts of you haven't changed." He turned his head and kissed West's shoulder. "Thank God."

"So, where should we put Granny's dresser, love? The TV would work on it."

Jeremy raised an eyebrow. "Oh, no. Clever, *love*, but no. I'm not letting you use this as an excuse to bring up that old argument again. A long dresser needs to go on a long wall." He grinned. He and West hadn't so much agreed about how to arrange the bedroom furniture when they'd moved in as called a truce on it.

West cackled, nice and loud. "Can we put the bed in the middle of the room and use the back of the dresser as the headboard?"

"Sure. And then you can sleep in the bathtub. Who floats a bed? Where did you even get that idea? It's nuts. Kiss me and promise me you'll never mention it again."

"You have my word, baby. You can put it anywhere you want if you fold my socks in those little balls."

"Count on it." He liked folding socks. It gave him a sense of order. West would tease him about it until the day he died and that was okay. He tugged on the front of West's sweatshirt. "Now where is that kiss?"

16

"Hey, honey? Can you feed the woodstove? It's getting chilly in here." Jeremy pulled a flannel shirt over his good arm and tucked it over his other shoulder. This cast thing was getting old. It was almost over though, next week he'd be done with it. He was perfectly capable of dealing with the fire when he had two hands, and he'd like to start doing things for himself again.

He'd been spoiled having West around; they all were. West was doing everything from repairs to cooking to driving...and Jeremy hadn't heard a single hint of complaint. West did like to keep busy, but this was kind of above and beyond busy.

"Sure, baby." West's phone rang again, and he answered it on the way to the fireplace, that earphone in again. "'Lo. Hey, lady. Yeah. Yeah, I know. Go ahead and set the camera crews up for me, see if you can't get me a spot on the radio with that one little girl that makes me laugh, and don't book too many autograph sessions. We want to go for accessible but not easy, right?" West fed a couple of logs in, stirring everything up. "Can you schedule a meeting with Pam and

Wilson—sure, supper is fine, if it's not too, too late. I'm hoping to have the whole family there."

Working West was still so weird. There were days, especially recently, when West had more calls than he did. He'd gotten pretty good at ignoring it; he had his own work to do after all, but his ears pricked up this time. Have the whole family where? The only place they were going was Estes for Thanksgiving. He was watching West now and listening with more interest.

"Yeah. Yeah, I'm fixin' to chat with the boss to make sure he's good with it, but go ahead with the suite, and make sure I keep at least two evenings free—one I'll need a babysitter for. Oh? Oh, honey, that's sweet. The kids would love that. Yeah, I want to take him somewhere nice, maybe go dancing or a show together like grown-ups. Maybe *Zumanity*? Yeah? Let me know. All right, Elle, I'll talk at you tomorrow. Tell Rick I said to take you to supper and kiss those babies for me. Bye."

Zumanity. Vegas.

He looked at his phone and kept his mouth shut, waiting to see how West decided to handle this. He wouldn't necessarily object to taking the family to Vegas, so he'd wait and see what West was proposing before he decided how he felt about it.

"It'll heat up here in a bit, baby. You got a second to chat?" West gave him a warm, happy smile, not even a hint of worry.

"I have several seconds for you. Come sit." Trey moved from his desk to the little den loveseat.

"Mmm..." West stole a kiss like it was the most natural, necessary thing ever. "I am going to have to go to the finals week in Vegas. There's no way around it with the business and the stock contractors and sponsors and all. Would you like to come with the kids? We'll have tickets for all the events, we'll have time to have a little fun with the babies, and we'll have a night out to ourselves. I'll have to work quite a bit, but it shouldn't be evil, and I'd love to have y'all there."

Well, that sounded both completely reasonable and like a lot of fun. "Is it during school? How much would Lukas miss? Not that he can't..." Lukas was only seven after all. And Jeremy could work from the hotel room if he had to, but he also had plenty of vacation time banked.

"We'd have to leave Thursday and be home the following Monday if we drove. If we flew? We could leave Saturday morning, spend the week, and be home Sunday afternoon."

"Can we fly? I think the shorter trip would be easier with Ava, don't you? She's going to be bored to tears in a hotel room." Yeah, he'd take vacation. There was no way he'd get any work done with the kids in the room.

He got another wildly happy kiss, that left him a little breathless. "Totally. Denver to Vegas is just a hop and would keep us from a fourteen-hour road trip. I checked the calendar, and we'll be coming back to the whirlwind of Christmas activities, but they won't be missing any."

He found he was all smiles too and looking forward to the break. "We haven't taken a vacation with both kids before, have we?" Ava had been tiny, and things were rocky before the divorce.

"Nope. I mean, we will have taken them up to Estes by then, but that'll be different."

"I'm excited." He squeezed West's fingers. Holidays, finals, a vacation...and he'd have his arm back soon. "I think the kids are going to love it. This is going to be a great winter."

"It is. And my horses are coming in the spring, so there will be riding up in the mountains this summer."

"There'll be some riding up in the bedroom tonight, if you're a—" The doorbell rang, interrupting his flirting. He sighed and stood. "Timing. Are you expecting anyone?"

"Nope. Maybe Lukas made some friends?"

"He does have a couple in the neighborhood, but usually their moms call..." Delivery maybe. He went to the door and opened it, getting hit with a blast of cold air.

And a couple of men in cowboy hats.

"Hey, there. Can West come out and play?"

"Can...?" Oh. Oh no. "West?" he called. "There are some cowboys here to see you!" Sure, West could go out and play. He really didn't want these guys to come in. He peered past them at the trailer in the driveway. "How many of you are there?"

"In total, in town, or in this trailer?"

One of the cowboys smacked the smartass on the ass. "Be nice, now. You don't remember me, do you, Mr. Trey? I'm Blake Whitehead. Me and Craig and Lowell wanted to stop by and see West."

Blake Whitehead? He had been a baby. A *baby*.

West came up to the door. "Well, lord have mercy. Hey, y'all! Come on in, you're letting the heat out."

"I think they wanted you—" *To go out?* Jeremy was forced to step back as the guys came in at West's invitation. He took a deep breath and closed the door behind them.

"Hey, family man!" One of the others—Craig or Lowell —took West's hand and pulled him into a bro-hug. "You look good."

"I feel pretty damn good, buddy. How are y'all? You just driving through or are you staying around for a couple days?"

"Our plans are pretty loose. Two or three days probably." Blake shook with West and smiled handsomely. "On our way to the next event."

"Weren't you about twelve the last time I saw you?" Jeremy shook his head. Blake had been nineteen or so, but he'd looked like a high school freshman.

Blake laughed. "Maybe thirteen. What happened to you? Do I need to break West's arm for him?"

"Tempting but no. I fell." He needed a better story.

"I hear that happens as y'all get older." There went the smartass again.

"Watch it, boy. I don't allow that sort of talk." West was immediately in the kid's face. Okay, that was hot.

The kid straightened up and tugged his hat down over his eyes. "Yes, sir. My bad."

Mmm. That was his man. "Go on in the den, guys. Anyone want Cokes?"

"Thank you, Mr. Trey, sir." Blake shot him a smile. "We was hoping we might could buy y'all supper and see the kiddos? It's been a while, and you know I miss my best girl."

"You can call me Jeremy." He smiled back at Blake— man, that kid was charming—then glanced over at West. "You want me to call the kids?"

"Of course. Ava and Blake here have quite the mutual admiration society going." West chuckled softly, shaking his head. "How're y'all riding?"

Mr. Rude grinned at West. "It's been good. Real good. I'm trying my hand at bareback. It's wild as hell."

"Lord, Craig, that makes my back hurt, just pondering on it."

Craig. Well, now at least he could tell them all apart. So, only one other thing to clear up before he went to the kitchen. He moved around Craig, caught West's face in his hand and kissed his lover's cheek. "You guys can go sit. I'll get drinks."

"Thank you, baby." Oh, he did love that expression on his husband's face.

He gave West a wink, then headed upstairs to find the kids. "Lukas? Ava? Daddy's got some cowboy friends downstairs that want to say hi."

"Cowboy Blake?" Ava came running.

"Yes, ma'am. Run on down to the den."

Lukas was right behind. "Thanks, Dad!"

Watching them run made him smile. Maybe having the boys around for a bit would be worth it. Maybe.

This new-old life was pretty damn good.

He followed them down the stairs, ducking into the kitchen for soda to hand out. No way was he giving this crew beer. If West decided that was a good idea later, that would be on him.

Ava was squealing, telling Blake about her life, her school, her friends.

He handed out drinks and then joined West on the loveseat, which, he noted, West had kept open for him. "I can't blame her for having a crush on Blake; he's adorable," he said softly for West's ears only.

"He thinks she's the cutest thing ever," West agreed quietly before asking the cowboys, "So are you hooligans staying out of trouble?

"Always!" they answered, in unison.

"So, that would be no." Jeremy grinned. "Business as usual?"

"Well, Lowell's keeping his nose clean," Craig said pointing at the quiet cowboy. "He's fixin' to be engaged."

Lowell blushed. "Maybe."

Craig snorted. "He wants a buckle first, thinks it will impress her."

"I need to be something worth marrying, don't I?"

Sweet kid. "What's her name?"

"Josie." Lowell looked right at him and smiled, face lighting up. "She's from up here, little town 'tween here and Denver."

"We're dropping him off in a couple of days so he can meet her parents." Poor Lowell. Craig was teasing so hard.

"Good for you, kid. She a barrel racer?" West let the teasing, the roughhousing, roll over like it wasn't even there.

"Yes, sir. And she's comin' up. Fast."

"She's really good," Blake agreed. "Fearless. Smart."

Lowell gave Blake a shy smile.

Lukas waved a deck of cards at Lowell. "Crazy Eights?"

"I'm in, kid."

Okay, so the guys were on their best behavior around the kids; that was cool.

The Craig guy, he just seemed to watch and tease, watch and tease. Every so often those eyes would land on West and linger.

Wishful thinking. Craig could look all he liked, but that wasn't happening. Jeremy felt bad for the kid. West wasn't interested, and it was hard to find someone who was, genuinely anyway, in their line of work.

Also, Jeremy was the jealous type. Always had been, and he couldn't help it. He'd made himself known earlier, and if Craig didn't pay attention, he'd be happy to make it crystal clear later.

"So what did you say was the dinner plan, Blake?"

"Whatever y'all want. We could go out, order in. We could fetch something and bring it back." Blake shrugged.

"We just wanted to say hello and see y'all. It's different, without you and Hank now."

He bet it was. "You guys should go do something fun tomorrow, honey. I can hang with the kiddos. Go skiing or something."

"No!" Ava frowned at him. "No, I go. I go with Cowboy Blake too. Daddy, please?"

West chuckled softly. "Me and Trey had plans to take the kids into Denver tomorrow, go shopping, maybe do something fun and then have supper. Sorry, guys."

Oh. West had remembered. West had remembered and cancelled plans with the guys.

"Your son is a card shark, West. He's killing me at Crazy Eights."

Lukas's snicker was everything, and Jeremy had to chuckle with him. "Lukas loves cards. And he's much smarter than we are."

Ava looked over at Blake. "Daddy is loving my dad again. That makes him not stupid anymore, right?"

Blake looked at West with wide eyes, and West snorted and gave Blake a bare nod.

He pretended to be shocked, but they'd both been a little stupid. "Ava, baby. Everybody makes mistakes. And we don't use words like stupid, remember?"

Ava looked at Blake, and Blake pointed at him. She looked over with sheepish eyes. "Sorry, Dad."

He gave her a wink and a smile.

"It's my fault, baby. I was explaining D-I-V-O-R-C-E, and my part in it."

Figured. Still.

"So..." Craig said. "Y'all are back together? Not just stickin' around until the arm heals?"

He opened his mouth to answer, but West beat him to it. "You know it. All the way."

"We're solid, yeah. Another week and my arm will be too."

"You fixin' to get rem—"

"Shut it, Craig," Blake cut Craig off with a hiss.

Jeremy glanced at West briefly. That was the million-dollar question, wasn't it?

West grinned, looking easy and relaxed in his skin. "That ain't our call, y'all. We could order from the Pizza Garage. They got great stuff."

"Sure, that sounds good." Blake grinned. "I hear you redid the basement. Can we see?"

"Sure! I built out a closet and redid the bathroom."

How had they heard that? Good grief cowboys were nosey. He was glad West wasn't living in it anymore; that would have been embarrassing and awkward.

"I show you!" Ava wiggled off Blake's lap and took a few steps toward the hall. "I show you Cowboy Blake."

"Are you allowed down all them stairs, little girl?" Blake swooped her up, airplaning her around.

West whispered in his ear, so quiet. "He lost his sister, the one that was all sick? She passed away last year, so he takes comfort in Miss Ava."

"Oh." He blinked at West and nodded. Blake was lovely, and Ava had enough love and energy in her for everyone.

"You fly me higher than Daddy!"

"Well, I'm taller than your daddy," he heard Blake say as they headed down the basement. He chuckled, though Blake hadn't meant it as a joke.

"Not saying much." He winked at West.

"Uh-huh. Butthead. I'm tall enough." West kissed him.

"Come on, y'all, I'll show off the basement, and then we'll talk pizza."

They all stood, but Craig lingered, gaze going between him and West.

He put a hand on West's back telling him to go ahead while he took his time. "You okay, Craig?"

"I am. I think you should know, I'm in love with him, and when you get tired of him again, I'll be there to pick up the pieces. This time he won't be crying because he misses his kids."

Oh. He understood what was happening now. He snorted and shook his head, staring Craig down. "If you really loved him, you'd want him to be happy. He's not a prize to be won, and those kids are more important to him than anyone. This is the last time you'll set foot in our house."

"We'll see about that. You'll fuck up again."

"Don't you talk like that to my dad!" Lukas stood there, lips tight. "You don't cuss my dad. I will tell Daddy on you, and he will kick your butt."

He held his temper in check for Lukas's sake. "That's my brave boy. Thank you, buddy. I've got this now. Okay? Go on down to the basement."

Lukas didn't look the least bit convinced, but he went. Jeremy assumed to tell West.

He turned on Craig. "Get out. Now."

"You can't throw me out." Craig sneered at him, lip curled. "I'm here for West."

"No you're not. You're here for yourself." He took a step closer. "Get the fuck out, Craig."

He could hear the sound of boots hitting the stairs like a thundering herd. Lowell hit the door first. "Craig, what the fu-fi-uh-hell?"

He raised an eyebrow at the asshole. "I warned you." He looked at Lowell. "I was just asking Craig to leave, Lowell. You think you could see him out for me before West breaks his jaw?"

"Yessir, Mr. Trey. Absolutely." Lowell grabbed Craig, talking hard under his breath while Blake stayed between the man and his West.

"Baby? You okay?" West glanced at him, then at Craig being hustled out of the house.

"He cussed at Dad!"

"I'll get him gone, man. I swear. Maybe y'all can meet me and Lowell for breakfast in the morning?" Blake asked. "Just the two of us?"

"That sounds great, Blake. Thanks." He nodded to West as the door closed behind Lowell. "I'm totally fine."

"What? What hap—"

Ava and Lukas both started to cry, and West held his arms open. "Easy. Easy, y'all."

"Naptime maybe, huh?" He waved Blake over. "Blake, I think we need—if you two can and want to come back for dinner later you're welcome. Otherwise we'll see you in the morning, okay?"

Blake nodded. "I'm real sorry about this."

"I promise you there's no way you could have known. He just needed to leave. Everything is fine now." He walked Blake to the door, leaving West with his arms full.

"You can't go with him, Daddy. You can't! You promised!"

West nodded, holding Lukas tight. "You're right. I did, and I'm staying with y'all. You and sister and Dad. I promise to God. I ain't going with anyone. If we go somewhere, we'll go as a family."

He saw Blake out, then hurried back over to his family.

"Hey, guys. Sorry that scared you." He took a deep breath. "He just wasn't a good guest, that's all. Everybody okay?"

Ava nodded and pushed into his arms. West though, he had Lukas, and was rocking and talking hard, working to reassure their son that all was well.

"Dad, are you okay? Did he scare you?" Ava whispered. "He made Lukas *cry*."

"I'm fine. I promise. Lukas was very brave, and I'm proud of him. It's hard to be brave." He hugged her close, then stood and took her hand. "It's naptime, baby. And when you get up, we'll all have pizza okay?"

"Okay. Can I lay down and just look at a book?" She'd look for five minutes, tops, then crash.

"Of course. You can always read, right?" He got her upstairs and into bed with her book, but she lay down to read before he'd even left the room.

West carried Lukas up the stairs, the little boy sound asleep. "Pull back his comforter, baby?" West whispered.

"Oh. Yeah, I got it." He ducked into Lukas's room and pulled back the covers, tugging them back up again once West got their son down.

Then they both walked back downstairs without a word. West put some more wood on the fire, then glanced at Jeremy. "What on God's green earth happened?"

He shrugged. "How well do you know that kid?"

"Craig?" West looked vaguely confused. "I pulled rope for him a couple times, had a beer with him once, maybe twice. He's a stupid kid, just one of Blake's friends. You know Blake's uncle and me were fast friends in high school, right?"

"Yeah, I remember." West had no idea what was up with Craig, obviously. "He's in love with you. He thought I should know that. He had plans to be there for you when this didn't work out."

"In love with...oh good lord. He's a baby. He's just a little boy. A stupid one. You ask, I never cheated on you. Not once. I wanted my family back."

"I didn't ask. I don't need to. Even if there had been someone, we were divorced, honey. But you said there was no one else and I believe you." He touched West's face. "I *believe* you. But he meant business. He tried to tell me I couldn't throw him out because he was here for you."

"Well, you showed him about that, didn't you?" West chuckled softly, pushing into his hand with a tiny sigh. "Jesus, Lukas was on *fire* coming down them steps. He was gonna protect you, and damn the consequences."

"He's got a strong sense of justice, for sure." But it was more than that. Lukas wanted his parents together. He understood what it meant that Trey and West had broken up. "We have to be careful with him. He's too smart for his own good sometimes."

"He's way smarter than me, that's for sure." West shook his head. "I ought to go kick that boy's ass."

He shrugged. "My guess is Blake has that handled. And Lowell may be quiet, but he's built like a tiny moose. Probably better you let them let Craig know you don't mess with someone else's man." He kissed West, knowing the possessive look in his lover's eyes. He loved it.

West pushed right in, taking his worry and stress and adrenaline out on Jeremy's lips, and Jeremy didn't mind a bit. He could take it.

Man, he couldn't wait until he had two hands again so he could push and pull the way he wanted to. He grabbed the fabric of West's shirt and held on, offering his lover whatever West wanted. He knew where he belonged, and he wanted to make sure West was clear on that. Like some wet behind the ears kid could give West what he needed. That was his job, dammit.

"I almost laughed at that kid, you know. He couldn't handle you. He should stick to the bulls. At least there he has a chance." He grinned against West's lips.

"Takes someone special to ride me. That what you're saying?" Those pretty eyes were laughing now, warm and happy, teasing him.

"You know it, cowboy." Jeremy chuckled, fingers moving to comb through West's hair. "You're a rare breed."

"Thank God for that, huh?" West shook his head. "Lord, baby. I hope you don't mind that I begged off tomorrow. I appreciate you offering to let me hang with the guys, but I've been looking forward to our day together all week."

"Are you kidding? You made us a priority over your friends. But I know things come up. I just wanted you to know you could decide whatever you wanted to. I'm looking forward to tomorrow too." And this nonsense with one jealous cowboy wasn't going to derail a good day. "Breakfast with the guys will be good. Blake will get some more time with Ava too. That's so sad about his sister, I didn't know."

"It was hard. She was so little. Her little body couldn't..." West firmed his lips as his voice shook. "We went to her funeral, me and Hank, and all I wanted in the whole world was to hold Ava and protect her."

He found West's gaze and held it firm. "We're all together now. We're as close to protected as anyone is going to get."

"I know. The heart don't care, baby. The heart just knows one little girl died, and it could have been ours."

"Honey." He put his arm around West and pulled him close. "It's scary, you're right. I'm so sorry."

"I feel bad for them. But tomorrow I want to just be us, run out to Denver, do some shopping, do something fun with the beasts, have a good supper, come home."

"Perfect." He kissed West's nose and grinned. "You want a beer? I need to get back to work, but you don't."

"No. No, I'm going to email Elle and tell her we're for sure coming, and then I need to put wood in the wood room for tonight." West winked at him. "You wouldn't want me beered up with an axe right there."

He blew West a kiss. Just a few years ago West might not have been so careful. "So we'll take advantage of nap time and then we'll order pizza. Love you, honey."

"Love you, baby. If you order, get me something greasy and wonderful."

"A salad. Got it!" He grabbed his flannel and tucked it back over his shoulder. Back to work. And then a weekend family day. He pinched himself and it stung. Yep. This was really real.

17

"I'm sorry, West. I didn't know. I'm sorry." Blake's eyes were devastated, the man having caught him when the kids and Trey went in the diner with Lowell.

"No worries. He overstepped, Trey dealt with it, and now we know." It wasn't no thing, and if Craig made it a thing, West would make things crystal clear.

Hell, it got him laid last night, didn't it?

"Well, we'll watch him. A guy like that usually has bigger issues. Thanks for being cool about it. Hopefully Trey's okay. Lukas was pretty clear on just what all was said."

"You just go let your best girl love on you over pancakes." Lukas was fine by last night, maybe even a little proud of himself.

Blake smiled brightly. "I will do that. Thank you, sir." Blake ducked inside as West held open the door. "Where is she? I just don't see her anywhere."

"Look down here!" Ava waved her hand.

"I know I hear her…"

Ava stomped her little foot like she knew there was no way he hadn't seen her. "I'm down here, cowboy!"

"Oh, my goodness. There you are!" Blake scooped her right up into his arms and she giggled and hugged his neck.

"My cowboy!" She patted his cheeks, just like she had when she was just wee. Sweet baby.

"We got a long wait, baby?" he asked.

"Nope. Less than five. She's putting some tables together."

"I'm *hungry*." Lukas rubbed his tummy.

Lowell was smiling at his phone. It didn't take a genius to know who was texting him.

West motioned over with his chin. "Puppy love, huh?" He'd never been so young.

Trey smiled at him. "I think we were born thirty."

"You know it. Maybe older." Today he was feeling every second.

They were seated quickly, and Trey asked for a round of coffee before his butt hit the chair. Ava sat between him and Blake, and Lukas between Trey and Lowell.

"French toast, please." Lukas said without even picking up a menu.

Lowell leaned over to him. "You've been here a few times, huh? Is it good?"

"So good." Lukas beamed at him. "It's big pieces too."

"The happy face pancakes are the best," Ava shot back. "Don't you think so, Daddy?"

"I like the Denver omelet here, baby girl, with wheat toast and hash browns." He wasn't going to lose the chance for an omelet from a flat top.

"Dad's boring. Eggs." Lukas made a face.

"What? I like eggs. Sunny-side up. Bacon, hash browns, rye toast..."

"Bo-rr-ring." Lukas sang, teasing.

Trey stuck his tongue out at Lukas and shook his head, grinning.

He chuckled softly. "You want to share a griddled cinnamon roll, baby?"

"Oh. That's evil. Yes, please."

Ava's eyes got huge. "Can I have a bite?"

"Of course, baby girl."

"You want a bite Cowboy Blake?" Ava patted his hand fondly.

"Oh, no thank you." Blake caught her little hand in his. "I have to watch what I eat so I can ride next weekend."

"You see they got an egg white omelet with a ton of veggies and jalapeno and sh—tuff? That's what I'm going to have. It looks good." Lowell shook his head at Lukas and grinned. "Are you going to rodeo like your daddy?"

Lukas blinked and suddenly looked terrified, like he didn't want to answer the question. He didn't, instead he shrugged and pushed his fork around on the table.

"Lukas was talking about being a vet the other day..." Trey offered.

"Oh, dude!" Lowell's eyes went wide. "Dude! That's *amazing*! Vets are so important."

"Right, and my girl here wants to be a safety man. I told her we'll start on the horse riding this spring." West winked at Ava. There was no way—none—that he was going to let a bunch of cowboys grab her, but she was four. He'd turn her to something less dangerous, like nuclear physics.

Lukas glanced at Trey and then looked at him. "Can I ride too?" he asked softly.

"Of course." Sweet boy. "I told you, I'm bringing four riding horses. You'll need to learn about horses to be a vet, and riding is fun as hell. We'll all ride up into the mountains and have a trail ride, once y'all are saddle ready."

Lukas got a nod from Trey and that seemed like it was the end of that. They put in their orders and sipped their coffee while Blake and Lowell filled him in on the news and the gossip.

The words poured over him—Sam Masters was on top in bareback, Ollie Hage took a hoof to the back of the head and he was out, the lead was spinning wildly in bull riding, but Gemini was taking bull of the year. All normal stuff— some good, some bad. Just rodeo news.

But the food was worth the wait. Lukas chewed happily, doing a little dance in his chair. Ava took a bite of her pancakes, a bite of Blake's bacon, a bite of Trey's hash browns, and several bites of his omelet.

"So you comin' to finals, West?" Blake asked, pausing before he stuffed another bite into his mouth. "Your outfit's gonna be there, right?"

"I am. I'm bringing the whole family. Thought we'd make it a vacation. I'm shooting a commercial, doing some signings, that sort of thing." He was actually looking forward to letting the whole family see this new part of his work.

"Good." Blake nodded once. "Wouldn't be the same without you."

"Vacation?" Lukas's ears perked up. "With us too?"

Trey laughed. "Well, we were going to tell you soon, but now that you've heard. Yes, we're all going to Las Vegas."

Lukas whooted, then covered his mouth, all wide eyes. "Oops."

"Oh, dude. Very cowboy." Lowell grinned. "We should all have breakfast one morning at the big buffet. After we ride."

"They have champagne on Sundays, but that's before y'all ride. We might have to have two breakfast buffets..."

West winked at Trey. They could spend a couple of hours getting slowly and pleasantly toasted.

"All we can eat, right?" Trey winked at him.

"Oh, man. I'm stuffed, y'all. I'm not going to eat again all day." Lowell leaned back in his chair, grinning. "That was so good."

"Right? I'm going to have to jog behind the car all the way to Denver." West waggled his eyebrows at Ava.

Ava giggled. "You can't run behind a car, you'll get runned over."

"You think? I'm pretty fast..." he teased. "And your dad drives slow."

"He drives like the old man he is." Trey winked at him. "Right?"

"Uh-huh." She looked to Blake. "My dad is old like the dinosaurs."

"And Jesus!" He loved this game. "Dad went to high school when Jesus was a *baby*."

Lukas nodded. "He's older than the *moon*."

"Man, maybe I'm too old to go to Denver..." Trey grinned at Lukas.

"Dad!" Lukas shook his head. "It's just a joke."

"Oh...well in that case."

West chuckled, winking at Lukas. "He's older than God, but he's pretty."

"You think Dad is pretty?" Lukas asked.

"I do. I think he's fine."

"Mhm. So like a cowboy. If he thinks he's in trouble he tells you how pretty you are." Trey rolled his eyes, playing.

Blake laughed. "He might have you there, West."

"You can take the cowboy out of Texas..." West shot back.

"Careful, or I'll send the cowboy back to Texas."

You've already done that once. He chuckled, but it wasn't funny yet. Maybe in a couple of years. Maybe in a couple of decades.

Not yet.

"No. No, if you send Daddy away, I will go with him, and you will cry." Ava stared at Trey, her little eyes flashing. "Daddy needs us. So bad."

Nothing like a four-year-old drawing a line in the sand.

"Oh, honey, I was teasing Daddy. And I guess it wasn't funny. I'm sorry. I'm not going to send him anywhere. I need him right here too."

"We're still learning about teasing," He murmured to Blake, and Blake grinned at him.

"God, I remember how hard that was, when I was a kid." Blake winked at Ava. "It's hard to tell, sometimes. Are you crazy excited about your family day in Denver?"

Oh, good kid. So good. West did like Blake a ton.

"Uh-huh." Ava jumped right on that, worry already forgotten. "We're going to the zoo!"

"You are? Cool!"

"And buying me a coat and boots and gloves, remember?" West wanted to remind her of the less fun bits too. Sometimes that prevented a meltdown.

If they were lucky.

Ava leaned over to Blake and whispered loudly, "Daddy needs a warm coat. He gets *cold*."

"Does he? You should give a ton of snuggles then." Blake whispered back. "What color coat is he getting?"

Ava looked him over critically, tilting her head. "Black. To go with his hat."

Trey nodded. "I approve, you have good taste, baby. Daddy needs help picking these things out. He's not as good at it as you are."

"No. No, he isn't real fashionisty."

"Fashionisty?"

She nodded. "Me and Dad watch *Project Runway*."

Blake glanced at Trey, and Trey shrugged. "Guilty pleasure. But Ava always has opinions."

"*Project Runway*." He grinned at Trey. "I bet she *loves* Christian Siriano."

"He's *fierce*, Daddy!"

Lowell laughed and elbowed him. "West, your four-year-old just said 'fierce'. You are in so much trouble."

"Tell me about it. They're both smart as whips, gorgeous, and talented as all get out. I'm either in big trouble or the luckiest father on earth." He tried real hard never to call one good-looking and one smart or anything like that. It was impossible to know what was fixin' to hurt someone's feelings.

Ava loved every single word of praise and sat up tall in her seat, smiling as she took another bite of her pancakes. At four, she was always seeking approval. Lukas played it way cooler and just gave him a little nod.

"You guys want more coffee?" The server stopped by with a pot in her hand.

"Mm. Yes, please, ma'am." Lowell pushed his mug over.

"Lord yes, thank you, ma'am." He could so use a warm-up.

She poured all around and stopped by him, leaning over as she filled his mug. "Good to see you back." She gave him a wink.

"It's damn fine to be back, Holly. Thank you." He grinned over at her, tickled as all get out. "I missed all this."

"Are you a big sponsor now? I thought I saw your name around. One of the outfitters?"

He felt Trey look over at them with interest.

"I got me a part-ownership, yeah. I'm fixin' to shoot a commercial next month in Vegas, even." It felt good, if he was honest, to be doing something, contributing.

"A commercial? Like on the TV?" She looked impressed. "You're doing good, huh?"

"I am. I'm retired from the circuit, I'm loving being here with my family, and I'm looking forward to celebrating everything from Thanksgiving to Valentine's day." It was stupidly normal, and he didn't mind a bit.

"Well good for you. Hope we see you a lot. You'll be a celebrity here soon enough." She put the check on the table before she walked away. "No rush, whenever you're ready."

Trey reached for it. "We're going to get this for you guys for helping us out yesterday."

"I—" Blake flushed a deep red. "I'm real sorry about that. I swear, we didn't know. We just wanted to stop by."

"Of course you didn't." West rolled his eyes. "The altitude obviously made him lose his goldurn mind."

"I thought maybe he wasn't sober, but he sure was." Lowell shook his head and sipped his coffee.

"Blake if you apologize again we really might have to make you run behind the car." Trey touched Blake's hand. "Thank you. Honestly. It wasn't your fault, but you two did take care of it. I appreciate it."

"No problem, Mr. Trey. None at all."

"Dad, why do cowboys call you 'Trey'?" Lukas asked, and West immediately had to fight a wicked smile.

"Well, for starters I have asked them all a dozen times to call me *Jeremy*." Trey eyeballed Blake, playing. "But your Daddy started calling me that when we first met to tease me. I'm Jeremy Dunn the Third, meaning my grandfather was Jeremy Dunn and my father was Jeremy Dunn...so I'm number three. Trey means three."

Oh, Trey left out the part about how he used to hate it. Maybe for the kids' sake? Maybe because he didn't hate it so much anymore?

Maybe he'd just given in to the inevitable. West liked that idea, he enjoyed winning. "And, because I adore you, son, I insisted I would call you Quad if we named you Jeremy the Fourth."

"So we didn't." Trey's tone was dry as dust.

Lowell snorted a laugh and covered it with his coffee mug.

"Nope. We most definitely didn't." He beamed at his lover.

"Are you teasing, Daddy?" Ava asked.

"Nope. I'm not." Although, had Trey insisted, he wouldn't have done that to his son. Mostly. After the first year or two.

"I like my name." Lukas said firmly.

"It's a good name," Blake agreed. "I like it too."

"It was my mother's father's name. That's the grandpa you never met, he died before you were born."

"And grandpa your dad lives in San... Fris...?"

"My father lives in San Francisco. Well, outside it." Trey nodded. "Very good memory, Lukas."

Lowell nodded and Blake hugged an arm around Ava. "We have to go, baby girl."

"Can't you stay, Cowboy Blake? You can stay in Daddy's downstairs room..."

"Rodeo cowboys have to ride, angel baby." West stood from the table. "And we have to go to the zoo. Hug Blake so you can run to the potty."

Ava hopped up and stood on her chair to hug Blake and he spun her around. "I'm going to miss you, but I'll see you in Vegas. You might get to watch me ride, okay?"

"Okay!"

Lukas hugged both the guys. "Vegas will be cool."

Trey shook hands. "Good to see you again, Blake. Nice to meet you Lowell. Good luck before finals."

"Thanks. We're not rocking it, but we didn't bust our melons like some." Lowell gave West a rolled eye.

"Shut up."

"I don't know, I think I like him better since he bonked his head." Trey gave him a wink and a happy smile. Happy enough to make it worth it. "I'm going to take Ava to the bathroom. Come on Lukas, you too."

"Okay, Dad. I'll see you later, Lowell."

They toodled off, and he signed Trey's name, snagging the credit card. "Thanks for joining us, boys."

"You really okay, West? Like for real?" Blake wouldn't quite meet his eyes. "We were real sorry about Hank."

"Yeah, him and me? We had some good talks, those last few weeks. I miss his face." And that was the God's honest truth. He'd never had a better friend, never would, and he had a hole inside him that wanted to reach out and ask advice, every goddamn day.

"He was the real deal, huh?" Blake squinted, eyes going past him. "Everybody misses him. His name comes up all the time."

"Good. I'd hate to believe he would fade away." He gave Blake a hard man-hug. "You know about that."

Blake returned the hug letting him feel some of that emotion. "Won't happen. As long as someone is thinking about them, they can't. Right?"

"Yessir. So long as we tell the stories. You and me, we'll tell all the stories." And dammit, he would start talking to his buddies about Hank, about the ones they'd lost.

"Thanks for letting us drop by. I'm happy for you, that

things worked out like you wanted." Blake elbowed Lowell. "I gotta get Lowell to his girl before they both drive me insane."

Lowell blushed. "It's been a minute since I seen her is all."

"Y'all be careful. Holler if you need me." He walked them out, shivering in the wind. Damn, he needed that coat.

By the time Trey joined them he had the truck all warmed up though, so his babies could climb into a warm car.

Trey rested a hand on his thigh. "I was happy with my eggs. How was everybody's breakfast?"

"Good!" Two voices called out from the back seat.

"Are we ready for a road trip?"

"Yeah!"

Trey looked over and grinned at him. "I think we're ready, Daddy."

"Let's do this, then." West sure hoped the snow held off until tomorrow. It wasn't a super long drive, but he didn't love driving in the bad weather. He turned on the radio, then headed out toward the highway.

"That was a nice visit. They seem like good kids." Trey leaned about as close as he could get with the console between them.

"They are. I mean, simple, straight-forward, raised right." He knew Lowell's folks some, and Blake's people dearly, and they were all decent, down home, country.

"A far cry from the cowboys that you used to have visit." Trey laughed. "I didn't know what to think when they walked in the door."

"Those kids aren't friends. I don't have a ton of friends left on the circuit." Everyone was dying or married or busy with their families. The days of wild parties were pretty much over.

He could feel Trey's eyes on him. "I'm sorry, honey. But you've got a new focus now, you'll make some new friends. We will. Together."

What would he say to that? They hadn't ever really made friends together. He wasn't sure how on earth he even would, but it wasn't worth arguing over. He got super bored, and he'd go get himself a job at the Lowe's for fun. Oh, wait, he was supposed to answer. "I got y'all."

"You do. And your work. Did I hear right? You're shooting a commercial in Vegas?"

"I am, yeah. I've got the day booked for a couple three promo shots for the stores and for the Tractor Supply spots on the big screen during the short-go at the finals."

"That sounds amazing. I didn't quite understand what a big deal this outfitters of yours is. Do you think I could bring the kids to watch? I wonder if Ava could behave long enough?"

"I told them that we would have the kids with us. I figure you could always take Ava swimming or upstairs if she gets frustrated. We're shooting in the hotel."

"Oh, perfect. Lukas will be fascinated I'm sure, but he's young too. We'll see how it goes. It sounds like fun."

West looked in the rearview, not surprised to find Ava asleep already and Lukas reading. "I wanted to make it as easy as I could." He shot Trey a wicked grin. "And as tempting."

"Did you think I'd say no?"

"I was worried. I didn't want to go without y'all." It was going to be tough, without Hank, with the memorials.

Trey squeezed his thigh. "We'll be there for you, honey. I wasn't before, but I will be now."

"Yeah...I just..." West cleared his throat. "Not now, baby. Later, but not while I'm driving." He couldn't get all misty.

"I love you." Trey ducked under his seatbelt long enough to lean over and kiss his cheek and then changed the subject. "Family road trip. I feel so domestic. I think we need to shop first while the kids have patience and before we try to do the zoo so you'll have a coat."

"Thank God. I would freeze to death out there. We don't have to do the whole zoo, either. Hit the highlights and go." He was easy.

"Ava won't have the patience for the cold long. We can do the indoor stuff and see the bears. I think they have a little movie. We'll see how it goes."

"Sure. I'm pretty sure she'd be happy with just going in, seeing one thing, and then getting a stuffed polar bear."

Trey laughed. "Lukas will not be. But since you'll be happy to buy that polar bear, we can split up if we need to."

"We'll figure it out. I can carry her if I need to. You know that."

"My strong cowboy."

Trey turned the music up, and they sang the rest of the way to Denver. They'd always shared music; they had the same taste, and Trey wasn't afraid to sing loud.

By the time they'd reached Cherry Creek Mall, West was exhausted, the stress of the drive making his jaw ache. "Okay, y'all. Let's do this thing. No bitching, okay?"

Trey pulled Ava out of the car, and she sidled right up to him. Lukas followed along with his book in his hands. "I'll drive home, honey. The weather's looking iffy and I'm better in snow."

"Your arm, though..." He could do it. He just wasn't used to the start and stop and all. He drove long hours on highways.

"Okay, maybe I'm not better left-handed." Trey stuck his tongue out playfully. "This should come off at the end of the week. I can't wait. I'm so sick of it."

"I bet. You'll have skinny, stinky arm!" He was ready for Trey to be better, just because he knew how much easier things would be, from showering to fucking.

"It won't stink for long because I am going to take a four-hour shower."

"You'll turn into a prune," Lukas said with all the wisdom of a seven-year-old.

"I'll be even more wrinkled than I already am." Trey hugged Lukas to his side as they walked into the mall. Ava had her little hand in his. "Coats. Hm."

"There's a Levi's store and a North Face. North Face ought to do it, don't you think?" That would be relatively affordable, not fancy, and washable. He liked shit that washed.

"Yeah, perfect. We can get boots and the whole thing there I bet. Let's get you warm, Daddy."

Once in the store, they traded kids. Trey and Ava went to wander and find him gloves and a hat and Lukas went with him to find a coat.

"You want to look cool Daddy. Like the snowboarders do."

"Do I? Okay. You'll have to help me. I want to be cozy." Cool. He had the cowboy chic thing down, but snowboarder fashion? Yeah, no.

Lukas's help was really no help at all, but it kept the kid busy. What was helpful was the salesperson who took one look at him and brought him a plain, hip-length parka with a zipper-out, down shell inside.

"Black, burgundy, and hunter green." She smiled and held out a black one for him to try on.

"Oh, that looks cozy." He shrugged the coat on, looking for Lukas. "You like?"

"Can you get the green one? I like the green one better."

He looked around for Trey. Really, his man was the one to decide. He saw Ava first, she came trotting over waving toasty looking gloves.

"Hey, that's nice. Is it comfy?" Trey circled him and tugged on the hem. "Is it long enough? It looks good."

"It's comfortable. Lukas thinks the green one is better." He took the gloves from Ava with a grin. "You got an opinion?"

"I think I agree with Lukas." Trey took a couple of steps back and looked at him. "You're not really a black kind of guy."

The salesperson laughed and traded him the green for the black.

He switched them out, spinning around so they could all see him in his finery. The coat was light and comfortable, but warm.

"There you go. I love it." Trey gave it another walk around. "Did you see the gloves? Do you want a hat?"

"I think I'd better get one for times when my Stetson won't work, huh? I love the gloves." He winked at Trey. "I bet Ava picked them out."

"Ava picked out some that were more...pink." Trey grinned at him. "But we discussed it and decided that you needed something that would go with everything. And also not get confused with her gloves. Right, baby?"

"That's impor-tant," Ava agreed, nodding seriously.

"It so is. I like these, very much." He shrugged the coat off and took it and the gloves up to the cash. "I just need a cap for my poor head. Nothing too tight."

That scar still ached.

Trey snagged a simple black beanie from a stack near the register. "Will this work? Hang on, that's a medium. Maybe you want a large."

"Can we see the bears now?" Ava tugged on his jeans.

"Let's go with the large, yeah. No squeezing." He scooped Ava up. "Two shakes, angel girl. Okay?"

"I have to go to the bathroom." Lukas was doing a little dance next to him.

"Oh." Trey swooped right in on that. "Uh... We'll be back okay? You got this?"

"On it." He settled Ava on his hip and grabbed his wallet. "Let's pay so we can enjoy the zoo, okay?"

"The bears!" she squealed, and the little cashier giggled.

"She's so cute. How old is she?"

"I'm four!" Ava held out her four grubby fingers.

"Four? My son just turned five. When do you turn five?" The cashier rang him up as she chatted with Ava like a total pro.

"My birthday is March two."

"Second. March second." He loved her so much, and she made him grin.

"Mine is March fifteenth. March rocks." She gave Ava a little fist bump and handed him his bag. "Have fun at the zoo."

"Thank you. Bears. Can you tell me where the closest bathroom is?" He looked up, seeing his son, who was crying and pale as milk. "Uh-oh."

And he didn't like the look on Trey's face either.

"He didn't have to pee; he had to throw up." Trey touched a hand to Lukas's forehead. "And I think he has a fever."

"Oh lord." He hurried over, touched Lukas's head. "Yeah. Okay."

Dammit.

"And that storm is here. It's snowing hard."

Trey shook his head. "Okay, what do you want to do? Head home? Stay in Denver...?"

"I want to see the bears!" Ava stepped right in front of him. "Can we go now?"

"Baby, Lukas is sick. Puking. He can't go if he's puking." Fuck a doodle doo.

"I'm okay, Daddy." The kid was turning green as they spoke.

They were so getting some Pepto on the way home.

"He can stay in the car with Dad!" She glared at Lukas. "Don't be sick, Lukas."

Trey shook his head meaningfully at West. "We better—"

Lukas covered his mouth, and Trey rushed him to a nearby garbage can.

Shit.

He knelt down and looked at Ava. "Baby girl, he's sick. I promise we'll come back, but he needs home and taking care of. You know that."

She wasn't going to be reasonable, and West was going to resort to bribery, but he had to try first. Eventually she'd develop reason, or he'd drown her.

To her four-year-old credit, she tried. Instead of screaming and throwing a tantrum, she burst into tears and plopped down on the ground. But she was still forty-five pounds of inconsolable dead-weight.

"Car?" Trey suggested, loud enough to be heard over Ava.

"Totally. I'll stop at the Walmart-Target-CVS-whathaveyou and get Pepto and chewable kid's Tylenol along with consolation prizes, hand sanitizer, and air freshener." Lord have mercy. He patted ye olde devastated child while Trey navigated the sickie.

"'M sorry." Lukas climbed into the truck, but not before they'd all gotten cold and snowy. "I'm really sorry."

"It's not your fault, Lukas. You're sick. Just close your eyes. Maybe you can sleep."

Fat chance of that with Ava wailing in her car seat beside him.

"Jesus, it's freezing out here." Trey closed the back door and climbed into the passenger seat. "Are you okay driving, honey?"

"Fine as frog hair." He was going to head from here to the nearest Walmart. And he was having them put every single item in its own bag. That way Lukas had somewhere to puke for the next hour or so.

"Crack his window a little?"

"This...sucks!"

"Ava!" Trey gave up wrestling with his seatbelt and turned around. "Enough."

"Daddy promised the bears!"

"Plans change, baby. The zoo isn't going anywhere. It's not as much fun in the snow anyway."

"I'm really sorry, Ava." Lukas sounded miserable.

"You did this on purpose!" she screamed, and West slammed on the brakes, right there in the parking lot.

"Young lady, do we scream in the car?" he snapped, whipping around to glare at her.

"No." She stared back and for a second he got a glimpse of the teenager she was going to become. Every bit as wild as he was. "Sir."

Damn straight. He held her gaze until she backed off. Then he got them moving again.

Lord have mercy, he was not going to survive until she

was grown. Of course, Trey would have it worse, because there was no way his Mary Poppins lover was going to know what to do with a hellion on wheels. He was going to have to buy stock in popcorn.

"Maybe don't slam on the brakes in the snow if you can help it. You're going to skid and hit somebody." Trey patted his knee.

"Right." He told himself to become Zen. Practice deep breathing. Peace and light and shit. All he needed was to get to a store to buy Pepto. *Oh look, a Target.* "I'm heading right there to get the sick-o what he needs."

"Sounds good. Thanks, honey. Leave it running for us." Trey smiled at him. "I'll hold down the fort."

"Yessir." He found a grin for his lover, then he sprinted into the Target. Time for meds, bribe toys, Sprite, and a soft sweater to wear in the house when he was cold.

18

J eremy looked out the sliding doors to the deck and watched West stack firewood in the snow. West had on his new coat, new boots...everything they'd bought yesterday, and he looked great. If not for the little grimace on his face anyone would think he belonged out there.

It looked like he was about done, and he'd be hauling in a load for the woodstove and another for the fireplace pretty soon, so Jeremy left him to it and went to the kitchen to put on a pot of coffee and start lunch. Grilled cheese was the plan, even for Lukas, who'd slept for fourteen hours and woke up feeling fine.

Like, fine. No fever, not grumpy, hungry for breakfast. He was glad; he hated when his kids were sick, but he couldn't help but roll his eyes a little after all the drama the day before. Thankfully Ava showed no sign of whatever Lukas had had, so it hopefully wasn't a virus. The last thing they needed was a full round of twenty-four-hour vomiting.

He found the filters and started the coffee, pulled out the griddle and went hunting in the fridge for cheese.

Ava came in, dragging her new teddy bear. "Where's Daddy?"

"He's out dealing with the wood. You can see him through the back door if you want to. How's Mister Bear? Is he feeling better?" Lukas was sick, and Mr. Bear had been under the weather last night too.

"Uh-huh. Can I go help him?"

He wasn't sure about that. West had a deep frown and wasn't talking much today. Jeremy thought headache more than bad mood, but there was no telling.

"No, it's very cold out and it's snowing. Would you like me to put on a movie for you? I'm making grilled cheese for everybody."

He could understand the headache. West had to drive in the snow and the traffic...and with Lukas puking in the back seat. It wasn't exactly the day they'd planned. They probably should have looked closer at the weather report, but West really did need that coat.

And it looked great on him. Even scowling West was as handsome as ever.

She stamped her little foot. "No, I want Daddy. Is it his weekend?"

Oh boy. "We don't have weekends anymore, Ava. Daddy lives here now, so we both get to see you guys all the time." He tried the first line of defense—distraction. "How about you help me with lunch? Daddy will be hungry when he comes in."

She pursed her lips, giving him a suspicious look, then she lit up. "Yes! Yes, I can help make Daddy's lunch!" She ran to the glass door and banged on it. "I'm making you lunch, Daddy!"

West blinked the snow away, eyes searching to make

sure Jeremy was in the kitchen with her, then he gave her a thumbs-up.

He reminded himself that Ava was just four, and of course her best friend was going to be the guy that had bought her a stuffed bear, not the guy who did three loads of her laundry this morning. He ought to be used to it, but sometimes it still got under his skin.

Also that thumbs-up for Ava was more enthusiastic than anything West had said to him all day. Not that it was rational to be jealous of a four-year-old.

"Okay. So we're going to butter the bread first. Can you get the bread out of the drawer?" He let Ava fuss with that while he moved the butter from the counter to the table and got them each a knife.

"Four for Dad and two for brother and two for me and four for Daddy!" She was just singing away. "Me and Dad are making the lunches 'cause we're so nice, and brother is sick, and Daddy is freezing his peanuts off!"

Those poor peanuts.

Jeremy managed not to laugh out loud, but he chuckled and smiled happily at Ava. "We are totally nice. But, better than that, they'll appreciate that we did the work, and you'll get a nice thank you. Which is pretty awesome."

She brought over the stack of bread. "What's preciate? Does Daddy preciate us?"

There was a time when he'd have said no to that question, but that had changed. A lot of things had changed. West's injury, losing Hank...they hadn't talked about any of it specifically, but he knew. Those things were profound. "He definitely does. Appreciate means that someone is thankful for the things you do for them. Like... I appreciate that Daddy is out there in the snow right now so we can have wood for our fire later and be warm."

He could see her little mind working. "And I preciate when you let me read a book and not nap. And brother preciates when we go to the library?"

He smiled. She was sharp as a tack, just like Lukas was at her age. He'd be lucky to keep up with either of them. "Just like that! Very good. That's a nice big word, huh?"

He put the sandwiches together on the griddle. "I'd pick you up to help, sweetie, but I can't with the one arm. I'm getting my cast off this week though!" He might as well be four himself, he was so excited and telling everyone he could.

"Will Daddy go away when you can use it again? I like when he stays with us. A very lot."

"No. Daddy lives here now with us. He's not going away."

God. Saying it out loud to a four-year-old somehow added weight to the decision. Like there'd be hell to pay if they fucked this up again.

"You promise? Promises mean you can't break them for nothing or you *die*."

See that? Hell to pay. "Yes." God help him. "I promise. I love your daddy very much, and I want him to stay forever."

Her eyes lit up like he'd just given her the best present. "Dad! Me *too*!"

"Yay!" He started to try to pick her up and was reminded that was a bad idea. *Ow.* He nuzzled her nose instead. "Oh! I have to flip the sandwiches. You want to go wave at Daddy and tell him lunch is ready?"

"Uh-huh!" She beamed at him, singing as she skipped. "Daddy is staying! Dad says so! Dad promiseded, and that's important and I preciate him so *bad*!" She banged on the glass. "DADDY! COME PRECIATE YOUR LUNCH!"

All Jeremy could do was laugh and shake his head. He was either super lucky, or really, really stupid. He decided to go with lucky. He scooped the sandwiches onto plates. "Lukas! Come preciate your lunch too!"

"Smells good." Lukas walked in, then went to the back door. "Why's Daddy sitting on the snowpile?"

"Why...?" *What?* He looked out over Lukas's head. West was...getting snowed on. "Have a seat, son. Ava? You too. Grilled cheese is better hot, right? Go sit." He shooed Ava away from the door and opened it slightly, hoping West would hear him. If not, Jeremy would slip into his boots and jog out there.

"Honey? You hungry? Ava and I made grilled cheese."

"Did you? Cool." West didn't sound right, but his lover stood up, closing his eyes a second. "I was trying to get some wood in."

"Thank you. I think there's plenty. Come in here and warm up." Did West have Lukas's fever? He'd check once West had eaten something. "Just leave your boots..." He shook his head. "You know where to leave your boots. You're not four."

That earned him a low chuckle. "No, sir, I am not. I do got me a bitch of a headache, though."

He knew Lukas was about to say something about the cursing, but he caught his son's eye and held up a finger, and Lukas went back to his lunch.

"I'll get you some Tylenol. Sit and eat." Should he worry? Was this just a cowboy with a headache thing, or a bull rider with an old head injury thing?

"Thanks." Did West stumble on his way in? Seriously?

"Hey." He stopped West with both hands, trying to check him out and hiding it by helping his lover get his coat off. "Anything other than a headache?"

"It's just my damn head. It ain't no thing."

He reached around to the scar, surprised to find it swollen and hot to the touch.

West hissed, shook his head. "Easy…"

"Hey, you guys, I'm going to get Daddy something for his headache. We'll be right back, okay?"

He didn't wait for an answer, leading West to the den where they could talk. He heard Ava start to fuss, and Lukas said something, and things got quiet again.

He didn't waste any time fussing over West either; he needed information first. "What do I need to know here, West?"

"It gets irritated. Doc says there was a lot of dirt up in there, and that the flap wasn't smooth. It just gets to hurting."

Doc. He remembered Doc. He was going to look the man up in Vegas and find out what West wasn't telling him.

"So you overdid it? How long were you just going to sit out there? Why didn't you come in?"

"I was hurting, dammit. I told you. I couldn't hardly breathe with it."

"Okay, honey. I get it." Deep breaths. West had downplayed the whole thing, told him it wasn't a big deal, but this wasn't a good time for twenty questions. Got it. Take care of him now, figure the rest out later. "I'm going to get you some Tylenol. Do you want to lie down? Or maybe just sit here and put your feet up?"

"After I appreciate Ava, huh? She was excited, and I hate to disappoint y'all." West cupped his jaw. "Then I'd love some Tylenol and a nap with you. We got any ice packs?"

"We have two kids, and my middle name is Klutz. Of course we have ice packs." He stayed close to West on their way back to the kitchen. "Appreciate is her new word."

"I hear you helped with lunch, little girl. It looks

amazing. Thank you." West patted her head, looking about green around the gills.

"I did! Because Dad said you were working hard and we preciate being warm!" Her volume level was hurting his head, he could only imagine what poor West was dealing with.

"Inside voice, baby," he whispered to her.

"I do appreciate that, my baby girl. Very much." West sat, and Lukas frowned at him.

"Daddy?"

"Yes, son?"

"Do you need me to put ice on your scar? You look like you're hurting."

Lukas knew more about this scar thing than he did. "I'll get it, Lukas. Are you done eating?" He didn't waste time letting that sink in, he just went for an ice pack in the freezer, wrapped it in a dishtowel and handed it to his son.

"Thanks, Dad." Lukas looked at West, so serious. "Don't throw up, okay?"

"Jeez, you puke once..." West braced himself against the table. "Ready."

Ava nodded. "I'll count. One. Two. Three."

Lukas put the ice pack to West's head, and West went gray.

Ava cheered for him. "Daddy! You didn't throw up!"

"Hooray." He bent and kissed West's cheek. "Done this a few times, huh? Keep breathing, Daddy."

"Yep. I know how to help. It gets all swole up." Lukas looked so proud.

"That's what he told me." He ducked out of the kitchen for a quick second to grab the Tylenol and set two on the table with a glass of water.

"Ava, are you all done with lunch? It's naptime."

"Can we make peanut butter cookies after naps?" Always negotiating, his daughter.

"If you actually sleep, yes." Selfish motive. He could go for some cookies.

"I will sleep, Dad." She nodded and stuck out her pinky for a promise.

He hooked his pinky in with hers. "Come on, I'll tuck you in."

"Oh, I would preciate that." She looked over at West. "Can I kiss you, Daddy?"

"Oh, angel girl. You can always kiss me. *Always.*"

She went and kissed his forehead. "Is that 'cause you preciate me?"

"No, baby. That's because I love you."

"I love you too! Be careful of your head."

So adorable. He looked at West. "You head up when you're ready. I'll clean up lunch and join you after. Lukas? You can nap or you can read, but you do it in your room. Deal?"

"Deal." Lukas nodded. "Do you need me to hold this still? I can do it upstairs until Dad comes up."

"Oh, I'm ok—"

"No. I'll walk upstairs and hold it until Dad comes." So serious. So much like him.

"You're a good boy, Lukas. Go on up with Daddy. He's a stubborn patient." He winked at West and headed off with Ava and her bear.

It didn't take him long to get her down, she was still pretty worn out from the epic tantrums the day before. Grilled cheese sandwiches didn't keep. He took three or four cold, rubbery bites of his trying not to waste it but gave up and tossed it along with West's.

Nothing had really gone as planned this weekend. It was

frustrating, probably for West most of all. He didn't think West would have much patience for being slowed down by a headache. He'd be there though, whether West wanted to sleep or talk or just pout for a while. He hadn't been for a long time and he wanted to make up for that.

He grabbed the Tylenol and a bottle of water from the fridge in case West needed more and headed upstairs.

———

IF WEST HADN'T BEEN SO DAMN stubborn, he would have taken a pain pill in the morning, but they were locked up downstairs and he'd been busy.

Now he was laying with his head in Trey's lap, Trey petting up on him. That was good, but it would have been better without the aching head.

Trey had traded out the first ice pack for a fresh one, but that was warming up now too. In all that time Trey hadn't really said a word, just sat there with him, kept him company.

He closed his eyes for a second, then turned to kiss Trey's leg. "Love you."

"Thank you, honey. Are you feeling any better?" Trey spoke softly and stroked a hand down his arm.

"I am, yeah. That stupid thing just gets to hurting."

"Is it because yesterday was a tough day, maybe?"

"Oh, I'm sure the stress didn't help. I was tugging my cap down a lot too, rubbing on it.

"Maybe we should have gotten you earmuffs instead. Those are sexy." Trey chuckled. "They come in leopard print, pink shag..."

"Oh, pink shag. That is so me..." He chuckled softly, pleased when that didn't hurt. "How does it look?"

Trey leaned back a little and shifted his hair aside. "Better. Less red, less like an alien is trying to take over your skull."

"Yeah, it pulls, all the damn time." He'd had a hell of a time keeping it closed up at first. Doc'd had to sew him up five different times.

"All the time? And there's nothing they can do about that? That sounds awful."

"I guess not. I'll stretch eventually, I reckon. It's just skin." How the hell would he know? He just kept getting headaches.

"That sucks." Trey tickled his chin. "I was watching you out there in the snow, dealing with the wood. All I kept thinking was how handsome you are."

He heated up, from the pit of his belly up. "Yeah? I like that."

Trey hummed low. "Mhm. Just as handsome as the day I met you. We're not those kids anymore, though."

"No." No, he would have done everything different, up to and including waiting for his career to be done before he pursued Trey so fiercely, but it was what it was. They weren't new to this anymore.

"I wish I'd been there for you when you did this to your head. I wish you—or anyone—had told me. I wish a lot of things. We can get past the regrets, right? Do it better this time?" Trey was still speaking gently, touches meant to soothe him.

"We're going to. I won't lose you again." He had committed to this. He would do it. "I couldn't tell you, you know. I didn't want to lose any time with the babies. I'd already missed so much, and I'd—" *Almost died this time.*

"I know. It doesn't stop me from wishing things were

different. I'm just glad that they...that *we* didn't lose you. I'm really in this now. You know that, right?"

"I do. You let me come upstairs." He winked up, teasing.

Trey snorted. "Oh, that? That's just because you're hotter than the sun, and I want you."

"I'll take it." He was easy. Whatever got him an in.

"Shut up, you." Trey found the little ticklish spot on his hip and tapped it, threatening but not tickling. "If it weren't for your head..."

"Mmm...and the fact that the second we got busy the kids would interrupt us." He chuckled softly, snuggling in. "I do like this, though, hanging out with your happy ass."

"Mmm and it is happy. Very, very happy." Trey gave his butt a pat. "We haven't just hung out since you moved back in, have we? We should take family nap time more often. When I was on my own, I had to use the time to get things done that I couldn't do when the kids were underfoot. I guess I'm used to having a naptime agenda."

The way he remembered it, Trey had always been busy, naptime or any time. It was an event if he could get Trey to sit and actually finish a beer.

Still, if Trey was willing to learn to enjoy downtime together, he was all over it. "I could learn to nap with you, baby."

"I'd just like to hug you properly. Four days. Four." Trey sighed. "And a few weeks of PT. But still. It will unbend."

"Yep. You'll have to tell the therapist that you're working to a long session doggie style!" Damn, he cracked himself up.

"Just for that I will. And I'll make sure you're picking me up that day."

Trey would never. *Never.* He was wound way too tight for that. But it was funny to picture it.

"Hell, I'll be in the waiting room for that." West started laughing, groaning as his head throbbed a little.

"Oh, easy baby. Hang on." Trey shifted and lay down with him. Putting that good arm under his head. "Comfy? This is good. Now I can kiss you." And Trey did. Just gentle, just sweet. "Am I allowed to say I don't like it when you're hurting? Or will you try to hide it from me again if I say that?"

"I don't like it either. It was way worse before. Now it comes in waves." He held Trey's gaze. "I love you, you know that, right?"

"I do. I like that you keep telling me though." Trey kissed him again. "Does that mean the next time you get a headache you'll tell me as soon as it starts and not do the tough cowboy thing?" Trey grinned. "Not that you're not my tough cowboy."

"I'll take it under advisement, yessir." He winked back, happy in his fucking soul. "I should have taken a biggie-wow pain pill last night, but I thought it would back off."

"Lesson learned for next—"

"Dad! Daaaaady! Daddo. Daddydoo." Ava's shout came from her room down the hall.

Trey froze. "Is that distress or boredom?"

He chuckled. "Avy-baby! My sweet baboo! My angel girl!"

She giggled. "Can I get out of bed now?"

"Are you done being ti-i-i-ired?" he sing-songed back.

"Are you done being head-ed-ed-achey?"

Her giggles were contagious, and Trey was laughing at both of them.

"I a-a-a-a-am. Lukey-Cukey?" He winked at Trey.

"Yes, Daddy-O? Oh Melonhead, oh Rodeo-O-Do-Daddy?"

"Lukey-Cukey? Are you serious?"

"Dad-o! You're not sing-ing-ing!" Ava yodeled from her room.

"Oh, good lord." Trey rolled his eyes.

"We have to tee-eee-eee-each Dad-O-Doody this ga-aa-ame!" He wasn't letting Trey off the hook.

"No. No, you don't really." Trey rolled onto his back. "I can just enjoy listening."

Ava appeared in their doorway and then launched herself onto the bed. "Daddo-doody! It's easy."

Trey's heavy sigh made him grin. "How about we put on a movie?"

"Sing with us, Dadolicious!" Lukas plopped down next to them. "Sing like you mean it!"

"Preach it, Duke Luke!" he cried, and Ava squealed, throwing her arms up.

"Pree-ee—each!"

He was having a ball.

Trey snorted. "I'm going to tickle you like I mean it. Lukey-Cukey."

Lukas beamed at Trey, obviously pleased as punch. "What if you make me pee?"

West hooted, tickled shitless. They'd been hanging out with him, and it was glorious. Lukas needed a little wicked in his life.

Ava came with that pre-installed.

"Lukey-Pukey!" Ava laughed.

"This is your fault." Trey was grinning at him though. "Daddio-dum-dum-daddoo..."

Lukas and Ava both squeaked. "Yay, Dad!"

He chuckled, taking the blame with pleasure. "Yes, sireedoodah."

"I will make pancakes for dinner if everyone will give me and Daddy fifteen more minutes to get up from our nap."

"Blueberry?" Lukas asked.

"Sure."

"Nutella!"

"Yes, Ava. Nutella if you want."

The kids scrambled off the bed. "Bye!"

Ava's little face peered back in. "Don't forget the cookies! Bye!"

The kids giggled all the way down the stairs.

God, he loved his life.

"Cookies." Trey looked at him. "I forgot about the cookies."

"We'll make magic peanut butter cookies. No worries." He could make those over a campfire, for fuck's sake.

Trey rolled back over and kissed him. "Not yet. I want my fifteen minutes, doo-doo-Daddio."

"I am completely yours, studmuffin." He took a kiss that was much more goofy and playful than erotic, but it got him the laugh he craved.

19

J eremy pulled the last suitcase down out of the attic and set it on the floor in the hallway. "That's the last of them. Man, this two-armed thing rocks." A couple of weeks of PT had really helped. Most of the time he felt like his arm actually belonged to him again.

He took his suitcase and West's into the bedroom and set them on the bed. "Lukas? Can you please put your sister's duffel in her room and put yours on your bed for me, buddy?"

"Sure! Can I bring some books and my pillow?" Lukas was in a lovely mood, both of the kids excited to show him 'Daddy's playhouse'.

"Yes. We're taking my SUV, so there is plenty of room for your books and a pillow." Two arms meant he could drive again. It was one of the first things he did after he got the cast off. His all-wheel drive was good in the snow, and so was he, so West didn't have to stress the driving. Plus, West was just better at entertaining the kids and made a decent DJ.

Hopefully it would be easy to convince West.

He heard West whistling outside, loading some random kitchen stuff in the SUV. The majority of the food they were picking up at City Market.

Somebody else was happy. If West was whistling out there in the cold it was a good day. He started pulling things out of drawers, warm things because Estes Park was often even colder than Boulder. He packed wool socks and long underwear and a bottle of lube.

Things to keep him warm.

He laughed to himself as he finished filling up his suitcase, overjoyed to be packing jeans and things with buttons and zippers because he had two hands to do up his own pants these days. Jesus, he was happy.

He started packing for West, not putting things in the suitcase yet, but laying them out on the bed: jeans, undies, long johns, socks. Just to help West get started.

And then it was on to the kids, who were much harder to pack than he was.

Both of them had 'helped'. Ava had packed her galoshes, a fairy costume, four baby dolls, twelve nightgowns and her bear. Lukas, on the other hand, had shoved in one pair of pants, eight books, three sweaters, and his pillow and comforter.

Their priorities were clear. And amusing. For Ava, he left everything but half the nightgowns and the galoshes, then added all the things she also needed. Like clothes. And a toothbrush. For Lukas, he pulled out the comforter and the pillow, which took up the whole bag, but he'd let them travel in the car.

"A-plus for remembering pants though, bud." Jeremy grinned over at his son who was digging out underwear at his direction.

"Pants are important. They keep your bits warm." Icy hands landed on his back under his shirt. "Hey, baby."

He gasped, shrinking away from his lover's frozen fingers. "Oh shi-ii-iver me timbers! Jesus, you're cold."

"Uh-huh. You're warm." Those icicles moved around to his belly and his balls tried to pull into his body. "Nice catch, by the way."

"Thanks," he squeaked. "You're killing me with those hands."

Lukas made a big show of counting his underwear and putting it in his bag. "And also two more pairs of pants."

"Socks, buddy. And some T-shirts to go under your sweaters." He turned toward West, letting those warming hands move to his back. The smile on West's face made his heart skip a beat. 'I took out a few things for you. They're next to your suitcase. Is the car good?"

"Perfect. I grabbed the things we talked about, plus some tools to do a little maintenance around the place." West kissed him quick. "I can't wait to show it off. It's not super fancy-pants, but it's absolutely not low-rent. It's a place for us to have fun, right son?"

"Yes! I love the condo! There's a pizza oven deal!"

"Ooh. Are we having pizza for dinner then?" He didn'-care if it was fancy, all he cared about was it was warm inside and surrounded by snow outside. He could count on both of those things at least. "Did you order the turkey and everything?"

"I did." West nodded, winked at him. "For tonight? Mexican. Then I got an order of pizza crusts and all the toppings for tomorrow night. Pizza is the ultimate pre-Thanksgiving meal, right? We'll have a feast and six days and five nights of games and reading and having fun. Right?"

"And it'll be together," Lukas whispered. "Like all four of us."

"You can say that louder, buddy." He opened one arm so Lukas could join them in their hug. "I'm excited too."

"I said all four of us!" Lukas hugged them and it wasn't a second before Ava was there too, squirming right into the middle of them.

"Ava helped me pack her things, Daddy." He grinned at West and winked. "She will not run out of nightgowns."

"Excellent. Nightgowns are important." West winked. "There is a washer-dryer combo there, though, should we need it."

"And there's all these games, Dad!" His son bounced— actually bounced. "Clue and Stratego and chess and Triominos and Guess Who and Sorry and Mousetrap!"

"Well geez. It really is a playhouse." Fun Daddy. That's what he'd always heard. Daddy was fun. He wondered sometimes what West heard about him.

"It is a vacation house, right? They're just for having fun together as a family." West shot him a look. "We went to a garage sale, and they had a whole shed of games and puzzles and stuff for a hundred dollars, and we decided to invest in it for the condo, right son?"

"Uh-huh. It was my job to make sure the games had all the pieces and throw away the ones that didn't."

"Very cool." He wasn't sure what that look meant, so he let it roll off and turned to Lukas. "Zip up your bag and put it in the hall with Ava's okay? You can take the comforter in the car if you really need it."

"Okay!" Lukas started fussing with the zipper.

"You all warmed up?" He gave West's butt a pat. "You want to go finish packing?"

"I do." West led the way to the bedroom. "Thanks for getting me started, baby."

"I pulled out what I knew...shirts and sweaters I had no idea." He laughed. "My chilly Texan."

"Yeah, well..." West chuckled. "The condo is toasty inside, and there's a covered area to sit outside with a little patio heater so you don't die when you're grilling or using the outside oven deal."

"It has an outside oven? Cool." He loved the idea of sitting outside with the heater. "Sounds like a great place. I can't wait to see it. I love that you just planned everything. I feel special." He tucked a finger into West's belt loop and tugged.

"You are. I want you to be able to relax. Just breathe with me and the kids." West stepped up into his space with a grin. "And you're driving."

He couldn't help the grin that practically took over his face. "I am *driving!*" He took a kiss, the quick and hard kind he liked, and resolved right then to leave his work laptop home.

"We have our own bedroom with a door that locks, and there's a hot tub outside. Tell me you packed lube."

"I packed lube." He laughed. "Three cheers for locks. A hot tub? You were just waiting to spring that on me. This is going to be the best Thanksgiving ever. Oh. Remind me to have the kids call my parents."

"Have you warned them that you're back with the evil rodeo cowboy?"

"Stop that. They liked you...eventually." His dad was a big fan. "You were only evil at first because you don't have a vagina."

"This is true. I am, honestly, vaginaless. Sans vagina? Con penis?"

"Avec dick. And I like it that way. They got over it because you, Mister West, can be very charming when you want to be." He gave West's chest a pat. "Personally I'm a fan of the less charming and more lurid tendencies, but to each his own."

"That's me—lurid tendency man. Hey, how do you feel about getting Lukas a Kindle this year for Christmas?"

"You think he'd use it? It sure would make things easier, he packed eight books for the weekend. Eight. Books." He shook his head.

"Can we like, make it so he can't download porn or empty the bank account?"

Oh no. Nope. He pretended to plug his ears. "Lalala you did not suggest our son would one day want to watch porn. Lalala I am not listening."

"He's a boy. There will be porn. Sooner than later." God, West was such a boy. "Possibly he'll sneak your Pornhub account. He's a smart kid."

"Ha! I don't have a Pornhub account. I've been stealing yours since before we got divorced." He had. He'd been stealing his ex-husband's porn.

"You're a porn thief?" West clapped his hands to his chest dramatically. "I'll never be the same!"

"You really need to change your passwords. I could have stolen a lot more than your porn, honey." He winked. "I'll look into parental controls. Let's do that for him." That was his area; parental controls.

"I think he'd be over the damn moon. Books at will." West started packing, and Jeremy was reminded that his lover was used to being on the road, being a go-baby.

"You feeling ready to be on the road? You haven't been anywhere in months." Well, except that awful trip to Denver.

Estes Park wouldn't be a long drive, an hour in good weather and no traffic, and he was hoping for both, but even if the traffic getting out was bad because of the holiday weekend they'd still be there by lunchtime.

"I'm ready for a little vacation. I'm ready for you to see the condo. I'm ready for an easy holiday altogether."

"We're taking our bags downstairs!" Lukas called from the hallway.

"Yeah! We'll be downstairs." Ava's little voice followed. "Hurry up, Daddos!"

"They don't really want to go. Maybe we should stay home?" He gave West a toothy grin and went to close up his suitcase.

"I'm sure Ava would eat your face. She told me yesterday that if Lukas got sick he could sleep in the garage."

He barked out a laugh. "Oh my God." He pulled his suitcase off the bed. "She's going to be voted most likely to kill someone in their sleep, isn't she?"

"In preschool. By high school, I'm voting serial killer."

Jeremy shook his head. "So much trouble. Are you packed, Daddo?"

"I am. Can we stop and grab doughnuts and coffee on the way out, Dad?" West grabbed him and spun him around. "Can we, Dad? Huh? Huh?"

"Yes!" He threw his arms around West's neck and hung on. "I vote Munchkins. And I'm driving so I win."

"Sounds like one hell of a plan. Let's go, Dad. I have a whole condo to show off." West set him down and they dragged their suitcases downstairs where two expectant faces were waiting for them with coats and boots on.

"Oh, are you guys coming too?" He winked at Ava.

"Dad!"

"Okay, let's get your stuff in the car. Daddy has talked me into Munchkins..."

Lukas approved. "Awesome!"

"I rock, I know." West beamed at him, then grabbed up Lukas and his suitcase all at once. "To the Mean Green Dad Machine!"

"It's black, Daddy," Ava said, rolling her eyes.

Jeremy snorted and scooped her up too. He wasn't quite at the point of trusting his arm enough to carry her suitcase too, but he knew West would trot back in and get it without him even having to ask.

He got Ava settled in her seat with her bear and a blanket. "All good, baby girl?"

"Good!" She gave him a loud, wet smack on the lips.

"Mm. I got a girl kiss!" He shouted out and closed her door.

"Lucky bastard." West winked at Lukas. "Ready to va-cay, my boy?"

"Bring it on, Daddy-O!"

Jeremy had missed how fun West was—how eager he was to explore, how much laughter and energy he brought with him.

He waited for West to lock the door and get Ava's suitcase into the truck. As soon as everyone was belted in, he started the car and called out, "Dunkin' Donuts or bust!"

He definitely needed coffee, and the kids were hungry. He leaned toward West after he pulled out of the driveway. "I'm actually thinking about one of those egg sandwich things."

"No more dieting for me. I want two apple fritters. Or an apple fritter and a blueberry doughnut." West cuddled into the seat, looking for all the world like the happiest man ever.

"I'm going to enjoy watching you eat that while I'm driving. Me. Driving." Jeremy grinned.

"I love you driving. I love you not driving. Which playlist?"

"Play the taco song!" Ave cheered as Lukas groaned.

"Okay. Taco song, then Lukas gets one. I will be DJ Daddy. Daddy DJ? Whichever."

"I'm not rubbing anything in, just glad I *can* drive." Oddly, it felt like the last piece of a complicated puzzle. West had moved back in because he'd needed help, so this new life couldn't really begin until he was whole again, and West was just staying because he wanted to.

"God, I am too. I hate driving in the snow. This is like the best vacation ever."

He snorted. "It's not snowing...*yet*." The forecast was for a good dump the day before Thanksgiving, but no one was going to have to drive. They could just stay inside and watch it come down and work their way through the piles of games.

"Maybe it'll be gorgeous the whole time." West didn't sound terribly nervous.

"It will be. Whatever it's doing outside, we'll be toasty." He pulled up to the drive-through and ordered all the goodies, plus two big coffees and two chocolate milks. That should keep everyone happy. They'd have sugared-up kids by the time they got there, but that was okay. They were going to be wound up in any case.

"I meant to ask you if you'd have friends that will be up there while we're there?"

"Who, me?" He got a totally confused look from West.

"Yeah, like in the area or anything? Anybody with kids. That kind of thing." He grabbed both coffees from the pass-through window and handed them to West.

"No, honey. Everybody I know is home for the holidays. There'll be a ton of folks in the condos though—last year the kids and I Thanksgiving'ed up there with Hank and stuff." For a second, West's smile dimmed, then it brightened back up. "Y'all need help with your donut holes?"

"M-m." Lukas's mouth was too full to answer with a "no".

He reached over and rubbed West's arm. He didn't know anything for sure because West hadn't talked much about Hank's last couple of months, but he had this feeling that he ought to be grateful for Hank this Thanksgiving. "We'll raise a glass to him. And we'll make our own new, amazing holiday memories."

"Hell yes." West caught his fingers, kissed them. "We'll grab some wine at the store, huh? Some Jiffy Pop?"

"Pop it on the stove and watch *The Wizard of Oz.*" Because that's what you did at Thanksgiving wasn't it? Football and the Wicked Witch of the West.

"Yep. The parade, the dog show, the football, the turkey. Christmas music on the way home." West chuckled softly. "Then Vegas and Christmas decorating! You want to invite Drew and his boy toy for tree trimming?"

He smiled at West. He'd been keeping Drew kind of off the radar. They'd had lunch and texted, but Drew was busy with his husband, so it had been easy to keep his little family kind of insulated for a while. "His *husband*. And... maybe. We might want to keep that just us and the kids. Let's see. It would be great to have them for some holiday cocktails at some point though."

"Whatever trips your trigger, baby. I'm easy." West shrugged. "I just want to make sure you know they're welcome up to the house."

"Thank you." He took a bite out of his breakfast as he turned onto Highway 36. It was a straight shot to Estes now, not that 36 was straight at all. It wound its way up and west, right up into the mountains. "Mmm. How's your fritter?"

"Delicious. You want your sandwich unwrapped?"

"That would be great, I'm kind of fumbling with it here." He handed it over and peeked into the back through the rearview at his quiet and happy kids. Ava would probably fall asleep soon, and Lukas would read or look out the window and start reading him any signs that zipped by. "This will be a better road trip than our last one. Because I said so."

"Amen." West stroked his thigh, eyes warm on him. "Love you, baby."

"Love you too. I'll love you more if you give me my breakfast back." He winked.

"I see how you are. All about the belly." West rolled his eyes and handed over the sandwich.

"Now you know that's not true. I'm all about you. I need my strength, right?" He shot West a knowing look before taking a big bite.

"Mmhmm..." West cleared his throat. "Door lock."

"Hallelujah!" He took another bite and chewed, grinning. They were going to use that lock tonight, damn it. He'd been a good boy in therapy and had been released to do it on his own already. He wanted to get both hands on his lover. Everywhere. West counted as a workout.

West seemed to relax more and more the higher they drove. The clouds gathered, heavier and thicker, like they were going to drive off into the sky.

The time flew by. They sang along to the radio and watched the pretty scenery go past. Even the kids behaved beautifully. "Man, it's been a long time since I was up this way. Where to, honey?"

"You want to go all the way through town and head north. You want to get unpacked, and come back for lunch and shopping?"

"Yeah, works for me. Let the kids pee and run around for a second." He was so ready to be there. He wanted this vacation even more than he'd realized. He drove slowly through the little downtown area with its cute restaurants and shopping. "This is great up here. It's adorable."

"Yeah, I love it." Jeremy could hear that in West's voice. "It's gorgeous in the summertime, and the condo has places to play for the babies. I rent it out when I'm not using it. You tell me when you want to come up, and we block off that time."

"I work from home. We can come up any time you want." Spring when it was all green, summer to escape the heat, fall to see the leaves change, winter to ski...any time was a good time. "So head north...oh, that way." He pointed, and then followed the road.

It twined up and up the mountain, and then there was a sweet little gated community and rustic, log-cabin style condos. "We're in building six, condo C. All the way in the back. We can park in the garage."

"We're here!" Lukas shouted from the back seat.

"Yay!" Ava clapped her hands and counted out the condos as they passed them. "One...two...four...six! That's six! That's Daddy's playhouse!"

"I love the log-cabin thing. And all the trees. So cozy." Jeremy pulled into the short driveway. "Does it have a clicky thing?"

"Uh, yeah. Hold up. I tossed the extra in the console." West dug it out and clicked, the garage door sliding up, exposing a line of plastic saucer-sleds, some snow shovels, and a bunch of smaller beach-type toys back along the wall.

"Right on." He pulled in and parked.

The car wasn't off two seconds before Lukas was out and running around to the back door. "Wait until you see the TV!"

"Dad! Dad! Let me out so I can go play!" Ava wailed.

"Remember, we have to unpack our special closet, right?" West said, sliding out of the car. "I've got the key."

Special closet. That sounded like fun.

"Me first!" Ava squirmed in her seat.

"Sit still, baby. I can't get your belt undone."

"Ugh!" Ava complained but she went still enough for him to get the straps undone. As soon as she was free though, she slid out and wiggled right past him.

He just shook his head, smiling to himself. The kids were excited; that was allowed. It was their holiday vacation too.

He left the suitcases for now and just grabbed all the garbage from their car breakfast before he went inside.

"Come *on*, Dad!" Lukas called from somewhere inside.

"On my way, Lukey-Cukey!" He snickered and followed the voice.

"Oh, very nice." West followed him, pinching his ass. "This is the mudroom and the laundry. Muddy, snowy boots go here."

"Daddy! The key!" Ava came to the door, hands on her hips.

"Hold on, I'm coming."

The laundry room opened up into a little kitchen and dining area, and then nice open living room with a fireplace. There were windows everywhere, showing off the huge wraparound deck and mountain view.

He wandered in, moving slowly, taking in the view and the feel of the place. "Oh, West. This is something special, huh?" He went to the window and looked at the mountains.

There was a hot tub out there, a propane deck heater, a table and chairs, and a grill.

"Daddy! The key!"

West chuckled. "Have a look around, huh? I'll open that closet for them."

He glanced back at West. "What closet is that? The games?"

"No. I put our personal things in the big linen closet—the kids' toys, books we care about, our movies, our laundry detergent, special dishes—you know, things that are *ours*."

"Oh right, rental. I forgot. Do you hire someone to clear the snow off the deck or is that a condo association thing? They did a really good job." He could run for that hot tub right now. No sweat.

"It's the condos. They do the management too. If I ever decide to stop renting it, I just let them know and we're good to go." West led him upstairs and unlocked the closet, the kids squealing over their toys and art supplies and goodies. There were three coffee cups—obviously hand-thrown pottery, one big, one purple, and one bright red. The back of the door had lines and names and dates on it, artwork taped to the back of the door. One silver buckle, a bottle of whiskey, and a pair of shattered sunglasses sitting together. It was like a snapshot of a weekend dad. "They do the cleaning, the upkeep. It's nice."

He didn't ask about the sunglasses yet, not with the kids still trying to get his attention. He helped them pull their things out, and they carried them into a bedroom and started making themselves comfortable. "This is cool, you guys just haul all this stuff out after the renters go? That's cool, it's like opening a present every time you open the closet."

"Yeah, it gives them a chance to have a permanent space with me. Somewhere special for us." West grabbed a pair of pillows and some pillowcases.

And West had turned something that could be a chore into something fun and special. It was thoughtful and sweet. "I think it's great." He pulled out a few more things at Lukas's direction and carried them into the kids' room. "You need help with your bed, Ava?"

"No, Dad. I've done this a mil-ee-on times."

Nothing like offending a four-year-old. "Got it. You're on your own then, girlie."

Lukas popped his head out. "I'll help her. I get the top bunk today and tomorrow, Ava can have it Friday and Saturday, and Thursday we'll sleep on the pull-out sofa."

"The sofa?" He looked at West curiously. "Why the sofa?"

"Two nights up for each of them. We're here an odd number of nights." West rolled his eyes dramatically. "We will sleep in our bed."

"Mhm. Some, I guess." He slid his fingers over West's hip as he went to explore the third floor, he wandered into the master bedroom. "I suppose we should unpack the car."

"After we make the bed." West pulled the comforter back and put on one side of the fitted sheets, offering him a wicked, naughty grin. He did like this whole Estes-Park-West. "That way we can...nap at will."

"I like how you think." He pulled his side down and helped West make the bed, laughing softly. "It's like playing house when we already have one. Can we hot tub tonight?"

"I'll get it turned on. I grabbed your trunks because I adore you. And there's a heated robe and towel warmer out there." West wiggled a little bit. "It's the best when it's snowing."

"That is super fancy. I was ready to run back inside frozen. I didn't even think about trunks. Thank you. Damn kids." He winked. "It's going to snow tomorrow afternoon I think."

"Yeah? I'm looking forward to soaking and napping and just having a quiet week." West lowered his voice. "Don't tell anyone."

"No?" He crawled across the newly made bed toward his ex-husband and amazing new lover and tugged on him. "Better kiss me to keep me quiet."

"Oh, that's a dangerous thing to ask a poor old cowboy." West bent to him, taking his mouth like there was nothing else West would ever want to do in his life.

Dangerous. He knew what he was doing. He had a plan to make sure his cowboy was chomping at the bit before they got the kids in bed. West was fun to seduce, and more fun to tease. He liked his man hungry.

He returned the kiss at first as if their bedroom door wasn't open, leaning into the kiss, fingers digging into the fabric of West's shirt. After he got that first little sound though, just the tiniest groan from West, he broke it off and smiled, breathless. "Suitcases."

"Uh-huh..." West wasn't listening to him.

It was the best thing ever, knowing West was still so into him. He climbed off the bed. "The kids need their stuff, lover." He took West's hand and tugged gently. "Shopping? Remember?"

"Mmm...evil man." West cupped his ass and squeezed. "Yeah, we'll take them out for lunch in town, huh? Maybe hit the toy store for a goodie?"

"You spoil them." He meant that fondly. It was vacation, and a little spoiling was in order.

"Uh-huh. I know." West dropped a gentle kiss on his neck. "Going to spoil you tonight."

"I can't wait." That put a little spring in his step for sure, and they got the bags inside in record time. "Hey, guys!" He called back up the stairs. "Come take your bags to your room okay?"

"Okay, Dad!" Ava sounded like a thousand thundering elephants running through the house.

They followed the kids up with their own bags. "Should I unpack? Where do you want my stuff?"

"Sure. Unpack away. I haven't claimed anything, so we can share the bureau. The chest of drawers has towels and linens."

He sat his suitcase on the bed. "Let's do this quick before the kids get hangry." He winked at West. "Ava is just like you when she's hungry. Or you're like a four-year-old. Take your pick."

"I'm totally a four-year-old." West unpacked quick as a bunny. "Oh, my shirt!"

West went out to the closet, taking a huge, burnt orange, fleece hoodie out and pulling it on with a happy moan.

Jeremy laughed. West reminded him of his first roommate out of college when she took off her bra. So cute. "It looks cozy but.. this is a thing? Your shirt?"

"It's my cozy, non-cowboy shirt. Now I fit right in."

"I do like it on you." He got hold of the fabric and tugged West toward him. "And you look warm."

"Cozy. Snug as a bug in a rug."

He pushed his hand under the heavy shirt, stroking West's belly. Nothing like making those hard muscles quiver. "Toasty. Hot even."

"Dad! I can't find the Munchkins!" Lukas called up from downstairs.

"Kitchen counter by the toaster!" He called back. He scritched his fingers against West's warm skin. "The natives are getting restless."

"You're scratching the bear." West groaned and cupped Jeremy's cock for a second, squeezing him.

His eyes crossed a little. "The bear likes it. And that's not fair."

West chuckled softly, fingers moving. "There are rules?"

"I guess not on vacation." He kissed West playfully and let him go. The suitcases on the bed would be in the way later. "He's going to finish those doughnut holes, and we're going to be sorry."

"Come on, gorgeous." West patted his butt. "Let's go feed the hooligans, then we'll pick up our goodies and get good and settled for the duration."

"Right on." Jeremy stuffed the last of his clothes into a drawer and set the suitcase on the floor next to it. "After you, stud."

"Come on, beasts. Let's go get some lunch and stop at the toy store!"

"Yay! Mac and Cheese!" Ava jumped up off the couch and ran for her coat.

"Do they need boots do you think?"

"They should be fine. The sidewalks will be clear." West's smile was pure joy as he watched the kids go.

"Daddy! You're wearing the shirt we bought you with Uncle Hank!" Lukas beamed at him. "Your favorite shirt!"

"Yep."

His heart hurt a little every time Hank came up unexpectedly like that. He thought he was hurting for West, and he was mostly, but what bothered him right now was regret. He'd known Hank was important to West, but he hadn't understood how much. Maybe West hadn't made it that clear to him or maybe he hadn't paid enough attention, he really didn't know. But he'd missed things—important things—in West's life the last two years and he regretted that. Deeply. There was nothing he could do to fix it, but he wasn't going to miss any more.

"Here's your coat, handsome." Jeremy grabbed his too and tugged on a hat he'd stuffed in the pocket. "Does your felt bother your scar less than the little beanie does?"

"I like the soft one. The one without any elastic or brim you brought me the other day from Target. It's perfect." West squeezed his hand. "Thanks."

Oh, good. He'd seen the little super soft hat in West's pocket, but he hadn't been sure if it had worked on that scar. He smiled, glad he'd helped a little. "Excellent. You're welcome. You want to drive? You know best where the parking is and everything." He dangled the keys at West on one finger.

"Sure, honey. I got you. Kiddos, load up! We're fixin' to ride."

"Woohoo!" Lukas boosted his sister up into her car seat and then climbed right in over her.

"I've got her seatbelt, buddy. Thank you."

"Toy store!" Ava was sugared up, eyes wild and happy.

"Lunch first. Then shopping. You never want to shop on an empty stomach." That didn't really apply to a toy store, but she didn't know that.

"Okay, Daddio!"

He got into the car and put on his own seatbelt. "Where are we eating? I could go for a burger maybe. Sounds like you guys have a place? Ava sounds like she has her heart set on mac and cheese."

"It's a local place right up here. Nice sized kiddos menu, burgers, some fancy shit, great desserts. I like the pie." West climbed up into the driver's seat. "The cherry is the best. Claire makes a great one."

"You and your cherry pie." He wondered if cherry was on the menu for Thanksgiving too. "Weird to be in the passenger seat of my own car."

"It's my favorite." West winked over. "Let's do this."

20

Wᴇꜱᴛ was going to beat Trey to death. All day there were a thousand little touches, little looks, teasing whispers.

All through lunch. Through the wild downtown toy store. And then at the grocery where West actually got a crazy stolen kiss while the kids chose cookies. Lord have mercy.

Now they were home with a store-bought pan of enchiladas ready to pop in the oven later, a fire going, and the snow beginning to fall, and his balls hurt.

"I'm so excited about that hot tub later. Maybe the snow will be falling. How cool would that be?" Trey was over at the window watching the sky, hands tucked into his back pockets and looking totally relaxed. Like this was just a regular, lazy afternoon.

"It's amazing." He walked over, wrapped his hands around Trey's waist and snuggled into that fine ass. "Nice view, huh?"

"It is." Trey pulled one hand out of a back pocket and slid it over to cup him through his jeans. "A great...view."

His breath huffed out of him in a hard rush. "Baby." He caught Trey's ear with his teeth and tugged.

"Mmm." Trey's hum escaped around a grin West could hear without having to see. "What's the matter, lover?"

"I will beat you." He chuckled softly, grinding into that touch. "I am going to tear your ass up later."

"It's yours for the taking." Trey pulled his hand back and turned in his arms. "Oh. This view is also really good." Trey's playful fingers slid into the hair at his temple.

"Dad, are you dancing with my Daddy?" Ava had her hands on her hips. "You're supposed to dance with me!"

"Oh, my goodness. Come here, baby girl. Let's all dance." Trey laughed, eyes lighting up. "Can you pick her up for me, Daddy?" Trey's arm was way better but a forty-pound kid was still a bit much.

"Always." He scooped his baby girl up. "You having a good day?"

"I am. I love my new baby and my puzzles." She'd carefully chosen a baby doll with some clothes and a big pack of jigsaw puzzles that weren't too hard or small for little fingers. Lukas had Lincoln Logs and some LEGO. It worked.

"What did you name her?" Trey looped an arm around them both and hummed something West almost recognized, dancing them in a slow circle.

"Lulu, like Ladybug Girl. Because she has a ladybug dress." Ava was starting to pronounce "L"s like they should be and less like "W"s every day.

"Oh, Lulu is my favorite. Good choice."

"Lulu is a grand name. I like it." West two-stepped her around, loving how she squealed and laughed for him.

He caught Trey taking pictures on his phone out of the corner of his eye. "Smile you two!"

Ava pressed her cheek to his, and they both smiled at Trey. "Cheese!"

"Oh my god. So cute." Trey took a couple, then stepped in close and got a selfie too.

"Dad, I need some help with—"

"Lukas! Good timing. Come here." Trey waved Lukas over and got a couple of family pictures. "There. Now it's a real vacation."

"Good. Come help me." Lukas dragged Trey upstairs, and West settled with Ava on the sofa. She was drooping, and they could both have a second's rest together.

"I like your house Daddy. It's fun." Ava leaned on him, almost ready for a nap.

"I like it too, baby girl. It's a good place to get away to." He stroked her back, feeling her get heavier and heavier.

By the time Trey came downstairs again, she was out. "Lukas is—"

He put a finger up to his lips and Trey went quiet and pointed up the stairs.

He crooked his finger, so Trey came and took Ava, and they all went up the stairs together. She went down easy and after Trey tucked her in, he peeked in at Lukas in the top bunk.

"Hey, man. Daddy and I are going to lie down for a bit while Ava is napping. You good with my iPad?"

Lukas nodded without even looking up from whatever he was watching.

"*Iron Man*. I know, he's a little young for it. I'm a bad father." Trey pinched his ass as they slipped through the bedroom door together. "I'm a good lover though."

"You're a wonderful lover, but an evil, evil tease." He grabbed Trey's ass and squeezed. Oh, that was a great double-handful.

"I have no idea what you mean," Trey said softly, even as he closed the bedroom door and turned the lock. "You mean evil, like bad? Like I shouldn't do everything I can to turn you on so you can't take your eyes off me?"

"I've never been real good about taking my eyes off you, baby." He sat on the edge of the bed and patted his lap. "C'mere to me."

Trey took slow steps toward him. "You want me to sit or kneel, cowboy?"

He whimpered, his cock trying to unzip his Wranglers, all on its own.

"I didn't hear you, honey. Did you say kneel?" Trey tugged his shirt off over his head and tossed it, then braced hot palms on West's knees and knelt, reaching for his fly.

"Jesus, I need you. So fucking bad." And that was the finest damn sight in the history of sights.

Trey's nimble fingers opened his belt, tugged on his waistband until they made enough room to open the top button of his jeans and lowered his zipper without wasting time. "Tell me again." Trey nuzzled into his lap, hot breath steaming up the fabric of his briefs.

His hips rolled like he was riding. Jesus, he was burning alive. "More than my next breath, I swear to God. I need you."

"Fuck." Trey tugged on West's jeans, helping him wiggle them down low on his hips and caught his cock in a firm hand. "I love you." That was the last thing his lover was able to say. Trey's tongue scrubbed along his length as he pushed his cock down Trey's throat.

He shoved his fist in his mouth, muffling the cry that wanted out, so bad. Heat flooded his belly, traveling down his thighs.

Trey's fingers worked his balls in one hand, and he let West move, let him rock his hips and arch, and didn't ease up. The wet heat and heavy suction driving him was meant to get him off.

"Don't stop. Don't stop, baby. I need this." He fought to keep his voice down, but he wanted to holler out with how friggin' good it felt.

He caught Trey's quick nod right before Trey's hands slipped around and dug into his ass, holding on tight. He humped up, feeling like a teenager, like an untried kid, but if he popped his cork, it was Trey's fault.

Not that it mattered one bit. Trey sucked in air through his nose and held him there, hands still tight against his ass, and swallowed over and over around him. West shot so hard his bones rattled, and he slumped back onto the mattress, totally spent.

Trey let West go with a wet-sounding pop and sucked in a harsh breath. Trey straightened up, hands going to his own jeans, roughly pulling them open. "Fuck...fuck." One hand dove in and freed that heavy prick, hard and standing away from Trey's body.

"Mine." He reached out and pulled Trey into his lap, hands working Trey like he'd loved the fine son of a bitch for years. He worked the tip, making sure Trey felt every stroke.

Trey threw an arm around his back and muffled a cry into his shoulder, nearly bucking right off his lap. Trey trembled against him, and he knew how close his lover was. It wouldn't take much to set Trey off.

"Mine," he groaned and sank his teeth into Trey's shoulder, digging into the slick slit.

Trey gasped, and there wasn't any muffling the sound this time. Wet spunk poured over his fingers and the musky scent filled his nostrils as Trey moaned into his neck. "Fuck. Oh, god."

Oh, hell yeah. Better. So much better. He hummed softly, holding on through the aftershocks.

There was no more teasing after that. Trey was downright snuggly, leaning on him hard while he caught his breath. "Jesus. You were on *fire*."

"You made me ache, baby. I was fixin' to lose my shit." He chuckled softly, shook his head. "So fucking hot."

"I'm not sorry." Trey kissed his neck. "Not one little bit. I'll do it again, promise. Maybe even later."

"After I loosen you up in the hot tub?" He nuzzled in. "You like our playhouse here?"

"I love it. It's cozy and the view is fantastic. The kids are so relaxed. It's really nice."

"I do too—it's just enough. Not big, not fancy, somewhere you can breathe." Somewhere he could be a single dad and rest.

Trey sat up on an elbow and looked at him. "You're going to keep it, right? I mean...not that you need to, if it's too much I get it but..."

"Why wouldn't we keep it, baby?" West didn't understand. "You like it. I like it. We've got at least five or six years before the kids start balking at sharing a room on vacation. Then we can figure that out—either upsize or just get a great sofa sleeper for one of them."

Or maybe he'd just pitch Ava a tent in the snow...

"Good, okay." Trey settled back down again. "It's just a little weird being the new guy here, and I guess I needed...I don't know. To hear you say that 'we', I guess."

"I'm not going anywhere, Trey. Not now. Not tomorrow. I'm yours, and you're stuck with me." He knew they weren't married. Hell, he didn't know that Trey wanted to marry him again, but as far as he was concerned, Trey was his husband, this was his family, and damn the consequences.

"I'm yours." Trey nodded. "I've got a new mark to prove it." He felt a soft snort against his skin. "Also, you're the hottest lay anywhere. Ever."

"By the time we head home, you'll be bowlegged." West laughed softly, dragging his lips over Trey's hair.

"Ooh. Promise?" Trey fingers slid over his still-bare hip. "We're going to have to clean up a little before Ava wakes up. I probably need to change. You think we can stay here for a little yet?"

"Yes. We're not heading out for a few days, so just get comfy. The kids are happy." West yawned. "We're twenty-five hundred feet higher here, after all."

"Oh yeah. So she'll sleep longer. I don't even feel it." Trey yawned too, as if it were on cue and laughed. "Much."

"Figures the Texan is good at seventy-five hundred feet," he teased, grabbing some tissues from the side of the bed to clean them up.

"Shut up. You yawned first, cowboy." Trey didn't help, just watched him, grinning like a fool. When he was done, Trey wiggled his jeans off entirely but kept his briefs on, and pulled the big, heavy blanket from the bottom of the bed up. "Snow...hot tub..."

"Uh-huh. Enchiladas. Nappage." He was all over that. He threw on some shorts, unlocked the door, and climbed into the bed.

21

J eremy added a couple of logs to the woodstove and stoked it up, loving how the fire roared inside, dangerous but contained. "This is a great stove, honey. I love the side load door option, it's so much easier than our front loader at home."

West was in the kitchen dealing with the enormous Thanksgiving food delivery that arrived early because the weather was expected to get ugly. Snow was normal for up here in the winter, but it was early in the season for the feet they were expecting—two feet they were saying—over the next twenty-four hours.

They had plenty of food, plenty of wood, and nowhere to be until Sunday, and by then, the plows would have run. It was perfect.

Lukas was reading and watching a movie on the couch, feet up and snuggled into a blanket. Ava was sitting at the dining room table working in her puzzles again. She loved them, and they were keeping her occupied. It didn't get any better than this.

"You good in there?" He dusted off his hands, closed the

stove door, and ducked into the kitchen. "The kids are quiet...busy busy."

"Good lord. We're gonna have a feast, aren't we?" West grinned at him, stole a kiss. "That storm's fixin' to—"

West's phone rang, and he glanced at it with a frown. "It's Blake." He answered it, hit speaker. "Hey, kiddo. What's up?"

"Mister West?" Oh, someone sounded shaky as hell.

West stopped. "What's wrong?"

"Lowell's girl's married. To someone else. And Craig left us sitting at a truck stop here in Denver."

"He what?" Jeremy glanced up from the phone to West. "A truck stop?"

"I'll come get y'all. Text me where you are." West shook his head at Jeremy, lips tight.

"Are you—"

"Boy, do as you're told. I'll be there in an hour and a half, two tops."

"Do you have cash? Do you guys need us to Venmo you something?" Trey reached out and touched West's shoulder, rubbing in circles.

"We got our cards. There's a restaurant. We'll eat. I'm sorry, Uncle West. Honest."

Oh, it was so easy to forget how very, very young Blake still was.

"No worries, kiddo. You just grab some food. We'll have a good holiday together." West hung up, then glanced at him. "I'm sorry, Trey. You know I can't leave them stranded."

"Of course not, poor kids. I'll go. Let me just get some jeans on." He wasn't going out in sweatpants, and West shouldn't be driving in snowy weather at all. No one should really.

"No. No, you haven't been driving a lot."

Yes, and he'd grown up here, driving in the snow, unlike a certain Texan.

"I took a few almost snowless weeks off for a broken arm. I'm fine. I know the roads and honestly, honey, I'm better with the weather that's coming than you are. Let me go, you stay here and keep the kids happy." What he didn't say was if it sucked, they could stop in Boulder for the night and come up in the morning. He didn't say it because he wanted to be here tonight. Oh, he didn't like that frown on West's face. "I'll take it slow. You can call and check on me any time. Okay?"

"I—Okay, but if you have to, you stop. Our feast won't be until later tomorrow afternoon anyway." West sighed. "I don't like it. What if you need me?"

He cupped West's cheek and kissed him. "I always need you. And what if you went and got stuck? It's no different. Just let me go and get them back here. We'll be fine, and if we have to stop, we will. Okay?"

It wasn't how he'd expected today to go, but he agreed with West; he couldn't leave those kids at a truck stop. "I'm going to throw that punch that I didn't before if I see that asshole again. Fair warning."

"I'd pay to see that, baby. It would be hot." West followed him up the stairs. "Do we have enough food? Should I order more?"

"I don't know, how much do these kids eat? We probably have plenty of turkey...you want to get a few more sides?" They probably had plenty, but it would give West something to think about.

"I'll get another order, if I can." West kissed him hard, his lover worrying this like a dog with a bone.

"Mm. That's a nice send off." He traded his sweats for

jeans, toasty socks, a warm sweater. "Did they text you where they are?"

"Uh. Yeah. Yeah, I'll send it to you so you can GPS. You want coffee? Are you sure you don't want me to go?"

Frantic West was adorable.

"Coffee would be good. Maybe a snack for the road? Something easy. I've got this. And I'll have plenty of company for the drive back. Don't worry."

He'd worry. West was going to worry.

That did mean, however, that he was so getting laid tonight. Comfort sex was the best.

"I worry, but—We'll have pizza here tonight. That's a great pre-Thanksgiving feast."

"Perfect." He grabbed his wallet and headed back downstairs with West on his heels. "Will you grab me a travel mug? I'm going to get my snow hikers on."

"Dad?" Lukas frowned at him. "Where are you going?"

"Can I come?" Ava asked.

"I'll be back in a few hours, guys. Cowboy Blake and his friend Lowell are stuck in Denver and need some help."

"I can help, Dad. I'll come."

He looked at Lukas seriously. "That is really kind of you buddy, but I need the room in the car for them on the way back. Plus..." He sat next to Lukas and talked quietly. "Daddy's going to need someone to keep him company. He's worried about his friends." And him. Probably more about him, but Lukas didn't need to know that.

"Are you picking up Uncle Hank too? He was here last year."

"Uh." Oh, Jesus Christ. Right now? West hadn't told them? "No. No, I'm...not. But we'll talk about Uncle Hank when I get home okay?" West needed to talk about Hank. He'd bottled it up, and that wasn't good.

And sure as anything the guys would mention Hank too. Dammit.

"You look after Daddy until I get back, okay?" He got up.

"Okay, Dad. I got it."

He popped out the back and opened the garage door, then grabbed his keys and started the car remotely to warm it up a little. "I better get rolling, honey. It's not going to get better out there." The storm wasn't too bad yet, and it would be a little lighter in Boulder and Denver, so he just needed to get down off the mountain before the snow got heavy.

He imagined he'd need chains coming back up.

"You be careful, baby. Please. I love you."

He stepped in close and put his arms around West's waist to hug him tight. "I will. I'm going to need my eyes and my mind on the road, but I'll check-in when I can. I love you."

"I love you." West was already about stressed within an inch of his life, so Jeremy knew it was time to go. It wouldn't be fun, but it wasn't scary. Just a little stressful.

He stepped away and grabbed his gloves and hat. He gave West a wink and left without another look, even though he could feel West's eyes on his back.

As he left the condo complex, he was glad to see the plows had made at least one pass and sanded, so the road wasn't too bad. He knew the worst of the drive would be coming home, but he had the guys to help put the chains on and be extra eyes. His goal was to make good time on the way to Denver so they wouldn't have to drive in the dark on the way home.

He thought he'd be able to check-in with West every half hour or so, but once he got going on the winding part of the highway, he didn't want to stop. It was turning into the kind of wet snow where as long as you kept moving you were okay. If he stopped it might get too slippery.

So he didn't get to call West until Boulder, an hour and a half or so later. The roads were plowed here, and the snow was falling, but lightly. He tapped his headset and told Siri to call West.

The phone rang and rang, but when West answered, the connection was for shit, all cracks and pops.

"Oh, crap. You're breaking up, honey. I'll text you. Love you!" He hung up and texted instead.

All good here. In Boulder. Took a little longer than I thought. OMW to Denver now, and the driving is much better down here. Xoxo

West didn't need to know that he slid a lot on that bit through Lyons. Going back would be hairy.

22

"Daddy?"

"What?" He was very, very busy obsessively watching this storm gather strength.

Lukas waited until West looked up from his phone. "Where's Uncle Hank?"

"What?" *Oh. Oh God, kid. Not now. Not yet. I'm not ready.*

He wasn't sure he ever would be.

"Uncle Hank. Isn't he coming this year?" Lukas looked disappointed. "I wanted to show him my LEGO."

"No, son. He's not coming." *Come on, tell him. You can't lie to the boy.* "He passed away this summer."

That was fair and true, and he was fixin' to puke.

Lukas looked at him, obviously confused. "He passed where?"

Oh, for fuck's sake. What did Trey say? Surely the kids had learned about this a little bit. "He passed away. He was real sick, and he went to Heaven."

"Kenny said his dog went to Heaven and isn't coming back. Is Uncle Hank not coming back too?" He had a feeling Trey hadn't talked with these kids about death at all.

"He can't. He got cancer and was super sick, and his body couldn't hold him no more. We'll all be together again someday, I believe that with all my heart, but it won't be on this earth. I'm sorry."

Lukas looked back down at his book, nodding. "I'm sorry he got sick." He thought for a second that might be the end of it. Lukas was only seven after all, and sometimes little kids didn't quite get it. But he heard a soft sniffle, and a tear dropped onto the pages of Lukas's book.

He nodded and held his arms open for his son. "He loved y'all, and he was so proud of you, you know. He loved how smart you are, and he loved your jokes. He was always telling people about you and Ava."

Hank was—had been—the best man he'd ever known. A good friend, a mentor, the kind of man West wanted to be.

Lukas leaned on him hard and sniffled into his sweatshirt for a while. "I made him a horse. It's red, and it has a blue saddle, and I wanted to show him."

West closed his eyes, swallowed against the pain that wanted to split him open. "I believe that, when you die, you get to peek in on the folks you loved, so maybe he got to see it. One way or the other, I want to see it, because it sounds like something he'd have loved."

"You really think he saw it?" Lukas looked up at him, watery eyes hopeful. "That would be cool. I can show you too."

"I really do. I believe that no one that we love is ever really gone. I believe that with all my heart."

"Like when I didn't get to see you, but you still loved me."

"Yes. Nothing can stop me from loving you, and nothing could stop Uncle Hank from loving you, either."

"I believe that too." Lukas tried out a smile. "I love you, Uncle Hank!" he called out to the ceiling.

"I love you too, old man." If his voice cracked, no one was going to mention it. "Show me the horse, boy. I made another food order that's on the way soon. I'll need your help with it and the pizza."

"Okay!" Lukas hopped up off the couch and ran for the stairs.

A text buzzed his phone. Trey. It didn't say much, just, *Coming back. Got the guys. Love you.*

He sent back, *Be careful. Love you.*, but it didn't make him feel better.

As he headed upstairs, he glanced out the back window. It was getting hard to see much past the deck, the hot tub already had six or eight inches on it, and his man was at least two or three hours away. He didn't like this. He didn't like this at all, and there was nothing he could do but pretend not to be terrified.

Dammit.

"Daddy!" Ava threw her arms open when he came into the bedroom, hair everywhere and not napping. "I'm awake!"

"Baby girl!" He scooped her up and squeezed her tight. "I love you!"

She was sheer joy.

"I love you too!" She kissed him on the cheek. "Lukas is playing LEGO."

"Here Daddy, see?" Lukas brought the horse over. It was boxy and had a long square head and long square legs and looked just like a LEGO horse should.

"Dude! You rock that. Seriously. I love it." He gave it the attention it deserved, because it was cool and his boy was smart as a whip.

"I'm keeping it. His name is Hank." Lukas walked over and sat it on the bedside table. "I'm going to leave him here and then every time we come back we can see Hank! He'll always be here."

He nodded, laughing softly. "I think that's perfect. Seriously. I love that. Hank loved being here with us."

One day, it would be all joy to think about his friend, he had faith. One day.

23

"Can you even see, Mister Trey?"

"You can call me Jeremy, guys." The windshield wipers weren't quite keeping up, but if Jeremy put them on high they just smeared the snow everywhere. He reached down and turned the defroster up to keep the windshield warm and help melt the falling snow. "And yes, I can see." He kind of wished Blake and Lowell couldn't, he could tell the weather was making them both nervous, even if Lowell hadn't said one word since they left Denver.

"Have I mentioned that I appreciate y'all letting us stay for Thanksgiving? We do. We'll help do whatever y'all need." Blake kept looking back at Lowell, then at him, then back.

"We're happy to have you. I'm sorry you're not home with your own families, but you're welcome with ours. I still can't believe that Craig guy just dumped you at a rest stop." He looked in the rearview. "You okay, Lowell? There's some water bottles back there if you need one. You want to put something on the radio?"

Lowell just shook his head.

They were through Boulder and had started up the mountain on Highway 34 about twenty minutes ago. The snow was getting heavier by the minute, and he played the drive back in his mind, trying to figure out the best spot to pull over and get the chains on.

There was a gift shop about halfway. He remembered seeing it. He could stop there, if he had to.

Christ, he hoped they didn't shut the highway down. West would be livid.

"Have either of you ever put chains on before?" He looked at Blake fully expecting a no.

"I can help." Lowell said confidently from the back.

"Really? Great." That was a bit of good news. It would go much faster with another set of hands.

"My daddy drove a truck. I used to go out with him when I wasn't in school. Winter break was all about chains."

"I'm going to pull into a parking lot a little way up the road. Blake, when we stop, you can try to text West and let him know where we are and what we're doing okay? Just the facts, don't get him worried."

Because West would flip out enough at the mention of "chains". The fewer details the better.

"Yes, sir. We're coming. We're okay. We're good." Blake was a good boy.

"We're going to be fine, guys. Okay? We just have to take it slow and be smart." And pray the goddamn road stayed open.

They stopped and got the chains on, Lowell working hard and quick, and they were back on the road in no time. By the time he got them moving up the mountain, the trucks were behind them.

"They just closed the road, Mr. Trey. Behind us." Blake sounded stunned.

He looked in the rearview and saw the flashing lights they'd just passed. He'd had no idea that was what was going on. He didn't like what that said about the rest of his drive, but he was committed now. At least it wasn't dark yet. "Damn. Do you think it's out on the radio?"

Would West know?

"I don't know. Are we—should we turn back?" Blake was turning gray around the edges.

"We got chains, buddy. We're close." Lowell managed to sound totally calm.

"We're ten miles from home. We're closer to home than anywhere else." He put a hand on Blake's shoulder and gave it a squeeze. "I've got this." He really had no choice, did he? There was no point in worrying now he just had to keep his eyes on the road.

He reached down and turned the radio up, mostly to give Blake something to concentrate on, but also to discourage any more talking while he navigated a road he literally couldn't see. He was tracking his route by the guard rails, the GPS, and the open space between the trees that lined the road.

It took him half an hour to drive those ten miles, it was nearly dark, and the only reason he knew he'd been breathing was he hadn't passed out.

But he got them home. He turned into the condo complex and it looked like a completely different place. It could have been the moon. The trees were bent and heavy with snow, the roofs were covered, there wasn't a single clear driveway...except for theirs.

"West fucking shoveled." He laughed. "No sign of life anywhere but my husband fucking shovels. Uh. Ex-husband. Whatever." Whatever? If he walked in the door and West proposed right now, he'd accept. That last ten miles had brought his priorities into very sharp focus.

"Mr. Trey, a man doesn't drive in snow like this to get home to an ex." Lowell chuckled softly as the garage door opened. "Someone's waiting for us."

No, one did not. "Lowell, you're absolutely right."

He stopped the car just at the edge of the garage figuring they should sweep some of the snow off the roof before he drove it in. But the sight of West, standing in his headlights in the middle of the garage wasn't one he was ever going to forget. He'd never been so happy to see anyone in his whole fucking life.

He left the car running and climbed out, playing it cool. "Hey, honey. Look who I found."

West came right to him, grabbed him up, and kissed him like West was storming the beach at Normandy. No hesitation, just pure intensity.

All Jeremy could do was hold on and let West have whatever he wanted, and that was just fine. Better than fine. He could stay with West on this little island of a moment forever, with the snow and the boys and the stress far away.

———

BY THE TIME the lights appeared, he'd fed the kids, put them to bed, made sure the sleeper sofa was okay and made up and put back together. Then he'd made coffee, shoveled the drive, and heated the jacuzzi.

Then he'd paced and fretted and prayed, talked to Hank, and fussed and bargained with God.

When Trey stepped out of that car, he'd never seen anything finer.

"We're okay," Trey whispered, holding onto him, still a little breathless from his kiss.

"Jesus. I was scared. I can't lose you again, baby. I will not." And thank you, God, he hadn't. "Come in. Come on, let's get you fed and warm. This storm is a cold, stone bitch."

They were going to be snowed in for a few days. Good thing he bought everything they could possibly need for a while.

"The car..."

But Blake and Lowell were already on it. They'd cleaned off the roof, and Blake pulled it into the garage behind them.

He hustled Trey into the house as if it wasn't real until the door closed behind them.

"I think I'd like a drink, honey." Trey blinked at him. "A strong one."

"Whiskey or tequila?" They had both, plus rum for a hot buttered drink tomorrow.

He sat Trey in front of the woodstove to defrost, wrapping his lover up.

"Whiskey. Blake, you joining me?"

"Yes," Blake said flatly, still looking pale. "I mean...I might could have a sip."

Lowell almost doubled over laughing. "Fuck, pour me a double. I got dumped twice today."

"Four glasses. I got it." Lord have mercy. What did it say that this was going to be the best Thanksgiving in four years?

"Okay. I didn't want to say anything on the road, West, but Blake was terrified."

"Shut up. Lowell didn't even speak most of the trip!" Blake flopped on the couch.

Lowell snorted. "Uh-huh. Well, Mister I Got This was a

little white-knuckled on that steering wheel the last few miles."

"Hey, you're here." Trey laughed. "Be nice, kid, or I'll dump you out on the deck tonight and you can call it a trifecta."

"There's a hot tub out there, so you wouldn't die," West offered up, and he poured four doubles and passed them out. "I fed the kids pizza and watched *Coco*. Twice."

"I don't know how to thank you enough for rescuing us from that truck stop in this weather." Blake looked at him, eyes serious. "Mister Trey is damn good in the snow, but that drive sucked."

"It did suck," Trey agreed. "No joke. I wouldn't let them text you and tell you how much. Did you hear they closed the road? We were the last car through, and probably only because we had chains."

He sat next to his lover—no, this was his husband. He'd made his promises to God, and he'd make them to Trey. "Yeah, this storm is big. We're all here, and in, and staying. We've got wood and food and games. We're solid."

"I'm not getting back in that car any time soon, that's for sure. We can have a bubble in the hot tub later, and you guys can tell me crazy stories." Trey leaned into him, warm now and definitely wanting his attention. "It's going to be a nice Thanksgiving."

"It's going to be perfect. I'm here with my kids, my husband, and my buddies." He held Trey's gaze, daring him to argue.

Trey's eyes twinkled at him. "A man doesn't drive in snow like that to get home to an ex."

"Oh, wise words." Lowell chuckled. "Hear, hear!"

"Yeah. Hear, hear." He took a soft kiss, then whispered. "I want to make it right."

"It's right," Trey whispered back "It just needs to be officially right."

"When we get home, we can go to the courthouse?" He didn't need a to-do. He just needed them to sign the papers.

"Perfect. Just redo what we undid. Take the kids, make it a family thing?"

"Yes." It wasn't this great romance, but maybe they didn't need that. Maybe the romance was the last few months and all the months to come.

Blake and Lowell were doing their best to act like part of the furniture, but someone's stomach growled, reminding him they were there.

"Sorry," Blake looked embarrassed.

"There's pizza. Lots of it. All sorts."

Trey squeezed his hand and stood, taking a few steps toward the kitchen. "Come on you guys, let's get you fed."

"You sit. I got this. You want pepperoni?" He eased Trey back down. "I made a veggie too."

Trey smiled up at him. "Veggie would be great, honey. Thank you."

"No problem." He got the guys set up, grabbed a piece of sausage for him and two veggie slices for Trey. His heart was starting to slow down, and he could feel his shoulders coming down from around his ears.

Trey leaned right back into him when he sat down, and he got the feeling his lov—*husband* had been more stressed than he'd let on. Trey had probably been putting on a game face for the guys on the drive. Even if they were grown, they were still young.

"Eat. Make with the chewing and all. It's good for you."

"Yes, sir." Trey glanced up at him and winked. "Did the kids go to bed okay? Were they worried?"

"Lukas and I had a couple of long talks. Ava was just

excited to make snowmen in the morning." Lukas had damn near broke his heart.

"Long talks? Is he okay?" He felt Trey's shoulders sag against his side. "Oh. Was this about Hank? He asked me a question right before I left and I...pushed it off."

"It was mine to answer." And he'd done his best. He was going to keep that horse forever. That horse, Hank's glasses, all the stuff in storage. Well, maybe not some of the stuff in storage.

"I thought that. I wasn't sure what the right time was, but it wasn't three minutes before I walked out the door." Trey put his plate down on the coffee table and took his hand. "Will you tell me about the things in the closet at some point? The belt and the glasses? When you're ready. Sometime before the weekend is over."

"Yeah. Yeah, we'll talk upstairs." He didn't want to share some of this with the guys and, more than that, he didn't want to rub in how little Trey knew.

"Jesus, West. Did you buy the grocery store?" Blake came in with another piece of pizza. "I never seen so much food."

"I wasn't sure how long the storm would last."

"And we've seen how you put away breakfast." Trey put his feet up on the table next to his plate. "Thanksgiving is meant to be a feast."

"Thanksgiving, and then cantaloupe for a week." Lowell nodded, looking into his empty glass.

"I'll put you to work shoveling snow." West looked over at Lowell. "So, married?"

"Yeah."

"Did the husband know what she was doing?"

"Nope."

"He still don't. Lowell shook the guy's hand, gave her

some folded up cash, and thanked her for lending him money." Blake shook his head. "She deserved worse."

Lowell shrugged, his jaw tight.

"You're classy, son."

West knew Blake. Blake would have that news to his momma, who would have it running through the circuit like wildfire. She'd been a barrel racing queen.

"There's beer and soda in the fridge if you want, guys. Lowell. Help yourself, okay?"

Lowell took Trey up on that offer. "Thank you, Mister Trey. Blake you, want a Coke while I'm up? Mister West?"

"I'm good. Thanks. Y'all call your folks, let them know you're safe and here?" He knew their people would worry.

"Oh. Sh—yeah. I better do that, huh?" Blake hopped up and pulled his phone out of his back pocket. "Momma's gonna love this story."

"Yeah. I'll call my folks tomorrow. I don't feel like explaining."

Yeah, that was gonna be...awkward. Married. Shit.

Blake took off for the kitchen with the phone to his ear, and Lowell followed him.

Trey shook his head, laughing gently. "Never a dull moment, huh?"

"That hasn't changed, baby. Texans love Colorado. Always have, always will."

"They better get some thicker skin then and enjoy the snow instead of freezing their balls off." Trey nipped at his chin, laughing.

"Hey, I do all right. I'm fixin' to get snowed in, and there's wood and food and booze and games for days."

"Nobody I'd rather be snowed in with. Speaking of which, where are we putting these cowboys tonight?"

"I have the hide a bed here made up, the extra pillows and blankets in the coat closet." He had this shit down.

"I hope the kids don't wake them early. Ava might run down here for Blake."

"If she does, they'll manage." He chuckled under his breath. "I wonder if I can set up a camera..."

"Mr. West, Momma wants to talk to you." Blake came back from the kitchen with Lowell on his heels and held out the phone dutifully. "She wants to say thank you."

"No problem." He took the phone. "Hey, girl, happy Thanksgiving."

"Good lord, y'all are getting one hell of a storm. Thank you for taking them in."

"You know I always will. You and yours are always welcome with me." West smiled at her so familiar voice.

"Blake was on his way here you know, when Lowell found out about that woman. And then they both would have come if not for... Craig is it? Oh, I have to find out who his people are," she muttered. "Anyway, I know they'll have a decent holiday with you."

"Sure they will. I got all the fixins and enough food to hold us a good while. I figure we'll play Uno for a few days before we move to Spades."

"You're a good man, West. And Blake says your Trey is there with you now..." she trailed off, leaving the question open-ended.

"Yes, ma'am. I got my family back, and I'm fixin' to keep them."

"Praise God." She actually sniffled. "Oh, I'm so happy for you, honey. Congratulations."

"Yeah. Yeah, thank you." He had good friends, close or not.

Trey gave his knee a squeeze. "Staying right here," Trey mouthed at him and made a stupid kissy face.

"You be sure and let me know when I can return the favor. We have lots of room and would love to have you all."

"You know it. My kids love y'all, and Trey does too." West winked at his husband. "Maybe we'll come down in the summer when it's ten thousand degrees."

"Give your snowbunny something to appreciate." She laughed. "Anytime you want, honey. We miss your face around here. Have a very nice turkey dinner, and thank you again for looking out for my boy."

"Anytime. Love you, lady."

"Love you too, West."

He handed the phone back to Blake with a chuckle. "Don't tell her about the dancing girls."

Blake rolled his eyes. "Yes, he was joking Momma. Yes, ma'am. I will. Yes, ma'am." Blake must have repeated "yes, ma'am" seven or eight times before he finally said, "I love you too. Bye, Momma."

Trey chuckled, and Blake gave West a mock-glare. "She loves you more than me."

"Nonsense. She's my friend; she's your momma." There was a huge difference. Vast.

Trey laughed louder. "Are we going to have a fight? Because I need to get some popcorn."

"That'd be something to see." Lowell snorted.

"Like I'd fight with my Uncle West." Blake sat down. "Y'all are the dads of my best girl. Does she know I'm coming?"

"She does. And she gets up early." Trey emphasized that last word carefully. "You can send her back up to us if we don't catch her before she gets to you."

"No problem. We'll watch cartoons. I love cartoons."

"This is why you're her best friend." Trey shifted, turning to look at him. "I'm ready for the hot tub."

"Boys, y'all want to join us?" Please say no.

"No, sir. We're going to eat pizza and watch a movie. It okay for us to pull out the sofa and all?"

"Go for it. Blankets and pillows are in the hall closet." Oh, thank goodness. He reached for Trey's hand.

"Night, boys." Trey took his hand, looking as relieved as he did, and followed him upstairs to change.

24

J eremy closed the bedroom door quietly and locked it, still trying not to giggle too loudly after creeping half-naked past the cowboys sleeping on the rollout.

"They're so cute." He stepped up close to West again, both of them still damp and a little chilly from the quick trip in the snow from the hot tub into the house.

"Uh-huh. Lowell's into boobies. Quit matchmaking." West tugged him into the bed, the electric blanket making it cozy.

He snuggled into West, grateful for the warmth. "I'm not matchmaking! They're about as far apart as people can be in the same bed. They're just so funny." He looked at West. "Wait, Blake's gay?"

"Duh." West rolled his eyes at him, and Jeremy could see Ava, clear as day.

"Honey, I wasn't sure you were, even after you came on to me. Twice." His gaydar was terrible, and his flirt meter could be even worse.

"You figured it out after I kissed your happy ass, though." West looked absolutely tickled.

Oh, he remembered that kiss. So hot it had him reeling, and he hadn't even been that drunk. "Yeah, your tongue snaking down my throat pretty much clarified things for me."

"I'm clear that way. I want to marry you. I want to be married to you forever. I want to watch our grandbabies grow up together. Just to be clear."

"That's very clear." He dropped a kiss on West's chest. "I want that too. It's what I wanted the first time I married you. We lost two years out of many...maybe we needed to so we could have this."

"I don't know that I needed it, but it happened, and it's not happening again." West hugged him, hard.

Okay. Well maybe he'd needed it. He wasn't going to apologize again. And West must have heard him because he was home now, wasn't he? "Nope."

Still, he needed to know about the things he'd missed. He needed to understand what had changed West so profoundly. And he thought he knew where that answer lay. "So your talk with Lukas went okay?"

"As okay as it could. I tried to explain without freaking him out. I love the idea of Hank looking down at us, but I didn't want to get him 'Jesus I'm being stalked' dreams."

He chuckled. "You know I'm terrible with that stuff, so I'm sure you did better than I would have. And it was good that you had some time to sit with him about it. Do you feel any better having told him?"

"It was hard." West closed his eyes. "He made a horse for Hank. He wanted to give it to him."

Damn. Jeremy sat up on one elbow so he could see West better. "Wow. I didn't know they were that close."

"They spent at least one visitation a month seeing him, sometimes more. He loved them dearly."

"I'm sorry I didn't know him better." In the early days he was always home with the kids when West traveled. West hadn't told him much about Hank at all, but it was obvious to him now that Hank had been West's chosen family. West had been estranged from his blood family as long as Jeremy had known him, and never talked about them either. "But I'm glad the kids knew him. Lukas especially. That's special between you guys, those memories."

"He loved Lukas to death. Thought he was brilliant." West closed his eyes, hiding away.

"He was right. We have a brilliant kid." He touched West's face, played with a lock of hair. "You loved him."

"Sure I did. He was my best friend. He took me in when I was sixteen and scared and lost, gave me a place to be, helped me learn how to cowboy. He was the best man I've ever known."

"Why didn't you talk about him more? I mean, I remember him being around sometimes, but I don't remember him...like that. How did you meet him?"

"I met him at a rodeo." West winked at him. "He signed my hat. I asked him how to become a bullfighter, and he said he didn't know. My dad, you know, was a roper, and I started traveling with him, so we saw each other again and again. When...things got bad, I called him. He put me up in a hotel, then he came to get me."

He nodded. "You were lucky. So when did he get sick?"

"They found the cancer on a Saturday night after a hit. He was dead twenty-five days later."

"Shit, honey." That was much too fast. No wonder West still seemed so dazed about it. "You haven't had much time to grieve have you?"

"I just...You don't understand. I got hurt, Hank got sick, Hank died, and you got hurt when I was working my way back here." West sighed softly. "I just got back up on the horse, so to speak."

"I'm sorry." That explained a lot. How busy West made sure he was, every minute out in the garage or working on fixing up the basement, keeping occupied. "You're right. I didn't understand. But I do now. You did everything you could, you know. You stayed with him, took care of him."

"I did. He was a good, good man. He left me everything. Like I was his son. We talked, right before he died. It was late, and he asked me what I wanted more than anything. I told him I wanted my family back." One single tear escaped West's eye. "He told me to go get you back, no matter what."

"And then I fell off a chair." He kissed the tear away, heart breaking for West. "Look at me, West. You can open your eyes and look at me. Your secrets are safe here with me. All of them. You can cry if you need to, and I'll hold you. Nobody will ever know but you and me." And Hank, if he was watching like West believed he was.

"I loved him, and I'm going to miss his face." West's lips went tight. "He was the closest thing I had to family, after y'all."

"I know. He was family, right? He made himself your family." Jeremy hooked an arm over West's chest and rested his head on that strongly beating heart. "You're not alone, honey. You have us."

"I know. Thank you. We're going to have the best Thanksgiving ever tomorrow. I have faith."

"We are. And we'll remember the people we wish were at the table with us." Like Hank. And Blake's sister. "Whoa. Blake's mother must be missing him like crazy, huh? Wow."

"I'm sure she is, but she knows he's with family and safe, not driving in this shit."

"Yeah. We're good." He still hurt for West. But it was

good to know, to understand. Losing family was hard, losing a career was hard on top of it. They were moving forward now, though, and his job was to make sure West knew he was loved. He needed to lighten things up, help his husband relax.

He inhaled deeply. "You smell good, honey. If Hank is really watching, it's time for him to get out of our bedroom."

West started to chuckle, deep, husky sounds that shook his lover's body, top to bottom.

25

"Daddy! Daddy, they're here!" Ava had the loudest whisper in the history of whispers. "And there's going to be a parade and breakfast and turkey!"

West chuckled and pulled her in under the covers snuggling her and loving on her. "Happy Turkey Day, my love."

"Mrpy-trrky," Trey mumbled. Poor man got a workout last night and was exhausted. West couldn't hide his grin Hell yeah.

"Shhh. Dad is sleeping." Ava snuggled right down between them. This wasn't their first rodeo; they'd pulled on PJs and unlocked their door before they fell asleep last night knowing the kids would be looking for them in the morning.

"Mhm." Trey's face was still mushed into the pillow, eyes stubbornly shut.

"Uh-huh. Did you already wake up Blake, my little potato?" He booped her nose.

"Nope! I was so good. I woke you up!"

"Yay." Trey's lack of enthusiasm was epic.

"Is it time yet?" Ava climbed over Trey to get a look at the alarm clock.

"Come on, my beautiful baboon. Let's go make cocoa and warm up cinnamon rolls." He swung out of bed, scooping her up, making monkey noises at her.

She giggled madly and tightened her arms around his neck. "Daddy!"

"M'comin'." Trey yawned and rolled over, groaning. "Moving slow, I'm...tired. Coffee?"

"Sleep, baby. I'll make sure you're up for the parade, okay?" He settled Ava on his hip. "We need to start a fire and see how much snow there is!"

"M'kay." Trey was out again, that quickly.

Ava's eyes went wide, and her tone was awed. "There is so much snow, Daddy. I saw it out the window. So much."

"So much? Let's go see." He went downstairs, his eyes going wide at the sight of the snow, piled against the sliding glass door. Jesus. That was a lot. Thank God the wood was covered, and the wood closet deal was totally full.

Thank God Trey got home.

"That's some snow."

"Right? I ain't never seen it like that," Blake said. His hair was wet, so he must have been coming from the shower.

"Cowboy Blake!" Ava wiggled in his arms to be put down, and West let her run.

"There's my best girl!" Blake caught her as she launched herself into the air.

"I'm fixin' to make coffee and hot chocolate, man, for our pre-parade goodies. You or Lowell want to start the fire going?"

"I'm on it." Lowell was putting the cushions back on the rollout.

"He's on it." Blake grinned, then kissed Ava's cheek. "It's so good to see you!"

Ava hugged Blake. "Parade is soon, and then turkey."

"Are you ready to see Santa?"

"Yeah!"

"Mister West, you want me to use the wood in here or bring in more?"

"Use the wood in that door by the fireplace. We'll bring in more later."

"Yes, sir." Lowell got right to it, stoking up the embers of last night's fire and adding wood.

"Should we help Daddy with the hot cocoa?"

"Okay." Blake set Ava down and she ran into the kitchen. "Did Mister Trey get some good sleep? I bet he was tired."

"He's still sleeping. He was wore." He started a pot of coffee, then set to warming up a big pot of milk.

Blake looked around the kitchen. "What can I do to help?"

"Heat up the cinnamon rolls while I get this going." He had a crockpot deal to keep it in during the day.

"You got it." Blake picked Ava up and sat her in a kitchen chair. "You sit right there, dumplin', and we'll have breakfast up in no time."

Ava smiled at Blake like he was sunshine itself. The four-year-old crush was real.

He'd bought four trays of sweet rolls. They could munch for a few days. He hated the idea of not having something if he needed it.

Blake turned on the oven and got out a tray. "These look yummy." Blake didn't understand snow, but he understood his way around a kitchen.

Lukas wandered in, wearing his PJs and scratching his wild hair. "Lowell has cartoons on, Ava."

Blake waved his hand, "Go on, girlie, we'll bring out the food when it's ready."

"Okay!" Ava hopped off her chair and followed Lukas back out.

"I am no competition for cartoons." Blake laughed.

"Just wait for the parade. They both love that." He grinned over, shook his head. "Glad to have y'all with us, you know. I know we're not your folks, but we're family."

"Yessir. Thanks for the rescue. This is gonna be one hell of a story, you know. I ain't never been in a blizzard before."

West heard that, and the damn stuff was still falling, just slow. Still, they had all they needed and nowhere to go, so he wasn't fixin' to bitch.

"This is your first holiday back with the family, right? That's got to be something."

"It's everything." West met Blake's gaze. "I wasn't whole without them. They're my soul, and I need them like air."

"Yessir. You did good, fighting for them. I'm real proud of you."

"I'm trying to be the best man I can for them."

"It's not my business, but I'm glad y'all worked it out. Ava's happy, she told me so." Blake put the pan in the oven. "Mugs are...oh. Found them."

"Grab four glass, two of the plastic ones, please." He was going for half cocoa, half coffee, because it was a holiday, dammit.

Blake set them all down on the counter. "I hope I can find someone before I get my ass kicked."

"I hear you. I hope so too." He'd gotten his ass kicked a lot.

"Right now it's just me and the bulls, and if that's what it's gonna be, that's cool. I just wish I knew." Blake shrugged.

"Kiddo, I tell you what, live in the now. There's nothing

that wondering about the future's gonna give you, you know that. The wrong bull could come at you tomorrow, and it's over. Just live." He reached up, rubbed his scar, but his mind was on Hank.

Blake nodded, brow furrowed and thinking hard. When the kid looked up again, the cloud lifted, and he got a smile. "You're right. That's the plan. And the now has sweet rolls, so that's all good."

"Sweet rolls, friends, a girl that adores you, and coffee." He finished the hot chocolate and poured it into the cooker to keep it warm. "It works for now."

"Ava will never break my heart, right? She's going to keep you on your toes, cowboy." Blake finished pouring the coffee.

"She's going to be a serial killer, I have no doubt." She was his amazing girl.

"People are going to follow her everywhere. Boys, girls, doesn't matter. They're going to love her. She's dangerous." Blake winked. "Better get that shotgun cleaned."

"I intend to sit on the front porch with it across my knees."

Blake laughed. "That should do it. At least until they leave the driveway."

"She'll be fine. She'll be a cowboy."

Blake picked up two coffees. "Ava?" he called as he left the kitchen. "Are you a cowboy?"

"Yes, sir!" she called back, and scooted over on the couch to make room for Blake.

"Coffee, Lowell." Blake handed one cup off to Lowell and sat with Ava. "Well, all right then."

"I'm going to take Trey his coffee, y'all. I'll be right back down." He headed upstairs, taking Trey his mug so he could get his tired husband up for the parade. "Wakey, sleepyhead."

"Mm. Or you come back in here." Trey reached for him, one arm shooting out from under the blankets.

"I have coffee," he warned, setting it aside, before sliding into the covers to get a little snuggle before they had to be social.

"You love me." Trey was warm and relaxed heavily against him with a sigh. "Good morning."

"Good morning, baby." He squeezed Trey's butt, chuckling as his lover groaned. Yeah, last night had been good.

"Is it parade time?" Trey stretched and groaned again. "Oh man. I call the squishy couch today."

He chuckled, tickled shitless, and he patted again. "Poor sweet little butt."

"Happy little butt. Happier husband. Lots to be thankful for today." Trey leaned up for a kiss.

West gave it, eagerly. He was where he wanted to be, with his family. Kisses just made it better.

Trey sat up and took his coffee, then leaned back against the headboard. "The guys slept okay? Did the kids let them sleep?"

"They seemed to do fine. Ava was trying so hard to be a good girl." He rubbed their noses together. "You should see the snow."

Trey's eyes lit up and he tangled their fingers. "Yeah? Is it pretty? Prettier than you?"

"You know it. It's sparkly."

"Mmm. You're more stiff than sparkly." Trey slid a hand into his sweats to grope him.

"Your hands are warm." West snuggled right in. "I love that."

"How much time before the parade?" Trey pushed his sweats over his hips and disappeared under the comforter.

"A-about fifteen...Trey!" His eyes rolled up in his head, the touch of Trey's lips on his belly making his balls draw up.

"I can work with that." Trey's voice was muffled against his skin, lips moving lower. Trey's hot tongue swept around the head of his cock and teased his slit. "Can you?"

"Jesus fucking Christ, Trey. Don't stop. Please." West could handle damn near anything but it stopping.

His cock slipped easily past Trey's eager lips, and Trey hummed around it, the vibration strong enough he could feel it in his balls. Hell, he could feel it in his goddamn pinky toe. Trey took him deeper, then pulled up again until those hot lips locked under the head again, the thick comforter rising and falling slowly over his hips.

"Need." He bit the word out. "Fuck, I need you."

Trey's fingers dug into his thighs in answer, and his cock nudged the back of his husband's throat several times in a row. Trey pulled his hands back and braced them on the bed, letting him move. West humped up swallowing back his cries as he drove into his lover.

"Fuck. Baby. Soon." He was right there.

Trey didn't ease up at all, if anything the heat and suction grew more intense as Trey pushed him toward the edge of the cliff. That clever tongue scrubbed over his length and drove across his head every time Trey pulled up.

He could no more hold back his orgasm than he could give up breathing, and he shot hard. Trey gripped his hips and stayed with him through it, devouring every drop before coming up for air. Trey dropped light kisses over his hip, across his belly and chest, reappearing from under the covers looking mussed, full lips pulled back in a grin.

"Mmm. Happy snow day."

"Uhn." He was fairly sure that worked as a thank you.

"There we go." Trey wiggled him back into his sweats and settled next to him again. "Now you have something to think about while I enjoy being perfectly sore all day."

"Uh-huh." He so had baby-head. "There's cinnamon rolls."

"Yummy." Trey chuckled and kissed him, slow and sweet, then reached across him and for his mug of coffee. "Thank you for bringing me coffee."

"Anytime." Lord, he couldn't hardly focus.

"Daddy! Dad! You got to hurry! Lukas says!"

"We're coming!" Trey chuckled at his joke. "The parade. Come on Daddy. Time to make your legs work." Trey nudged him gently.

"You are evil. Ee-vile." He stole one more kiss. "Come on. I need to see the marching bands."

"Broadway shows. Al Roker!" Trey groaned again as they got out of bed. "Damn, honey."

He patted Trey's butt. "Grab your coffee."

"Got it right here." Trey followed him down the stairs, hovering close.

"Morning, Mister Trey," Blake and Lowell said at the same time.

"You're here!" Lukas hopped up and gave them each a hug. "It's going to start, come on."

"I'll grab us breakfast, babe. You go sit." *On your tender little butt.*

Trey kissed his cheek, then let Lukas drag him to the couch. Without groaning. He could hear them all getting settled in to watch, and Trey asking people to move around so there'd be a space for him when he got back.

Two plates, four cinnamon rolls, one husband, two babies. Friends, snow, everyone fixin' to watch the parade.

"Sit. It's just starting." Trey took the plates and let West get comfy next to him. "See? Al Roker." Trey winked. "Thanks for breakfast. These look so good."

Ava crawled into his lap, snuggling in. "Daddy, it's Thanksgiving!"

"It so is, baby girl."

They watched the parade. There were marching bands and the Rockettes, Broadway singers and pop singers, Sesame Street and Clifford the Big Red Dog. It was everything it always was, only just a little better for the company enjoying it with them.

And then it was...

"Santa!" Both kids, Blake, and Lowell jumped to their feet.

"Now it's *really* Thanksgiving," Blake said, scooping Ava up in his arms. West watched him hug her tight, and he was a little teary-eyed when he put her down.

"Now I can listen to Christmas music for hours and make your dad nuts!" He needed to lighten things up.

"Bonkers. From now until New Years. I think there are sixteen versions of Jingle Bells on your playlist." Trey was playing along nicely.

"There aren't that many versions of Jingle Bells." Lukas said dryly, like he was the holiday music expert.

"Dashing through the snow..." Lowell, of all people, started to sing. He had a decent baritone too. Who knew?

"Wanna bet?" he whispered to his son, then tickled Lukas's belly.

"Daddy!" Lukas giggled, squirming.

"Don't take that bet, Lukas!" Trey called out over the giggling.

"It's a sucker bet, right, Daddy?"

"Right, son. Never bet against me. That's a sucker bet."

"Time to start warming up dinner?" Trey got up off the couch.

"Cowboy Blake, can you take us sledding?" Ava looked up at Blake, her little head cocked back as far as it would go.

Blake looked at him. "Can I take them out, West?"

"You don't have to do that, Blake," Trey tried to let Blake off the hook.

"Oh. I'd love to, if it's okay."

"Go for it, man. The sleds are in the garage. I'll put out the cheese ball and stuff." West grinned wide. "Someone take pictures."

Lukas jumped up. "Yay! Come on Ava. We need socks and stuff."

"You need more than socks, buddy!" Trey called after them as they tore up the stairs.

"I got this." Blake went after them.

"I'll dig up the sleds!" Lowell headed for the garage.

Trey hustled him into the kitchen. "All the kids are going out to play, Daddy."

"No shit on that. I'll get the food started, but I'm going to want video."

Trey laughed. "We're so having a race. I have skill, and you're crazy. It'll be a good match up."

"Are we going to play in the snow?" He loved that laugh, more than anything.

"Of course. And then we'll eat and watch *The Wizard of Oz*, and then we'll hop in the hot tub. That's the plan, cowboy."

He closed his eyes. *Thank you, Hank. I love you, man.*

Time to go start his holiday season.

WANT MORE BA & JODI?

Interested in learning more about our East Meets Westerns?

Join BA & Jodi's Newsletter
https://lp.constantcontactpages.com/sl/nzvRTTy

Patreon: https://www.patreon.com/BATortuga
There are lots of tiers to chose from, and also free serial stories.
Discord: https://discord.gg/Vba5P5Qv
BA's Discord server has a channel for BA/Jodi related chat and info.

Hey, Y'all!

We want to thank you for giving Keeping Promises a try. We hope you enjoyed the story and want to check out the rest of the series.

If you can spare a few minutes to post a review at the retail website where you made your purchase, we'd very much appreciate it!

Yeehaw and thanks for reading!

BA & Jodi

ABOUT JODI

JODI takes herself way too seriously and has been known to randomly break out in song. Her queer MCs are imperfect but genuine, stubborn but likable, often kinky, and frequently their own worst enemies. They are characters you can't help but fall in love with while they stumble along the path to their happily ever after. For those looking to get on her good side, Jodi's obsessions include nonfat lattes, basketball (go Celtics!), and tequila any way you pour it.

Website: jodipayne.net

Newsletter: https://readerlinks.com/l/2317334

All Jodi's Social Links: <u>linktr.ee/jodipayne</u>

ABOUT BA

Western to the bone and an unrepentant Daddy's Girl, BA Tortuga spends her days with her hounds and her beloved wife, having mother-daughter dates, and eating Mexican food. When she's not doing that, she's writing. She spends her days off watching rodeo, knitting, and surfing Pinterest in the name of research. Following their own personal joys, BA and Julia heard the call of the high desert and they now live in the New Mexico mountains. BA's personal saviors include her wife, her best friends, and coffee. Lots of coffee. Really good coffee.

Having written everything from fist-fighting cowboys to rural single dads to werewolves, BA does her damnedest to tell the stories of her heart, which is committed to giving everyone their happily ever after. With books ranging from heart-warming stories of found families, to rodeo cowboys that are fighting to make a mark, to fiery passionate love affairs, BA refuses to be pigeon-holed by anyone but the voices in her head.

BA loves to talk to her readers and can be found at http:// batortuga.com/ and her newsletter signup link is http://bit. ly/BAJulianews

AVAILABLE FROM JODI & BA

East Meets Westerns

The On the Ranch Series

Tending Tyler

Roped In

Diamonds in the Rough

Outfoxed

The Wrecked Universe

Wrecked

Flying Blind

Special Delivery, A Wrecked Holiday Novel

Seeds and Sunshine

Pickup Man

Cowboy for Sale

The Merry Everything Series

Window Dressing

Cowboy Protection

Cowboys and Cupcakes

Thawed Out

A Present for Parker - Coming January 2026!

The Higher Elevation Series

Heart of a Cowboy

Keeping Promises

Bigger Than Us

Home Free

BDSM/Kink

The Cowboy and the Dom Trilogy

First Rodeo, Book One

Razor's Edge, Book Two

No Ghosts, Book Three

The Soldier and the Angel, a Cowboy and Dom Novel

The Sin Deep Series

(set in The Cowboy and the Dom Universe)

Sin Deep

Trouble with Cowboys

The Triskelion Series

Breaking the Rules

Making a Mark

Making the Rules

Les's Bar Series

Just Dex

Hide Bound

Wholly Trinity

New Tricks

Lost Boy

The Barn Series

Zeke & Wesley

Other Titles

The Collaborations Series

Refraction

Syncopation

Puzzles Series

Cryptic

Single Titles

Temptation Ranch

Land of Enchantment

———

Summit Springs Sapphic (F/F) Romance

Christmas Bizarre

Honeymoon in the Cards